The Cruel Trade

The Cruel Trade

Clifford Peacock

ROBERT HALE · LONDON

© Clifford Peacock 2012
First published in Great Britain 2012

ISBN 978-0-7090-9583-5

Robert Hale Limited
Clerkenwell House
Clerkenwell Green
London EC1R 0HT

www.halebooks.com

2 4 6 8 10 9 7 5 3 1

Typeset in 10.5/14pt Sabon
Printed and bound in Great Britain by
Biddles Limited, King's Lynn

Prologue

Dawn was breaking when the fisherman, returning to port after a night at sea, saw the naked body floating face down in the slight swell of the bay. Looping a rope round the legs, he dragged the dead man onto the canoe's out-rigger. The young Arab had not been long in the water but the sea had already claimed him, matting his hair and beard with salt and bleaching his swollen face the colour of mottled marble.

The fisherman was disappointed not to find a ring or other jewellery on the body to compensate for his trouble. There was a necklace of sorts: the cord used to strangle him was embedded in a deep groove of bruised flesh around the man's throat. The fisherman retrieved his rope and shoved the corpse back into the water. A scavenging shark surfaced, crunched it in its jaws and sank silently back into the depths.

The man who had been watching from the harbour wall hurried away to report what he had seen.

Chapter One

The Chief Minister of Zanzibar waited patiently in an elegant stateroom in the palace. He had requested an audience with the sultan that morning in order to deliver important news but his highness seemed in no hurry to receive it. Soon after arrival the minister was informed, with due deference by a senior eunuch, that his master was busy in his harem so a delay must be expected. The minister thanked the eunuch and politely dismissed him.

With time unexpectedly placed at his disposal, he turned his attention to the elegant furnishings of the stateroom. There were numerous Arabian artefacts which, as a knowledgeable collector, he greatly admired. A matching pair of camphor-wood chests, 400 years old and delicately carved with birds and sea monsters, stood on either side of the foot of a curved flight of marble steps at one end of the room. A wonderful green, pink and blue Heriz carpet, with a vine trellis and medallion design, lay on a floor of richly decorated tiles brought two centuries before by dhow from ancient Persian potteries. Above, on the high arched ceiling, eight exquisitely painted panels depicted voluptuous maidens cavorting in heavenly glades of brilliant flowers. Graceful white screens, intricately pierced to form classic Arabic motifs, stood between the seven tall windows through which slanted shafts of bright morning sunlight.

The minister drew aside one of the fine silk curtains and looked out across the harbour. It was a familiar scene, and an indication of the island's continuing prosperity in which he had played a great part. In the bay a dozen or more local trading dhows, blown in that morning by the new monsoon, lay at anchor. Three tall, square-rigged foreign merchantmen lay alongside the quay. After rounding the Cape of Good Hope far to the south, they had come up the east coast of the continent to take on cargoes of ivory, hides, rhino horn, coconuts and cloves for ports in Britain, Europe and America. There was no sign in the port that morning of Zanzibar's principal export, newly captured slaves from the mainland. A Brazilian ship had sailed for Recife the previous day with over 5000 crammed below her decks.

The minister's erstwhile name was Hemedi bin Mohammad el Marjabi but he was known throughout the island by his preferred name of Tippu Tip. It was an onomatopoeic reminder of the musket-fire that long ago had accompanied the exciting slave-raiding adventures of his youth. His official title, that of Chief Minister, was equally obfuscating. Zanzibar had no government in the accepted sense, Tippu was the chief, and only, minister. The ship of state sailed with his hand firmly on the tiller whilst the Sultan pursued hedonistic pleasures below. Second only to his highness in wealth, power and authority, Tippu had risen from minor slave-trader to his prestigious position through a combination of ruthless ambition and the opportunistic manipulation of others. It was he who now ordered the island's affairs. He ruled without compassion or mercy, his word was final and his judgements undisputable. His staff comprised lowly clerks, spies, and informers whilst a gang of ruffians maimed or killed in accordance with his orders.

Hated and feared in equal measure, Tippu perpetrated unspeakable cruelties, routinely ordering torture as a penalty for even small transgressions. Women and children were not immune from his punishments. It was often whispered that he went down to the dank windowless room below the gaol to observe his victims' agonies; many a prisoner's last sight on earth must have been Tippu, smiling at him from the flickering shadows. There was, without doubt, more than a whiff of metaphysical brimstone and sulphur about the chief minister. Yet, despite his tyrannical rule, he was invariably polite to those loyal to him. Indeed, when it was in his own interest, he could be most gracious. Astute, softly spoken, and highly dangerous, he was a most loving husband to his four wives and an adored father to his innumerable children.

*

The sultan entered the stateroom silently, emerging from behind a curtain at the top of the marble steps. Short and fat, with a bad-tempered face, his elaborate gold and scarlet *kanzu* reached to his feet. His fingers were richly jewelled, the gold chain at his neck carried a large mounted emerald.

For centuries his family had ruled the island of Zanzibar and an adjacent thousand mile stretch of the east African mainland coast. He was wealthy beyond meaningful description, holding an absolute monopoly on the island's immensely rich trade. Every year more than 40,000 slaves were seized by Arab traders in the African interior and driven, in brutal forced marches lasting two months or more, back to the coast. They carried the ivory dragged from the rotting carcasses of elephants previously killed by the traders during their long journey inland. On arrival at the coast the surviving captives and the tusks were crammed into dhows and transported across the twenty-mile wide channel to Zanzibar, an island prison from which escape was impossible. A tax was imposed on traders for every slave landed and, after auction, a similar amount was collected from the new owner when the slave was shipped abroad. These charges alone brought the sultan an annual income of more than one million thaler. The import and subsequent export of the ivory brought him as much again. On the island, and on the mainland, he owned vast plantations of cloves, worked by thousands of slaves. His four wives lived in separate pala-tial palaces with countless servants in attendance. His harem accommodated 200 concubines and his eunuchs boasted of presenting him with a young virgin every night.

Tippu stood in respectful silence until the sultan settled his ungainly figure on the elaborate couch at the top of the marble steps and nodded to indicate his readiness to listen to the report.

'Your Highness,' Tippu began without ceremony, the sultan had long since waived the need for formal preliminaries from his chief minister. 'Last night a young man, son of the slave trader Muammar, was arrested on my orders. On being questioned he confessed that during a recent expedition his father had discovered a hidden valley deep in the interior. He claimed it is inhabited by an unusual tribe

8

who are tall, handsome and very black. It seems the valley may never have been previously raided. Naturally, my immediate thought was to advise Your Highness of this discovery.'

'The man confessed under torture,' the sultan declared, well aware of Tippu's favoured method of extracting information. His piggy eyes stared down at his chief minister. 'He was probably lying.'

Tippu, ever careful to keep one step ahead of his master, had his response ready. But, to convey the impression of giving the matter a final consideration, he paused before bowing and again speaking with calm self-assurance. 'There is no doubt the young man told the truth, Your Highness. I was present throughout his examination and satisfied myself he did not lie.'

Glancing at a paper in his hand, he read out a section: '"*My father said the people in the valley were tall and black and very attractive in appearance. Especially the women. I swear this in the name of Allah, the most gracious, the most ...*" and so on and so on, Your Highness. Those were his exact words, I wrote them down as he spoke. Lying would have been of no avail as Allah took him into His loving arms soon after my examination ended.'

The sultan grunted; the death of a prisoner was the usual sequel to an interrogation by Tippu and of no interest. He sat with his plump hands clasped over his ample stomach. 'Tall, black, attractive women,' he murmured wistfully. 'They could be descendants of Sheba.'

Tippu, aware of the sultan's fascination with the fabled queen, had presented his report in a manner that ensured even he could not fail to make the connection. 'Quite possibly, Your Highness,' he replied cautiously. He nursed grave doubts as to whether Sheba had ever existed but wisely never ventured to say so.

'She too was tall, and very beautiful,' the sultan went on dreamily. It was pure speculation on his part since the only images of her were fanciful depictions produced by romanticists centuries after her supposed death.

'Apart from a connection with the Great Queen, Your Highness will have seen other possibilities arising from this discovery,' Tippu murmured respectfully, well knowing he had not.

'Of course,' the sultan snapped, switching his piggish gaze back to the chief minister. 'Give me your opinion.'

'The valley was discovered by the slave trader Muammar, a most loyal subject of Your Highness. It is therefore, without dispute, part of your realm. An outpost, as it were, of Zanzibar.'

'I was about to say so when you interrupted.'

'A thousand apologies, Your Highness! I suggest also that you see the valley as much more than a mere outpost. It has potential as a stepping stone in the fulfilment of your great plan. From the valley a campaign could be launched to extend your rule across the breadth of Africa. To the great ocean far to the west.'

The sultan said nothing. He closed his eyes and drummed his fingers on his knee. A full minute of silence passed before he sat bolt upright. 'Allah has spoken to me,' he declared. 'It was He who guided the footsteps of the slaver Muammar to the valley. It will become a stepping-stone towards the fulfilment of my great plan. From there a campaign will be launched to extend my rule to the far ocean on the west.'

'With Allah's blessing there is nothing Your Highness cannot achieve,' Tippu murmured, noting that Allah had voiced similar words as himself.

'He also assures me the people living there are truly descendants of Sheba.'

'Precisely as you said, Your Highness.'

The sultan nodded absent-mindedly. Tippu knew his mind was already in thrall to a vision of countless nubile young descendants of Sheba awaiting his lewd attentions. Sensing he had captured his master's interest, Tippu now cautiously fed him further information. Holding up a scrap of paper he said, 'This map was in the young man's possession when he was arrested, Your Highness. It is crude, but he claimed it shows where the valley lies. He swore his father drew it and gave it to him on his deathbed. With Your Highness's permission...?'

With great deference, Tippu advanced up the marble steps with his arm extended. The scrap of paper was snatched from his hand and he quickly retreated back to the lower level. The sultan peered at the crumpled fragment, twisting it this way and that.

'It lacks detail,' he grumbled. 'But a dying man would have thoughts of eternity on his mind. A skilled navigator may be able to interpret it.'

'An excellent idea, Your Highness.'

Naturally Tippu had a plan ready in anticipation of this suggestion. One of his numerous and highly lucrative posts was that of collector of harbour taxes. He possessed a phenomenal memory and retained a mental record of all impending shipping movements in and out of the port of Zanzibar.

'As Your Highness is aware, it is five weeks since the northern monsoon began,' he said. 'The dhow *Salwa* is always among the first to arrive from Musqat. Allah permitting, she will enter port within the next few days. Her captain, Khalil, has a high reputation as a navigator.'

'He is to command an armed expedition to seize this valley in my name,' the sultan ordered decisively. 'Give him this map. He is to set out immediately. As soon as the valley is captured, he is to bring back fifty of the young women for my harem.'

Tippu bowed. 'I shall speak to him as soon as *Salwa* arrives.' The order to bring women from the valley had come as a surprise so a careful comment was necessary. 'Captain Khalil has no experience of slavery, Your Highness,' he said cautiously. 'Bringing women for your pleasure will be a new venture for him.'

'He is to take care they are not interfered with by the guards during the return march,' the sultan warned sternly, narrowing his eyes. He added, in a surprised voice, 'No slaving experience, you say? Is he opposed to the trade?'

'He is employed by the Wafulu brothers, Your Highness. They interpret the Holy Qur'an in a strange way and refuse to carry slaves in their ships. But Khalil's personal views are of no consequence. He will be honoured to serve in whatever capacity Your Highness desires.'

'I shall send some of the women to my brother in Musqat,' the sultan declared. 'Their primitive attitudes may amuse him for a while.'

Tippu bowed yet again. 'I am sure the royal prince will fully appreciate your great generosity, Your Highness.'

The sultan nodded and dismissed the chief minister with a wave of his hand. He waddled back to his harem where matters of more immediate interest occupied his attention for the remainder of the morning.

*

The dhow *Salwa*, homeward bound across the Arabian Sea from Musqat to Zanzibar, dipped and rose in stately swoops. Dazzling white foam erupted under the stem and swept along her sides, creaming the azure sea far astern. These were enchanted waters. To the west they washed the shores of dark mysterious Africa whilst on the east they reached to India, land of the Raj and untold riches. To the north lay Arabia, birthplace of the Prophet, land of Omar Khayyam, poet and astronomer, and of the tales of Scheherazade.

Salwa was as much a part of the Arabian Sea as the shoals of flying fish and leaping dolphins that accompanied her. Following a design little changed in three centuries, a forward-raking mast carried a single curved yard as long as the ship herself; its triangular sail bellied majestically before the steady north-east monsoon. Captain Khalil stood bare-footed on the gently pitching after-deck, his thigh pressed against the tiller bar to counteract the steady force of the wind on the port quarter. Apart from a gaudily striped length of cloth tucked around his waist like a sarong, he was naked. A strong, muscular man in his mid-forties, there was a firm set to his mouth. Staring at tropical horizons for the past thirty years had etched deep lines around his eyes, his curly black beard showed a scattering of grey hairs. A scar, its paleness accentuated by his dark skin, extended from his left shoulder to lower sternum, the legacy of a scimitar slash sustained many years before when a swarm of Somali pirates had boarded his ship in a futile attempt to seize her.

The outward voyage had begun in May when Khalil had sailed from Zanzibar. On arrival in Musqat, after the unloading of *Salwa*'s cargo of ivory and timber, she was moved to a bay on the east side of the harbour. With her lateen rig she could only sail before the wind and was now trapped for the next five months, one of the great fleet of dhows blown north every year by the southern monsoon. Only in October, when the wind reversed direction, would they be set free. *Salwa* was invariably one of the first to leave as her owners, the immensely rich Wafulu brothers, demanded strict adherence to the company timetable. Within days she was followed by the remainder of the fleet, speckling the northern Arabian Sea with bleached sails as they headed south with the first trade goods of the season.

Khalil had been away from home eight months, an unavoidable consequence of being a professional mariner. He had long since trained himself to thrust all thoughts of his family firmly to the back of his mind during his absence from them since they could impose an additional burden of worry which he was helpless to resolve. It was only now, with Zanzibar merely a day's sailing away, that he allowed himself the luxury of thinking of his four wives. A powerful physical desire, long subdued, surged through him. It was heightened by the knowledge that they would each be eagerly awaiting his return and the physical comfort he would bring them.

Musqat had hundreds of brothels catering for all tastes, a situation inevitable in a port packed with sailors unable to put to sea. In the larger establishments opium and alcohol, as well as women and young boys, were readily available under the one roof. But to Khalil, an orthodox Muslim and law-abiding family man, such diversions held no attraction.

It was mid-morning, five weeks and one day after leaving Musqat, when the lookout called down to the deck that Ras Nungwi, the northerly tip of Zanzibar island, was in sight. Khalil ordered the steersman to alter course a couple of points to enter the channel between the island and the east African mainland. By late afternoon *Salwa* was abeam of Zanzibar and heading towards the passage through the reef. As she made the final turn into the harbour, a familiar and long-awaited sound reached the ears of her crew. The ancient watchtower drum, made from the dried ear of an elephant and audible across the island, was being beaten once at half-minute intervals to announce her arrival from the north. A vessel coming up from the south was accorded two beats. As the last of the tide carried *Salwa* into the harbour, the warm evening air was heavy with the tang of cloves from the sultan's plantations. When she was securely tied up at the long quay, Khalil packed his possessions into a bundle and, leaving the mate and two hands on board overnight, set off, with a spring in his step, to walk home.

*

The following morning he left his modest house on the northern outskirts of town to return to *Salwa*. Despite the outwardly bluff manner of a tough, professional ship's master, accustomed to giving orders and having them obeyed without question, he was at heart a pleasant and easy-going family man. A head-dress, habitually perched slightly askew, revealed to even the most casual observer that here was a man of good humour and genial nature. A gleaming white *kanzu* and leather sandals completed his attire. He was happy and content since his senior wife, Haleema, had as usual been most welcoming after his eight month absence. Umma, his second wife, and Haboosh and Khadija, the two youngest (collectively he called them his Jewels), were equally overjoyed at his safe return. His happiness was complete when Haboosh presented him with her first child, his fifth son, born just two weeks previously. With Haleema's approval she had named him Ali. It had been a truly wonderful homecoming and Khalil regretted having to leave them that morning. But, as he had cheerfully explained, once *Salwa*'s cargo was unloaded and the necessary paperwork completed, he would have a whole month with them before returning to sea once more.

He reached the mosque. Its golden minarets glinted in the morning sun and behind them glowed the pink parapets of the sultan's coral palace. His route to the port now descended through a maze of narrow, crooked alleys lined with mud-brick hovels roofed with dried palm fronds. Africans, Indians, Arabs and Persians crowded the passages, the air buzzed with the chatter of a dozen languages. Hurrying about their owners' businesses, domesticated slaves aggressively forced their way through the congestion. Swahili prostitutes in red silk pantaloons, the traditional badge of their profession, lounged at the entrances to rubbish-filled yards, saucily pouting in time-honoured fashion. From shadowy doorways merchants of all nationalities called out their wares as leprous beggars plucked at the robes of passers-by, crying for alms.

When Khalil reached Hunain Street his progress was temporarily arrested by a procession. It was being led by an elderly Arab; he stooped over his stick whilst limping along, chanting '*Bazar khush*' in a tremulous voice. A Swahili youth, in a white gown and blue waistcoat, followed, banging loudly on a side drum. Behind him, flanked by two guards carrying muskets, shuffled a line of twenty slaves of both sexes, shackled at the ankles. The market was primarily for the convenience of those buying slaves in bulk whilst a man wishing to make a single purchase often found a street procession more convenient. The slaves made a colourful spectacle and invariably attracted attention. Following an old custom, their faces were painted in broad red and white vertical stripes; apart from narrow loincloths about their waists they were naked. Their skins glistened in the morning sun due to the Arab earlier having rubbed them all over with coconut oil to give an impression of glowing health.

As the procession was passing, Khalil's eyes were drawn to a young girl. She was perhaps eighteen years old although it was difficult to be precise with her face so grotesquely striped. Despite her degradation she bore herself with a quiet dignity. When she drew level her eyes looked directly at him, mutely appealing. Her gaze remained fixed on his face and he stared back at her. Her Arab owner, alert for potential buyers, noticed Khalil's interest and waved his stick, calling out an invitation to him to step forward and examine her more closely. Khalil shook his head and, turning back to the girl, gave a shrug of helplessness. As the procession passed, her eyes remained on him.

The memory of the girl's silent entreaty disturbed Khalil as he strode on to the port. His unease arose from the contrast of his great happiness that morning with her profound misery. *Was I right to ignore her plea? A minute's haggling with the old Arab and she would have been mine for a few thaler. But what could I have done with her? Turned her loose, to join the swarms of diseased beggars in the port? She would have been worse off than in her present circumstances. Taken her home? The Holy Qur'an allows me, as a Muslim, to undergo a form of marriage in addition to taking four legal wives. But Haleema would have been furious, and Umma and the Jewels would have supported her by their shocked silence....*

He shook his head. No, he had been wise not to get involved. How he hated slavery! He sighed and continued on his way to the harbour.

15

Behind him the beat of the processional drum receded into the distance.

Salwa lay at the far end of the quay. Her mate and two deck hands stood along the rail awaiting Khalil's arrival and, as he came striding towards them, they greeted him cheerfully. He checked that the hatch seals had remained intact then gave orders for unloading to begin. Under the mate's supervision, the two seamen removed the covers and lowered a ladder into the hold. The smell of warm camphor, built up in the tropical heat of the unventilated cargo space, wafted across the dock, a scent redolent of every past homecoming. A rope was passed through a pulley attached to the yard and snaked below into the hold. The crewmen loaded items of cargo into a large net then, on the mate's signal, hauled on the rope. The yard was swung round and the bulging net lowered carefully onto the wharf. The securing ties were undone and a team of shore porters carried the merchandise across the quay into the Wafulu brothers' warehouse. Khalil stood at the open doors beside the company's agent and together they checked the incoming goods against the ship's manifest.

Musqat, where *Salwa*'s voyage had originated, stood at the junction of two ancient caravan trails. For centuries laden camel trains had followed long routes south from the lands of the eastern Mediterranean and Egypt along the shores of the Red Sea. Another trail reached back more than 2000 miles along an old silk road through Persia and northern India to China. This convergence of trade routes was reflected in the variety and quality of cargo *Salwa* had brought to Zanzibar. Her hold contained bundles of Smyrna carpets, rolls of Chinese silk and bales of printed Egyptian muslin. There was a quantity of delicate Peking porcelain packed in straw baskets. Elaborate brass-studded doors and fretted screens testified to the skill of Persian cabinetmakers. From Lebanon came a hundred beautifully carved aromatic camphor-wood chests. More mundane cargo included boxes of Egyptian writing paper and barrels of Palestinian dates and figs. And, returned from Musqat for re-use in Zanzibar's slave market, were two heavy crates containing sets of leg-irons and shackles made in Birmingham, England.

By noon *Salwa*'s hold was empty except for her ballast of large smooth stones lining her bottom timbers. Later that day she would be towed across the harbour and laid up for five months before the southerly monsoon returned to carry her back to Musqat. Long before then the Wafulus' agent would have sold every item of the cargo to export merchants for shipment to ports as distant and far apart as Calcutta, Liverpool and New York.

Khalil paid off the ship's crew and wished them the blessings of Allah. He picked up the bag of money given him by the agent and set off along the quay. There was only one more job to be done; after that he could go home to the family and begin his well-earned rest ashore.

In a street on the far side of the harbour he stopped by a high wall, put down the bag and shuffled his head-dress more firmly onto his head. He pushed open a heavy wooden door and stepped into a wide walled courtyard. As he had done on every other previous visit, he stood for a few moments surveying the scene before him and wondering if Allah would ever see fit to bestow upon him the considerable wealth necessary to buy a similar property.

The courtyard was a cool oasis, paved with patterned tiles and shaded by palms. Around the base of a graceful jacaranda a thick carpet of fallen purple flowers lay in a perfect circle. There was a rocky pool, with white and pink lilies and brightly coloured fish, into which sparkling water cascaded from an ornate fountain. Facing him was an elegant two-storey cream-coloured villa with deep, shaded verandas. The upper windows had graceful balconies with profuse blooms of scarlet climbing hibiscus covering their supporting pillars. Against the duck-egg blue of the afternoon sky, a low-pitched red-tiled roof added a splash of vivid colour. To Khalil, the villa looked even more beautiful than he had remembered. He sensed a deep yearning, a feeling bordering on sexual passion, as he imagined bringing Haleema and Umma, and the two Jewels, to live here. *If an earthly paradise exists, it is in this villa, with my four beautiful wives.* He sighed wistfully, and crossed the courtyard.

The building, no longer used as a dwelling, was the town office of Tippu Tip, the sultan's chief minister. It was here, as dhow captain, Khalil was required to pay the import dues on the cargo *Salwa* had brought from Musqat. The tax office occupied a room on the ground floor, ruled over by Baba, the cashier, one of Tippu's oldest and most reliable employees. A large sum in coin was paid into the tax office daily so a trustworthy collector was essential. A constant stream of foreign sea captains, from all parts of the globe, arrived at the office to pay their ships' dues. Baba spoke not only Arabic and ki-Swahili, in common with all Arabs on the island, but over the years, thanks to the cosmopolitan constitution of his clientele, he had gained an excellent grasp of English and Spanish. He knew German and French reasonably well, and was even making headway with Mandarin. Before condescending to conduct business, Baba made a point of questioning every captain who appeared at his counter, probing for details of his recent voyage and ports of call. Facts were sought regarding the captain's homeland, its cities, principal rivers and mountain ranges, its citizens and their customs. Baba's thirst for knowledge was insatiable and over the years he had accumulated an encyclopaedic knowledge of the world and its ways.

Khalil was an old friend and Baba greeted him effusively, eagerly enquiring after the success of his voyage. Khalil assured him it had been trouble-free. Anxious to get home to the family, he stopped further discussion by handing Baba *Salwa*'s cargo manifest. The old man read it through, consulted his tables of charges and, after much muttering to himself, scribbled a column of figures on a slate and added up the total.

'Eight hundred and twenty-six thaler, Captain,' he announced in his crisp, dry voice.

'Eight two six!' Khalil exclaimed. 'Are you sure, Baba? That's sixty more than last time! Have the charges gone up again?'

It was a token complaint. The Wafulu brothers personally inspected each of their captains' accounts line by line. They would be very concerned at the increase in dues but there was nothing they could do in the face of the sultan's monopoly over the island's entire trade. Baba smiled ruefully, hunched his shoulders and displayed both hands in a gesture of helplessness. Khalil spilled a river of coins from his bag onto the counter. Baba picked one up between his thumb and forefinger.

'Ah, the wonderful silver thaler,' he murmured. 'I count hundreds of these every day, Captain Khalil, yet I'm continually surprised at the incongruity of them being the recognized currency of commerce across the whole of East Africa.' Khalil nodded wearily; Baba delivered the same pedantic discourse every time they met. From past experience he knew it was pointless to try to hurry him as all attempts to shorten the transaction would be ignored until he had delivered his exposition in full. 'It is truly amazing, is it not, that these coins, struck in Vienna, a great city thousands of miles away, should be used from Khartoum in the north to as far south as here in Zanzibar?'

Baba pointed to the head of the Empress Maria Theresa on the coin. 'Some people mistakenly believe that is a likeness of the Christian woman Virgin Mary,' he said, shaking his head in disbelief at such ignorance. 'Now, I must warn you, Captain, only unworn, undamaged coins bearing the date 1780 are acceptable at the full rate.' He gave his characteristic shrug. 'Why that is, I do not know. The image of that year depicts the woman displaying an unusually large area of her titties. Perhaps that is the attraction.'

His homily concluded, Baba set about inspecting each coin to ensure it met the stated criteria, rejecting any that did not. It took a great deal of time but finally, sweeping those deemed acceptable into a slot in the counter, he returned the remainder to Khalil, wrote a receipt and handed it to him. 'Thank you, Captain,' he said. 'Enjoy your time ashore.'

As Khalil left the office, the final task of his voyage completed, out of the shade of the adjoining veranda stepped the chief minister, Tippu Tip.

Chapter Two

For Khalil the encounter was as sudden as it was alarming. The Chief Minister came towards him, smiling in a friendly fashion, his arms held wide open in greeting. '*Assalam-o-alaikum*, Captain Khalil,' Tippu murmured.

'*Alaikum-o-assalam, effendi*,' Khalil replied.

As they formally embraced and kissed cheeks a cold hand gripped Khalil's heart. *This is no chance meeting. I've been coming here to pay Salwa's harbour dues for five years but have never received a welcome like this* ... Tippu bowed his head and, holding out both hands with palms uppermost, gestured to Khalil to sit at a table in the shade beside the pool. A servant appeared, bowed respectfully, served coffee and silently disappeared.

'How was your recent voyage, Captain?' Tippu enquired politely.

'A smooth passage, *effendi*,' Khalil said warily, wondering if there was a query about the payment of dues. 'Thirty-six days from Musqat. No pirates. Cargo intact. Tax eight hundred and twenty-six.' *Should I mention that's a lot more than last year? The manifest was almost identical. But Tippu sets the rate and it may be unwise to query his judgement.* 'All unloaded and the crew paid off,' he added.

'Excellent,' Tippu said. 'You have done well, Captain.'

Khalil slurped his coffee and wiped his mouth with the back of his hand. Like a shadow, the servant reappeared and bent his head close to Tippu's ear, whispering. The distraction gave Khalil an opportunity to study his host more closely. Undoubtedly Arab in origin, there were obvious traces of an African ancestry in his full lips and broad nose. He was elegantly dressed; his *kanzu* was a delicate shade of mauve and his *fez* was embellished with a silver-mounted emerald.

His slippers were of the finest leather, decorated with gold leaf and semi-precious stones.

Tippu dismissed the servant with a nod. 'A trifling matter,' he assured Khalil. 'Please accept my apologies for the interruption.' He leaned back in his chair, pressed his fingertips together and smiled across the table. 'Captain,' he said warmly, 'I have a most important mission for you. On the orders of his highness himself.'

Khalil was astonished to hear the Sultan knew of his existence. He was aloof, isolated from his people and so far as anyone knew, never left his coral palace. Tippu's reputation made Khalil shiver; a ripple of ice-cold fear ran through his body. *Is he teasing me? Playing a game before snapping his fingers for askaris to appear and drag me off to be tortured? But for what? I've done nothing wrong!*

'You will, of course, be well rewarded for your work,' Tippu added, breaking into his thoughts.

'You are generous, *effendi*,' Khalil murmured. 'May Allah bless you.' Relief flooded through him. *Tippu wouldn't speak in such a friendly way if the mission wasn't genuine. Perhaps a special voyage is involved. The sultan may be planning a visit to Musqat and wishes to travel on* Salwa *on her next voyage!* Dismissing his earlier concerns, he sat forward, anxious to hear the details.

'In the strictest confidence, Captain, I can tell you his highness has recently become aware of a hitherto unknown valley, situated deep in the interior of the mainland.' Tippu spoke gravely, his voice was quiet yet most commanding. 'The inhabitants of this valley are tall and handsome and very dark-skinned. As black as a moonless night, in fact.' The ghost of a smile played about his lips, his eyes glittered strangely. 'His highness is of the opinion they descend from the union of King Solomon and the Queen of Sheba,' he added softly.

Khalil gaped at the chief minister. *Descended from Solomon and Sheba! That's impossible. Surely the sultan can't believe that. Everyone knows of the couple's legendary meeting, 3000 years ago, when they were the world's two greatest rulers, but the story's long been recognized as nothing more than a colourful myth.* He was about to say so but changed his mind when he saw Tippu was still looking at him in that unnerving way. It would be dangerous to contradict him so he raked his mind for an alternative comment.

'They must have come down from the north,' he said finally. 'From Ethiopia.' *It's not an unreasonable assumption. Ethiopians are usually tall and black, and say they are descended from Prince Menelik, the natural son of Solomon and Sheba. If the people living in this valley have Ethiopian links, they may well claim a royal connection.*

'Whatever the origins of its inhabitants,' Tippu went on, ignoring this clever response, 'the sultan wishes to take possession of the valley. He plans to extend his rule across Africa and this will be a stepping-stone in achieving this. You, Captain Khalil, have been awarded the great honour of leading the expedition to seize the valley in the name of his highness.' Khalil struggled to remain calm in the face of such devastating news and he had to force himself to look Tippu straight in the eye.

'Me, *effendi*?' he queried. 'Take command of a land expedition? Me? I cannot accept such a responsibility. I do not have the necessary experience. There must be some mistake.'

Tippu smiled. 'There is no mistake, Captain,' he said quietly. 'His highness has ordered command of the expedition be put in the hands of an outstanding leader. A man of strength, of resolution and courage. Someone capable of taking decisions on the spot, of seizing every advantage presented to him. A man who can travel with confidence across unknown territory. You are a master mariner, a renowned navigator and suitable in every respect. It was I who personally recommended you to the sultan.'

'*Effendi*, please! I have spent the last eight months away from home. My wives were without me all that time. One of them bore me a son during my absence and I saw him for the very first time only last night when I arrived back from Musqat. This mission would mean yet another immediate and lengthy absence. You ask the impossible of me.'

Tippu shook his head. 'The sultan has agreed your appointment. I cannot now go to him and say, "Your Highness, Captain Khalil refuses to undertake command of the expedition to the valley. He prefers to stay at home with his wives and children." That is plainly impossible. You must undertake this mission. You have no alternative.'

'But, *effendi*, I am a sailor, not a soldier! I know nothing of commanding men on land. I have no experience in organizing such an enterprise.'

Tippu ignored his protest. 'His highness also orders you to bring him fifty of the most attractive young women from the valley.'

The sultan must be mad. No sane person could devise such a scheme. Or I'm dreaming! Perhaps in a few minutes I'll wake with Haleema asleep beside me. He heard himself say, 'Effendi, I have never worked in the slave trade. My conscience does not let me. I know nothing of guarding or feeding captives on a long march. There are many local men far better qualified than myself for such work.'

'Slave trade, Captain?' Tippu shook his head. 'I made no mention of that. On the contrary, the valley women will welcome the honour of serving his highness. And your idea of the mission being carried out by a common slaver is preposterous. This is a matter of the greatest secrecy. There is plenty of expert advice available on every aspect of your appointment; I shall ensure you receive it. Did not our Prophet Muhammad, May Peace Be Upon Him, tell us experience is the best teacher?'

'But, *effendi*, my wives, my new son, my other children....'

'Your objections are pointless.' Tippu's voice was suddenly harsh, his smile sinister. 'His highness has confirmed your appointment. There is no possibility of it being revoked. You will undertake this mission and that is an end to this discussion. With regard to your family, I shall arrange for them to be properly looked after during your absence. And I repeat, Captain, you will be well rewarded.'

Ignoring Tippu's obvious irritation, Khalil courageously persisted with his protest. 'Excuse me, *effendi*, but, with the greatest respect, money cannot recompense me for another long absence so soon after my return. Also, I have responsibilities to my employers. They are expecting me to command a schooner on a trading voyage to India in a month's time.'

'There are other captains, Captain,' Tippu said, in a voice heavy with sarcasm. 'And the Wafulu brothers are wealthy. They will not go out of business simply because you are temporarily unavailable to take a cargo of stinking rhinoceros hides to Bombay. The situation will be explained to them. The mate Raschid will command the schooner *Bahira* on her Indian voyage. And he will sail *Salwa* to Musqat if you have not returned by the time the monsoon changes. But have no fear, I guarantee your job is safe. Provided, of course, that you satisfactorily complete this mission for his highness.'

Khalil felt his skin crawl. *Allah! They say Tippu knows everything, and this is confirmation. His tentacles even reach down to the details of the Wafulu brothers' business. He knows the names of their ships, of forthcoming cargoes, even that Raschid is Salwa's mate! An army of agents are said to feed him a continuous stream of information. It must include details of people's lives, their most intimate secrets and trivial misdemeanours. And the threat in his last sentence is plain and brutal. Carry out this mission or never command another ship.*

Khalil sat rigid as the earlier joy of his homecoming crumbled. He would have to tell Haleema and Umma and the two Jewels he was leaving again, all too soon. Explain that the month they had been eagerly anticipating having him at home was about to be snatched from them.

'There are several other matters requiring your attention,' Tippu went on calmly. 'Firstly, you will ensure the women you bring back are not molested by the *askaris* in the course of the return march.'

'*Effendi*, I must protest! How can I prevent—'

'No arguments, Captain! That is an order!' Tippu hissed. He banged his fist on the table and glowered through narrowed eyes. Then his smile returned and he continued speaking in his normal, quiet voice. 'Secondly, you will make a comprehensive chart of your route to the valley. It is a new part of his highness's realm and he naturally wishes to know its exact location. You will be given a small map to guide you but it contains insufficient detail. Your chart will rectify this omission. It is a simple task for a skilled navigator like yourself.'

'Yes, *effendi*,' Khalil mumbled. Tippu continued to fix him with that disconcerting look, boring into his very soul. Khalil shifted uneasily in his chair and wondered what else would be demanded of him.

'There is one final matter requiring your attention, Captain. You may regard it as a personal favour to myself.' Tippu smiled agreeably and nodded across the table in a friendly fashion. 'I own a small business exporting ivory. I confess it is a favourite hobby of mine. Elephants are plentiful on the mainland so you will bring me forty tusks of the finest quality.'

Arab traders, heading inland in search of slaves, butchered herds of elephants, leaving their carcasses to rot out on the savannah. Months later, on the return march, the newly captured slaves were made to drag the tusks out of the stinking remains and carry them back to the coast.

Khalil gathered himself for another, undoubtedly futile, protest. 'Effendi, I know even less about killing elephants than I do about capturing slaves.'

'Advice on the subject is readily available,' Tippu said smoothly. 'Be grateful for the invention of the modern musket. In the old days tuskers had to be shot with poisoned arrows and trailed for days until they died.'

It was time to make one final, heroic plea. 'Effendi, I thank you most sincerely for the honour of recommending me to his highness. But with the deepest respect, I am totally unsuited to command this mission. I know in my heart I shall fail. Please, in the name of Allah, I implore you to find someone else for the task.'

Tippu shook his head. 'You will not fail, Captain,' he said coldly. 'On the contrary, you possess every quality necessary to ensure your complete success. You are brave, resourceful and a proven leader of men. You will receive the best possible advice, your team will consist of highly trained and experienced askaris, the cream of the sultan's personal bodyguard. They will be armed with new weapons and equipment of the very best quality. I have made you aware of the importance of this mission to his highness. I have also explained it cannot be entrusted to a common slaver since it must be carried out with the utmost secrecy and discretion. You will go, Captain. You have no choice. Especially now you are aware of the facts.'

Tippu spoke this final sentence slowly and quietly. The consequences of further objection were unstated, but terrifyingly apparent. Go, or suffer. After a pause, he spread his hands and murmured, in a voice like a silken caress, 'Captain, what is it you wish for most in this world? If I were to offer you anything, anything at all, for what would you ask? Do not be reticent, or afraid. Tell me.'

A long silence followed during which Khalil felt the minister's black eyes fixed steadily on him. *All I ask for is your acceptance that in selecting me you have made a small error of judgement, easily rectified by appointing someone more suitable. But it would be a pointless request. He has made sure I know too many secrets ever to be reprieved....*

It was then that Allah came to Khalil's aid. It was as if he had been locked in a dark room, surrounded by unseen horrors, when mercifully a door had swung open, allowing light to flood in and show a means of escape. Of a sort. He could achieve a great ambition and, simultaneously, cushion the shock to the family when he broke the news that he was having to leave them again so soon. But the situation needed very careful handling, he must mind his words. He cleared his throat, sat up and met Tippu's eye.

'You will not be displeased at my request, *effendi*?' he asked politely.

'I have said you are free to speak, Captain. I shall take no offence, whatever you ask of me.'

'I would like to own all of this, *effendi*.'

Khalil swept his arm in a dramatic arc, embracing in a single sweep the courtyard and the villa, the jacaranda and the fountain. If Tippu was surprised he gave no sign. He simply spread his hands and shook his head sorrowfully, assuming the attitude of a man beaten fairly and squarely in argument.

'You strike a hard bargain, Captain,' he said mournfully. 'I no longer live here, but it continues to serve as my official headquarters. It is conveniently sited to the sultan's palace and the port, the two places where my principal responsibilities lie. But, as is well known, I am a man of my word. If your price for leading the expedition to success is ownership of these premises, then they are yours.'

Khalil struggled to contain his excitement. 'Thank you, *effendi*,' he replied, as solemnly as he could in the thrill of his unexpected success. 'This will go some way to compensating my wives and children for my premature departure and extended absence. I have made you aware of my limitations, but I shall do my best not to disappoint you.'

'I would not have recommended you had I thought there was even the remotest possibility of failure, Captain. His highness would be most displeased were I to choose someone who ultimately proved inadequate. And as far as this villa is concerned, I am confident Haleema and your three little Jewels will be delighted with your choice.'

Khalil noted the chief minister's information was, for once, wrong. He had only two Jewels, Haboosh and Khadija. Umma was not one of them, she was his second wife. That Tippu's spies were not infallible was a fact he found oddly cheering.

'I shall instruct my lawyer to arrange the transfer of ownership of the villa to you,' Tippu went on. 'But you must leave for the mainland without delay. And remember your orders: seize the valley at all costs. Bring fifty of the young women back to Zanzibar for his highness, taking special care of them at all times. Make a detailed map of your route inland from the coast. And bring me forty tusks of the highest quality.'

'Yes, *effendi*.'

Khalil was only half listening, the fears and trepidations that had filled his mind only minutes before were swept away by the excitement of his unforeseen victory. He could not resist looking round the courtyard. *This is all mine. The house of my dreams! By appearing reluctant initially, I have wrung it from Tippu's hands. What a marvellous place for the family. Haleema will be thrilled. Allah is watching over me, and I'll pray to Him daily to continue to do so throughout the expedition.*

'Go and see Slave Master Abdul tomorrow,' Tippu was saying. 'He has the small map showing roughly where the valley lies. No one must be told of it. Abdul is already recruiting a team of African *askaris* from the sultan's army and gathering the equipment and supplies needed. He will also give you any advice you require and will arrange for the proper welfare of your family during your absence.'

'Thank you, *effendi*.'

'One final thing, Captain. His highness wishes to send a selection of the valley women to the prince, his royal brother in Musqat. He has ordered that they sail immediately the monsoon changes to the south. Therefore you will return, with the various requirements of the mission totally fulfilled, no later than four months from today. This is an important condition of your mission. See that you comply with it.'

'Return within four months. I understand, *effendi*.'

The significance of the order slipped past him as some words in the Holy Qur'an came to mind: *He who does good for girls will find it as a curtain, shielding him from the fires of hell.*

'*Effendi*, there is a small favour I would beg of you,' he said suddenly. 'On my way to the harbour this morning I saw a young slave girl in a procession.' He gave a dismissive shrug. 'I have no use for her myself, but I wonder if there is a place for her in your household?'

Tippu smiled. 'If she is suitable I shall take her into my harem. If not she can work in the kitchens. Have her delivered to my steward.'

'Thank you, *effendi*.'

'May the blessings of Allah be with you on your journey, Captain Khalil.' In a final act of hypocrisy Tippu added, 'I shall remember you in my prayers.'

Chapter Three

'So you see, my dears,' Khalil said in conclusion, 'All I have to do is round up some unarmed natives and shoot a few elephants.'

His wives sat opposite, side by side on a long couch, facing him across the magnificent red and blue Turkish carpet he had brought from Musqat on a previous voyage. He had decided there was no point in telling them the whole story; in particular he had not mentioned the captives would be female.

The senior of his four wives, Haleema, was a handsome, passionate woman of forty. She was the mother of his four sons, all of whom had followed in his footsteps to become sailors and were presently at sea. Haleema was a true Arabian beauty with lovely eyes, a full figure and a flawless skin the colour of golden honey. Their formally arranged marriage of twenty years had been happy despite Khalil's frequent lengthy absences. It was a good match as his parents were comfortably off but socially inferior whilst hers were well connected although not wealthy. Only occasionally, at times of great stress, was Haleema prone to declare she had married below herself. As senior wife naturally she was the first to respond to his news.

'Why must you become involved in such a mission?' she demanded, immediately capturing the high ground of the discussion. 'You have been a sailor all your working life. Capturing slaves is for slavers.'

'It's a special assignment, my dear,' Khalil replied patiently. 'There is no one else Tippu feels he can trust.'

'Bah! You mean he can't find anyone else to do his dirty work.'

'The sultan himself chose me. On Tippu's recommendation.'

'And you say he's going to hand over this lovely villa you've been telling us about? For a few slaves and some tusks? There's something very odd about this whole thing in my opinion.' She folded her arms and sat back, scowling. The prospect of moving into a larger house had failed to impress her as much as Khalil had hoped.

Umma, his second wife and mother of his twin daughters, was different to Haleema in every way. She was small and dainty, with delicate oriental features. She had been privately educated in India where her mother was distantly related to a maharajah. She was artistic, and discussed poetry and music at length with Khalil, subjects dear to his heart although he knew much less about them than Umma. She was also an excellent chess player and during his last spell at home had beaten him in four successive games. The intimacy of these activities caused Haleema much irritation since her sole interests were looking after the children and management of the household.

'You must have been put under a great deal of pressure to accept this appointment,' Umma said quietly. 'Bringing people back from the valley means you will have to take them captive, surely? I cannot imagine they'll come willingly. And we all know how much you abhor slavery!'

It was exactly the perceptive sort of remark he expected from Umma. She was truly a pearl among women and invariably a solace at times of trouble. 'I'm going to see Abdul the slave master tomorrow morning,' he told her. 'I should get a clearer idea from him of exactly what is involved.'

He smiled, knowing she would have noted he had avoided giving a direct answer but would not press the subject with the others present.

The first of his two Jewels, and third wife, was Haboosh. Plump and jolly, still bemused at having become a mother, she sat nursing baby Ali on her knee. 'Can my little one have his own room in the new house when he gets bigger?' she asked, kissing his small dark head.

'Yes,' Khalil said confidently. 'There's a lovely room for everyone.'

He knew the villa wasn't big enough to accommodate separately all four wives and even the present number of children but he hoped, when the time came, this assurance would be forgotten in the excitement of moving.

'When will you be leaving us?'

It was Khadija, his second Jewel. She was only sixteen, impish and pert, the youngest of the four wives. She was the only one of the four yet to have a child, an omission Khalil hoped to begin to amend before he left.

'In a week or so, Khadija. The sooner I go, the sooner I shall return.'

He tried to convey his longing but, with Haleema in a truculent pose on one side of her and Ali now noisily suckling on the other, it was impossible.

All four wives having made their comments, Haleema clicked her tongue, a sure sign of irritation. 'This is all so typical of you, Khalil,' she snapped, with surprising vehemence. 'Home for a few days then away again. You'll arrive back just as the monsoon's turning. Then you'll be off to Musqat for another eight months. We'll hardly see you for well over a year. That's what you're really telling us, isn't it?' She held up her arms in supplication. 'Allah, why did I have to marry a sailor?' she exclaimed. 'My parents must have been quite mad to agree to it.'

Khalil sat looking across at her helplessly. He loved her so much but there were times when her prickly temper, and a stubborn refusal to accept that she could ever be wrong, made him yearn for the peace and solitude of *Salwa* and the sea. An instruction in the Holy Qur'an came to mind: *"Do not slap your wife; admonish her with kindness"*.

'Think of the new house, my dear,' he said soothingly. 'The fish pond and the fountain. All those lovely rooms, each with its own balcony. I know you'll adore it. You all will.'

He beamed across at them genially. *They are all so beautiful, each in her own special way. It's impossible to decide which I love most. I'm glad it will be a while before I have to say goodbye.*

Next morning Khalil walked down to the slave market. The two *askaris* lounging in the narrow band of shade beside the outer wall reluctantly got to their feet as he approached. 'I have business with the slave master,' he announced curtly. 'Take me to him at once.'

One of the men shouldered his musket, unlocked the heavy wooden door and pushed it open. Although Khalil had lived in

Zanzibar all his life it was the first time he had ever set foot inside the slave market. It was a grim, gloomy place, feared and shunned by all but those involved in the trade. The guard led the way into an open yard, past the infamous stone dais piled high with iron shackles and chains. It was here that slaves were paraded before auction and potential buyers were allowed to examine females, often crudely, in full view of the assembled spectators.

On the fouled, sun-baked earthen surface of the yard fifty or more women captives squatted or lay. Khalil guessed they were newly arrived from the interior and still recovering from their long march. All were pitifully thin, their ribs stood out like rows of hoops. Some had malnourished infants clawing at their flat, exhausted breasts whilst a pathetic group of emaciated older children, pot-bellied and with arms and legs like brown sticks, played in the dust. Empty food bowls, swarming with flies, lay scattered about. An open barrel of slimy green water stood under a couple of palm trees; their withered fronds offered the only shade against the sun, now directly overhead and beating down with blistering intensity.

Against the high stone walls of the yard three iron cages were crowded with naked African males. Khalil felt rather than saw their eyes fixed on him, watching in sullen silence through the rusting bars as he followed the guard across the yard. He felt deeply ashamed to be in such a terrible place where misery seeped from every stone.

Abdul, slave master to his highness, had an office in one corner of the yard. In contrast to the grim conditions outside it was clean and bright; the window faced north towards low green hills. Inside the rough stone walls had been freshly lime-washed but the stink of humanity pervaded every corner. A gaudy floor rug added an incongruous splash of colour.

Abdul was tall and lean. With his cruel face, piercing close-set eyes and large hooked nose he resembled a vulture. Years before, during a raid on a village in the mainland interior to capture slaves, an African tribesman desperately defending his family with a *panga* had chopped off Abdul's left arm above the elbow. Thanks to the ministrations of the village witchdoctor – extended incantations over the spilled intestines of a sacrificial goat and daily applications of fresh rhino-dung poultices – Abdul had survived the long return march to the coast. His empty sleeve was pinned across his chest, to Arab eyes the visible sign of an old and highly honourable wound.

He was flamboyant in nature and in dress. His blue *kanzu* was embroidered with the sultan's green and gold palm-tree emblem. On his remaining wrist he wore a gold bracelet, heavy rings adorned each of his four fingers. He was a lover of order and method. On appointment as official slave master three years previously he had set about introducing a proper system of book-keeping to replace the chaotic arrangement left by his predecessor. Leather-bound ledgers with pages ruled in lines and columns were ordered from India. The entries, written in his beautiful Arabic script, recorded all slave purchases including the date, name of the new owner, price paid and amount of tax collected on behalf of the sultan. The accounts were correct in every detail and accurate to the last thaler. Abdul's concern for the care of his ledgers far exceeded that for the welfare of the slaves in his charge. They were transient, arriving in large numbers and leaving soon afterwards but the ledgers were testaments to his organizing skills and wonderful penmanship. His life had been spent in the slave trade; no form of brutality or barbarism, no act of inhumanity or degradation was unknown to him.

He and Khalil greeted each other with a brief embrace and exchange of formal kisses. They were distantly related, their cousins had married the previous year, but they had little else in common. They met at the mosque occasionally and at family gatherings. Haleema had always hated him, and his deep involvement in slavery was a barrier to a close relationship with Khalil. Sitting on opposite sides of the plain table that served as Abdul's desk they exchanged items of family news; Khalil told him of the birth of Ali.

'This isn't a social call, Abdul,' he said without warmth when their small talk was exhausted. 'You know I've been appointed leader of the expedition to the interior. Tippu told me you are organizing the soldiers and supplies and will give me all the advice I need.'

'Yes, and I'm happy to do all that I can.' In spite of Khalil's less than friendly tone, Abdul smiled and nodded amiably. 'To be honest, I'm envious. I'd love to be going off on a really worthwhile job like you, instead of sitting in this rotten hole.'

'I can't understand why Tippu has chosen me,' Khalil told him. 'You're the best man for the job surely, with your knowledge and vast experience. I'm a simple sailor, more at home at sea than on land.'

Abdul shook his head. 'Ask yourself, Khalil, what use would I be in the bush? A man with only one hand?'

His empty sleeve suddenly rose and waved in the air; Khalil jerked back in surprise, he had forgotten Abdul could still move the stump of his mutilated arm. 'I'd be pure decoration. Like nipples on a bull camel.'

'But I'm not qualified for the job in any way,' Khalil insisted. 'Although I tried to refuse, Tippu wouldn't hear of it.'

Abdul nodded sympathetically. 'I understand your concern, Khalil. But the chief minister is knowledgeable in these matters and can judge a man well. If he thinks you are capable then you will succeed.'

'He has greater confidence in my abilities than I do myself,' Khalil said drily. 'All he told me is that a valley deep in the interior, is occupied by a handsome tribe who may be descended from the Queen of Sheba. I find that hard to believe. He said you have a map showing its approximate location. I have to find the valley and take possession of it in the name of his highness. I have to bring fifty of the women back here to join his harem. I presume they won't volunteer to come. And make sure the guards don't interfere with them on the journey. Twenty or more elephants have to be shot for ivory for Tippu. And I'm ordered to make an accurate map of the route.'

Abdul leaned across the table in a conspiratorial manner and began speaking in a half-whisper. 'There's even more to it than that, Khalil. Tippu told you his highness sees the valley as a stepping stone to conquering the whole of Africa. That's something I doubt he'll ever achieve. But one thing is certain: this valley will become a marvellous new centre for the slave trade.' Abdul's rapacious face was suddenly alight with excitement. 'The country has been stripped bare of slaves for hundreds of miles inland. March for days and you'll see nothing but burnt and abandoned villages. But, beyond this new valley, are vast areas never raided before. There are slaves living there in their thousands, just waiting to be marched back to the coast.'

Khalil stared in disbelief. 'Tippu said I was to bring back women for the harem. He denied the mission had anything to do with the main trade.'

'His only interest is the taxes slaves bring,' Abdul continued. 'He wants to see them arriving in droves, as they did in the old days.'

Khalil sat back. This was a new and even more revolting aspect of the mission. *I smothered my objection to slavery to accommodate the women demanded by the sultan. I even had a faint hope a few may feel honoured to serve him. But seizing the valley to become a means of capturing thousands more slaves is not what I agreed to.*

'It's an enormous responsibility you've been given, Khalil,' Abdul went on. 'And you've got a long journey ahead of you. A thousand miles there and back. It will take you all of eight months, even more.'

'Eight months?' Khalil gasped. 'Tippu told me to be back in four. The sultan wants some of the women sent to the prince in Musqat as soon as the monsoon changes.'

A worried look spread across Abdul's vulturish face. 'Four months?' he echoed, shaking his head. 'It'll take three months to reach the Mutumwa river. And no one knows how far the valley is beyond that. You've got to find and capture it, then bring captives back. Four months? I'd say eight, or more likely nine. Tippu's up to his old tricks again.'

Khalil stared at him. 'Old tricks? What do you mean?'

Abdul shuffled awkwardly, embarrassed at having let slip a secret. 'He enjoys giving orders that are impossible to carry out,' he muttered. 'Then he punishes the man responsible for failing.'

'He promised me the villa by the harbour when I return.'

'His office? He'll never give that up, my friend. The loss of that will be your punishment for not returning inside four months.'

Khalil spread his hands in despair. 'But I've promised my wives they can move in when I come home!'

Abdul shrugged. 'When you get back, assuming you do, they'll be so relieved to see you that not moving won't matter to them in the least.'

'But he gave me his word, Abdul.' Khalil said angrily. 'I made it plain I was reluctant to take the job and he asked what I wanted most in the world. I've always liked that villa and thought it would help to soften the blow to the family at leaving them again so soon. If he's not prepared to keep his promise I'll refuse to carry out the mission. He'll have to find someone else to do it.'

Abdul face became a stony mask as he stared across the table. After a long silence he said, in a voice that was hushed yet threatening, 'Are you really so stupid, Khalil? So innocent that you can't recognize the guile in Tippu's words? You have no alternative but to go.' The dark, cold eyes were unwavering. 'If you refuse, Tippu will have you killed. But let me tell you what will happen before that. Your four lovely wives will be dragged down to the prison. You'll be forced to watch each of them raped, again and again and again, by the bully boys. Can you hear their screams? See their faces? Listen to their curses? They'll damn you to Hell for all eternity.'

A sudden chest pain almost stopped Khalil breathing but Abdul ignored his obvious distress and continued in his soft voice. 'You have a new son. Ali, I think you said? You'll see him picked up by the heels and his little head smashed against the slimy wall of your cell. Can you, a man of honour and principle, allow such things to happen? Bear to watch those you love most dearly in the whole world being subjected to such horrors? All for the sake of some half-witted natives and a few dumb elephants? I think not. If you don't bring women back for the sultan, and ivory for Tippu, there are plenty of others more than willing to do so. They'll be sent to the valley to fulfil the orders you refused so the sufferings of your family, and the unspeakable death you yourself will finally suffer, will all have been in vain.'

Abdul reached out, caught a passing fly in his one hand and slapped it onto the table. He peered down at the squashed remains for a few moments then, raising his head, again fixed his cold eyes on Khalil's face. 'You'll pray a thousand times for such instant oblivion, my friend.'

Afterwards Khalil wondered how long he had sat with Abdul's unblinking eyes on his face. It may have been minutes, it seemed as long as an hour.

Eventually the slave master said softly, 'Go home, Khalil. Enjoy your wives in the last few days before you leave. I'll write notes to explain all you need to know. I'll send word when everything is ready.'

Khalil pressed his hands on the table and pushed himself upright. He lurched and almost fell as he got to his feet.

'Take care, my friend,' Abdul said, holding out a steadying hand. 'Tippu has told me to call on your family every week whilst you are away. They'll be safe and want for nothing. Trust me.'

Khalil nodded and stumbled out into the blazing sun and overpowering stink of the slave market yard. *Abdul, the foulest of men, is to be the protector of Haleema and Umma and the Jewels during my absence!* The horror of the thought was almost immediately eclipsed by another, even more terrible. *What will become of them if I don't come back...?*

He had no recollection of walking home. Umma came running as he stepped wearily through the outer door into the courtyard.

'Thank God you've come,' she gasped. 'Haleema is very ill.'

He thrust her roughly aside and rushed into the house. The Jewels were standing in the hall, clutching each other and sobbing. 'Where is she?' he shouted at their tear-stained faces. Haboosh pointed at the ceiling and he stumbled up the staircase. As he reached the top a bearded man in a white gown came out of the bedroom. Seeing Khalil rushing towards him he spread his arms, barring his progress.

'I am Doctor Talut,' the man said gravely. 'I am sorry, there is nothing you can do. Your wife has passed into the merciful arms of Allah.'

Khalil tried to get past him but the doctor, though slight of build, was immensely strong. He wrapped his arms round Khalil and pinned him against the wall. 'Wait, please, just for a few moments,' he said gently. 'A woman is with her, doing what is necessary. Then you can see her.'

'What happened? Why has she died?'

'She had an apoplexy. I came as soon as I was called from the hospital but she died before I arrived. Nothing could have saved her. It's Allah's will that she has been taken without suffering pain herself. Sadly, it is you and your family who must now bear the agony. May I ask, Captain Khalil, did your wife suffer a great shock recently? Such a thing can bring on an apoplexy which results in sudden death.'

*

The funeral, a quiet family affair, was held next day. Four African servants, originally slaves but long since domesticated and now almost family members, carried the coffin up to the small cemetery. Khalil walked alone behind it. Umma, holding her twin daughters' hands, came next, then the Jewels with Haboosh cradling baby Ali in her arms. Haleema was laid to rest in a grave on a clifftop over-looking the bay. Khalil drew solace from knowing she would approve of this simple but dignified arrangement. She disliked the traditional public displays of emotion at funerals. So far no one outside the immediate household had been told of the tragedy.

For the rest of the day Khalil sat alone in the courtyard. First Umma, then the Jewels one by one, came to him, each in her turn desperate to alleviate his distress. But he silently waved them away. He had no words to say, no wish to see anyone. He neither drank nor ate; as night fell a servant silently placed a lantern on the table beside him. Out of the surrounding darkness only the distant sound of Ali, crying briefly as he was laid in his cot, reached him.

He awoke, very cold, after a dreamless sleep sitting in the chair, his head resting on his folded arms on the table. Dawn was just breaking; the eastern sky was tinted in exquisite shades of pink and green. He stood up, stiff and exhausted, and slowly walked across the court-yard and out of the gate. He retraced his steps of the previous day up to the cemetery. Sitting by the mound of white coral sand that was Haleema's grave he watched the sun rise out of the Indian Ocean. It was a majestic sight, one he had seen thousands of times since he first went to sea at the age of thirteen. It had never before failed to stir emotion in him but that morning he felt nothing; no grief, no sense of loss. His world had shrunk to an empty pit in a desert of worth-lessness.

A thought briefly crossed his mind. It was like the sudden whisper of wind that momentarily ruffles the surface of a calm sea to give warning of the approach of a storm. Its significance failed to seize his attention at that moment and several minutes passed before he began to wonder why the doctor had asked if Haleema had suffered a recent shock. He recalled how truculent she had been, exceptionally so, when he had broken the news of his early departure. Invariably forthright, she had nevertheless surprised him by the strength of her protest following his meeting with Tippu. He had assumed that, as a mature woman and loving wife, she was naturally distressed at the prospect of his long-awaited physical presence being taken from her again so soon. *But could the shock of being suddenly deprived of my body be sufficient to bring about her death? A bullet, or a knife, killed. But a disappointment, however great? Surely not. Haleema was a strong healthy woman who had never been ill in her life.*

It was his recollection a few moments later of the death of her elder sister Fatima which began the chain of events that followed. Several years ago she had also succumbed to an apoplexy. According to her doctor the cause had been sudden shock although her circumstances had been very different to those of Haleema. Fatima's husband had long desired a son but her first four children, produced in successive years, were daughters. Then, after a problematic fifth pregnancy and difficult labour, she gave birth to a male child. He lived only minutes and soon afterwards Fatima had a major convulsion from which she had failed to recover.

Ever since the entire family – her husband and her parents, Haleema and her two younger sisters – had held an unshakeable conviction that the shock of the baby's death killed Fatima. They were united in their belief that if he had lived she too would still be with them. They accepted without question the doctor's assurance that shock at her son's death caused her apoplexy. Khalil did not agree with this explanation but he kept his opinion to himself. It was no concern of his, Fatima was merely his sister-in-law and he had only met her once, at her wedding. He suspected her doctor, in declaring apoplexy rather than a mishandled delivery as the cause of death, had been excusing his own professional incompetence.

Fatima's death marked the beginning of a tragic period for Haleema and her sisters. A month later their elderly father had had a fatal fall; within days their mother, stricken with grief, died very suddenly. And now, Khalil thought grimly, Haleema too has gone, just as unexpectedly. Three deaths, a mother and two sisters. Perhaps it is a gruesome inheritance, a family trait passed down through the generations from mother to daughter, like beauty or an artistic talent. It may have happened in earlier generations, no one now living knew why Haleema's grandmother had died. Three deaths, each following a great shock ... As the chain of consequences came together the full horror of the thesis burst upon him. Her father's death had killed her mother. The baby's death had killed Fatima. Tippu had killed Haleema!

The thought seized Khalil's mind. *Tippu forced me to take command of the mission knowing I had just come home after a long absence. That was the cause of her death, shock at the destruction of her joy of having me with her again. She died just hours after I had condemned her to more months of unnatural widowhood. It was not something over which she could have openly grieved, or discussed with me. She would think it unseemly to describe how much she would miss my physical attentions. Instead she would prepare herself to suffer in silence yet another long loneliness.*

Tippu Tip! Khalil cursed his name. *He doesn't care about the harm he does. He tortures. He lies. He'll cheat me out of the villa. And now he has killed Haleema. He's as guilty as if I had found him crouching over her body with a bloody dagger in his hand.* Khalil strode up and down the paths between the graves, pounding his fist into his palm, hate and anger boiling in his veins. *Tippu! I'll make him pay for this terrible thing he has done to me.* The words of the Holy Qur'an screamed in his head: 'Vengeance is Allah's. A Muslim cannot punish, he must forgive'.

He turned his face upwards and extended his arms. 'It is an impossible command,' he roared at the sky. 'Damn you! I shall never forgive!'

Chapter Four

Two nights later, after supper, Khalil sat at the table in the courtyard with Umma. He had sent the Jewels to bed early. 'You are now my senior wife,' he said quietly; Umma acknowledged his words by bowing her head. 'There are things I have to tell you. Things only you must know. No one else …'

He began by giving her an almost full account of his interview with Tippu, describing his dismay on hearing what the expedition entailed and what would be the consequences of refusing to go, or failing to carry out the full requirements of the mission. Umma listened in silence, her face solemn; she kept her eyes constantly on his face. He was very much aware, painfully so, of how impossible it would have been to talk to Haleema in this way. She would have constantly interrupted, demanding to know why he hadn't said this, or told Tippu that … He could not bring himself to speak to Umma of the horrors Abdul had described – the rapes, Ali's head smashed against the wall, the unspeakable death he himself would undoubtedly suffer. These were things too terrible to repeat, and so evil he felt he would demean himself just by speaking of them to her. He merely said Abdul had warned that if he refused to go, or failed in the attempt, he could be imprisoned for years and, on release, would not be allowed to continue as a ship's master. The whole family would suffer as a result. He did not tell her about the loss of the villa.

'There is one more thing I wish you to know.' He looked at her steadily across the table and said quietly, 'Tippu killed Haleema.'

On hearing this Umma stared at him in shock, eyebrows raised, her hand over her mouth. 'Tippu?' she gasped. 'Tippu killed Haleema? How can that be, Khalil? It's impossible!'

41

'He killed her by sending me on the expedition. It was the shock of that which brought about the apoplexy from which she died.'

'Tippu could not have known that would happen.'

'If he had, would it have made any difference? He would still have ordered me to command the mission. He is guilty.'

'How can you be so sure?'

'Shock killed Haleema's sister Fatima, then her mother. You know the story, the "double tragedy" she used to call it. Now she too has gone and it's become a triple tragedy. The cause is the same. Shock. If Tippu hadn't forced me to go, she would still be alive.'

Umma sat, hands clasped in her lap, head bowed in silence. 'I find it impossible to believe Tippu can be blamed for Haleema's death,' she said eventually. 'Haleema often told us the story, it was something she could not forget. But surely Fatima died because of a haemorrhage following childbirth. Her body must have been weakened by earlier pregnancies. As for their mother, I am sure she died of old age, not shock at the death of her husband. She was over fifty and had been in poor health for years. Doctor Talut said Haleema died of apoplexy. I think he is right. You do not know it but at times she became breathless for no apparent reason. Last year she often had to sit for long periods in order to recover. Clearly she was suffering from a hidden problem but ordered myself and the Jewels never to tell you. She did not want you to worry whilst you were at sea.'

Khalil bowed his head in acknowledgement of these logical replies from Umma. But they did not change his conviction of where the blame truly lay.

'Because you are my husband,' Umma went on quietly, 'I accept you believe Tippu was responsible for Haleema's death. But, I beg of you, do not harbour resentment. If what you have told me is true then Allah will know. Tippu will receive a just punishment when he dies.'

'That is not enough, Umma. I am determined to make him suffer here on earth.'

'Forgive me, Khalil, but you are still distraught. When you say you wish to make him suffer, do you mean you wish to murder him?'

'Yes.'

Umma shook her head. 'That's not possible. To do so you would

42

have to get near him. It's almost certain he now knows of Haleema's death. If you ask for another meeting with him, he will assume you again wish to beg him to replace you as expedition leader, or postpone your departure, to take time to mourn. He will therefore refuse to see you. If you are intent on murder, and I pray you are not, you must wait until you return from the expedition and are able to get close to him. By then you may think differently.'

'I shall never change my mind,' he said. 'But you are right about the impossibility of getting close to Tippu. Very well, Umma. You are intelligent, educated, familiar with the classics. You are also an expert chess player, and see moves further ahead than I ever can. Try to imagine this is a similar sort of game. Tell me what I can do to win.'

The shadow cast by the lantern picked out the exquisite arch of Umma's brow, the perfect sweep of her chin. She spread her fingers like a delicate fan. 'This is a strange game,' she said softly. 'A husband asking a wife, who respects him beyond all measure, how he can commit murder.'

'You are my senior wife, Umma, whom I respect equally in return. I wish I could spare you this request but I have no alternative. Can you imagine me seeking advice from the Jewels? Of course not! That is why I am forced to burden you with my problem. There is no one else I can turn to.'

She placed her hand in his and he felt its warm softness, as if a little bird had nestled there. 'I will do my duty, as you ask,' she said softly. She sat silent for a few moments, her brow creased in thought.

'Very well, Khalil, I will make a suggestion although it gives me no pleasure to do so.' She paused; a cicada burred somewhere close by, all else was silent. 'The murder of Tippu is out of the question, as you have accepted. But in any case, assassination is too blunt an instrument of punishment for such a man. He is a politician and the greatest penalty you could inflict on him would be to bring down his world of power. There is no reason for you to kill, others will do that once that power is taken from him.'

Khalil's excitement rose. *She knows me so well. She's putting my exact feelings in her words! Describing them better than I could myself*!

'Such a plan will demand great cunning,' Umma went on. 'From

43

what you say, that is something Tippu himself possesses in great measure. You must better him in it.'

'With your help I will.'

'You cannot destroy him yourself, that is clear. But as chief minister he is close to a man who can.'

'The sultan!' Khalil exclaimed. 'Of course! He can do it!'

'Yes. The sultan must be given sufficient cause to dismiss him in disgrace. Strip him of his high position, reduce him to begging in the port.'

'He would not live long. There are too many like me who wish to take revenge on him.'

'Let them do as they wish. You will have had your revenge.'

'How can I bring about his downfall? Do you have you a plan?'

'Only an idea at the moment, Khalil. There is so much I do not know, many details we shall have to discuss.'

'Tell me your idea, I'll supply the details!'

Yet again Umma paused, collecting her thoughts. 'You spoke of the sultan's plan to extend his rule across Africa. He sees the valley as a first stepping stone in achieving this dream.'

'That is why I'm being sent. To take possession in his name.'

'Perhaps that is where the solution lies. Suppose you begin by doing as he has ordered. Lead the mission to the valley and take possession of it. But not for the sultan. For yourself.'

Khalil sat back and stared in amazement at his wife. 'For myself?' he echoed. 'Myself? I don't understand. What purpose would that serve?'

'You return to Zanzibar and report the valley has been taken and awaits occupation by the new ruler.'

'But I have seized the valley on my own behalf. I am the new ruler!'

Umma shook her head and smiled. 'Only temporarily, King Khalil! You make the report I have just described not to the sultan, but to the British Resident here in Zanzibar. You pass ownership of the valley to him. The valley will then become a British possession.'

Has the woman gone mad, Khalil wondered? A score of questions crowded his mind and he was still struggling to organize them in a sensible way when Umma spoke again.

'If the British assume control of the valley, it will for ever stand in the way of the sultan's grand plan to rule Africa. His dream will be over. And he will blame Tippu for sending the expedition that failed to capture it for him. The sultan will destroy him. His position, his authority, his wealth, will all be taken from him. You will have your revenge.'

Khalil shook his head. 'This is fancy, Umma. Tippu will brand me as a traitor. He'll explain to the sultan I took the valley and gave it to the British. Their combined wrath will fall on me, on you, on the rest of the family. You cannot begin to imagine the horrors that would follow.'

'I said at the beginning you must be cunning, Khalil. Neither Tippu nor the sultan will ever know who gave the valley to the British. You will make it a condition that the Resident swears not to mention your name if he wishes his government to take possession.'

Khalil sat back in amazement. Was Umma insane, or a brilliant strategist? She seemed to sense his thoughts. 'It's not an original idea,' she said, smiling. 'I may occasionally beat you at chess but I am not so clever as to think of this solution unaided. I remember reading about a Persian soldier whose army captured a great city from the Greeks. For the love of a woman, he gave it back to them.'

'I'm full of admiration, Umma. It's a wonderful plan!'

'It's not a plan, Khalil, merely an idea at present. But there are certain advantages already in place for you. First, the British are great empire builders as I learned when I was at school in Madras. They conquered our country through the East India Company and our teachers said it would not be long before they came to rule Africa in the same way. Another thing in your favour is that the British are now opposed to slavery after being one of its greatest supporters for centuries. Abdul told you the valley would become a place from which to launch slaving raids further west. The British will not want that to happen, nor wish to see the sultan building a rival empire under their very noses. These things are greatly to your advantage. The Resident will recognize that.'

'It will not be easy to meet him, Umma. Tippu's spies are every-where, and I must not be seen near the Residency. And there are a thousand other details to settle! What about the young women I am expected to bring back for the sultan? And the ivory for Tippu? What do I tell the *askaris* under my command? What if your plan doesn't work? What if they discover that I am working for the British? What if...?'

Their discussion went on long after midnight.

The following morning dawned bright and clear; the northerly monsoon ensured a brilliant sky with a scattering of white cotton-puff clouds. Khalil walked down to the mosque and offered prayers for Haleema. News of her death had spread; servants were inveterate gossips and quickly passed on news to each other and it soon reached the ears of their masters. Friends clustered around, embracing him, kissing his cheeks, offering condolences. He drew comfort from their attentions and compassion, and resisted his first inclination to hurry away before they had all spoken to him. When he finally emerged alone into the afternoon sunshine he hesitated indecisively at the bottom of the mosque steps for a few moments before turning left to walk towards the waterfront.

Anyone watching him would merely see a grieving widower, going for a solitary stroll to contemplate his tragic loss. It was partly true; having carried out his religious and social duties in the accepted form he now wished to be left to himself. But he could make use of this opportunity to take a stroll past the plain white two-storeyed building which served as the office and official residence of Lieutenant-Colonel Atkins Hamerton, the British Resident on Zanzibar. He was a well-liked man, highly respected by all who knew him. Khalil had spoken to him several times in the port. Apart from his consular duties, Colonel Hamerton made a practice of paying an informal visit to the captain of every British ship calling at Zanzibar. He spoke fluent Arabic and when down in the port always took the opportunity to stop and chat to dhow masters working on their vessels at the long quay. He showed a keen interest in their recent voyages, asking knowledgeable questions about cargoes and the current state of business. The British Government, of which he was the sole representative on the island, was now strongly opposed to slavery. Nevertheless Colonel Hamerton spoke with equal courtesy to captains he knew were involved in the shipping of captives to Arabian ports. He made a point of urging them to do what they could to ease the conditions of the wretches crammed below the decks. As a result many dhows now took on extra water and food supplies for the slaves before leaving for the Gulf, essentials which previously had often been lacking.

Khalil felt instinctively that Umma had been right. If he could speak to the Resident for only a few minutes he would appreciate the situation. He was, without doubt, a man who could be trusted and would give him a fair hearing, especially when he realized the importance of his proposal. Meeting him for such a conversation would, however, be difficult. Colonel Hamerton's visits to the port were unannounced and occurred at irregular intervals. Khalil was sure that, until he left for the mainland, he himself would be watched by Tippu's agents. His movements would be noted and reported. If he was seen at the Residency his arrest would soon follow. He would be questioned and tortured to reveal the reason for his visit. The spectre of Abdul's warning of the fate of his wives and children rose in his mind but he dismissed it. There was no risk this afternoon, he was simply out for a solitary saunter and it would appear that it was only by chance he passed the Residency.

The front door to the building stood invitingly open as he strolled past. He was strongly tempted to walk up the short path, knock and ask to see the colonel. But the presence of two boys, each in a white *kanzu* and red *fez*, larking about on a bench in front of the building, stopped him. They were two of the local messengers employed to carry the constant flow of notes passing between the Resident and officials up at the palace. It was highly probable the boys were junior members of Tippu's regiment of informers, reporting daily on the identity of all visitors to the Residency. Khalil continued past with his head low, giving the building no more than a cursory glance before walking down to the beach and wending his way slowly home. As he had suspected, meeting the colonel was not going to be easy.

The following morning he woke with the sun already high, a brilliant shaft of light streamed through a gap in the curtains. It was long after his usual time for rising but, until the period of mourning was over, no one would come to rouse him. This suited him; he wanted to be left alone. Haleema's presence lingered. Her clothes hung in the wardrobes and lay neatly folded in the drawers, her silver-backed hair brushes and combs lay where she had left them on the morning of her death, on the shelf below the large mirror. The silk sheets on which her body had lain briefly had gone, they had served as her shroud, but traces of her perfume remained in the room, suddenly apparent at moments when he least expected it. Khalil had instructed Umma that nothing in the room was to be touched until he had left with the expedition; only then could clearance begin. Haleema's clothes and other personal possession were to be taken to the mosque to be sold and the proceeds distributed to the needy. On his return there was to be nothing of hers remaining, no keepsakes or mementos. He had no need of trinkets to remind him of her; treasured recollections of their years together were locked for ever in his mind. They would suffice until they were reunited in Paradise.

He lay staring up at the ceiling, thinking over Umma's startling plan to bring down Tippu. It was essential to speak to the Resident without delay as any day now sailing orders would arrive from Abdul. But how could he speak to Colonel Hamerton without being seen and the fact reported to Tippu? Yesterday's walk had shown how difficult it was going to be. Would it be better to go to the Residency at night? The boy messengers would have finished for the day; there would certainly be guards but in the dark his identity would be less obvious. He decided to take the risk. He would go to the Residency that very night and speak to the colonel. His excitement grew as the day passed.

After supper he put on a servant's dark *kanzu*, armed himself with two pistols, ready loaded and primed. He left the house, telling no one he where he was going. Zanzibar was a dangerous place after sunset; no respectable person ventured out if it could be avoided. Gangs of wild, ownerless slaves and ruthless criminals roamed the narrow streets, raping, robbing and murdering. Every door and window was barred and close-shuttered against them. There was a perfunctory official watch, made up of pairs of *askaris* from the sultan's army, but it was a futile arrangement. On patrol the soldiers themselves engaged in thieving, often working with the very thugs they were under orders to seize.

Khalil moved silently, every sense alert for movement. There was no moon but the stars give a surprising amount of light, sufficient to illuminate open spaces and cast deep shadows. He made slow progress, watching motionless from one dark spot before slipping silently to the next. He avoided the slums, keeping to the higher inland side of town until he was able to make his way down to the southern end of the port. It was an area less frequented by thieves and cut-throats; at night the warehouses were heavily barred and patrolled by their owners' men. Dhows containing cargo were manned by their crews who would not hesitate to bundle an intruder over the side into the shark infested waters of the harbour.

The last stretch was the easiest of all. He kept in the shadow of the low waterfront embankment, walking on the fine white sand. On his left the surf washing up the beach muffled any noise he made. The Residency loomed out of the darkness; a faint light glinted through a closed shutter on the ground floor. How is the place guarded at night, he wondered? He lay flat on the embankment and peered through his telescope at the front of the house. All was silent; if there were guards they did not seem to be carrying out foot patrols. He crawled forward on his hands and knees until he reached the beginning of the path he had seen the previous afternoon. This was a critical moment. *What shall I do now? Walk boldly up to the door and knock? If there's a guard I'm certain to be challenged. Instead of walking, would it be wiser to crawl up the path then tap on the shutter to draw attention from inside? It would be less obvious, but there's a greater risk of being shot as an intruder. I'll walk. Better to be accosted than killed.*

He stood up. At precisely the same moment the dark shape of a man rounded the corner of the house and strode past the door. He propped what appeared to be a musket against the wall and sat down on the bench the messenger boys had been larking about on that morning. Khalil froze. The man was no more than twenty paces away but luckily had not yet seen him; standing in his dark *kanzu* against the background of moonless sky he was almost invisible. Cautiously he drew out the telescope and lifted it to his eye. Despite the darkness

49

he was able to pick out the details of the man quite clearly. His face was pale, with a thick moustache and bushy eyebrows; he wore a red military uniform with brass buttons ... of course! The Residency would need to be well guarded, so who better for the task than a contingent of trained British soldiers! Khalil had never seen them in town, they must live permanently in a camp in the Residency grounds. They were probably sent across from India on short spells of duty. They would be infinitely more reliable than a squad of drunken thieving *askaris*. This assessment suffered a slight correction a moment later when through his telescope he saw the soldier take a flask from his pocket and raise it to his lips.

Khalil suddenly became aware of the danger in which he had unwittingly placed himself. *Two minutes ago I was perfectly safe, lying flat, a hundred yards from the front of the house. Now I'm standing no more than twenty paces from an armed British soldier drinking on duty! Allah! What a predicament! What should I do? Step forward, hands up, calling out that I come in peace? But the soldier might panic, grab his musket and fire at me. He's been drinking, but from such a short range there's every chance he'll hit his target. The best thing I can do is retreat, and reconsider my plan. But the soldier's eyes may have become accustomed to the gloom. The slightest movement could draw his attention. How can I distract him?*

It was impossible to bend and search for a pebble to throw; the man mght see him. The only available missiles Khalil had were his telescope and two pistols. He slowly drew the smaller weapon from his belt, held it by the barrel and threw it underhand to the right of the guard. Instantly there was a bright flash and a bang as the pistol went off. Khalil turned and fled as, from behind, came a sudden confusion of whistles and shouts. He reached the embankment, leapt over and lay panting and cursing in the sand. In his haste he had stupidly left the pistol cocked so on hitting the ground it had gone off. Instead of surreptitiously gaining entrance to the Residency, introducing himself and apologizing to Colonel Hamerton for the intrusion, he could well have shot a British soldier dead.

Lying flat, his telescope to his eye, he watched men with muskets and lanterns combing the Residency grounds. The clamour of their voices reached him. Soon they would extend their search and he would be discovered. The door of the Residency suddenly opened and a figure in a white European suit emerged, holding up a lantern. It could only be Colonel Hamerton, come to investigate the cause of the disturbance. Here was an opportunity not to be missed; there was a risk of being shot on sight but in this desperate situation it was a danger to be faced.

Quickly, Khalil buried his remaining pistol in the soft sand; he must not be caught approaching the Residency carrying a weapon whilst a search was in progress for an armed man. Climbing the embankment he held his hands above his head and boldly advanced, calling '*Salaam.*'

In the hubbub in front of the Residency his presence went unnoticed at first and he had almost reached the path before a shouted 'Halt!' rang out and men came running towards him.

'*Salaam,*' he called loudly in return. '*Salaam.* I am a dhow captain and wish to speak to the Resident.'

He spoke in Arabic as his knowledge of English was restricted to a few basic phrases and the main navigational terms. Hopefully the Resident would hear him above the shouting. His arms were roughly grabbed by two red-coated soldiers and a pistol muzzle jabbed against his head. Stumbling between the men he was roughly dragged up the path and thrust in front of Colonel Hamerton.

'*Assalam-o-alaikum*, Your Excellency,' he panted.' I am Khalil, master of the dhow *Salwa*. We have spoken together in the port several times.'

'Indeed? May I ask why you have chosen to come here at night and fire a shot at one of my guards?'

The Resident's Arabic was clipped, precise and fluent, typical of that spoken by Cambridge-taught Englishmen.

'I assure you it was an accident, Excellency,' Khalil replied. 'You have my abject apologies. I had no intention of shooting your soldier. My pistol exploded unexpectedly. I wish to speak to you in strict confidence.'

The Resident stared at him hard. 'As a Zanzibarian you must address yourself to the chief minister, not to me.'

Khalil knew that arguing his case on the doorstep whilst

surrounded by British soldiers was a dangerous situation. Local servants may appear at any moment, he could be recognized and his presence reported.

'Please, Your Excellency, let me speak to you alone, for a few minutes only. I cannot risk being seen here. My life is at stake.'

Colonel Hamerton seemed undecided for a moment; then his attitude relaxed and he spoke rapidly in English to the soldiers.

'Very well, Captain,' he said, not unkindly, turning to Khalil. 'You may enter. But if I decide you are wasting my time, you will be immediately turned over to the *askaris* of the night watch.'

A few minutes later they were sitting opposite each other in the Residency office across a handsome desk. The red leather chairs were deep and the carpet thick and luxurious; graceful brass oil lamps with tall green glass chimneys stood on each corner of the desk giving a pleasant glow. Khalil, dirty and dishevelled in a servant's mud-streaked *kanzu*, felt ill at ease in such elegant surroundings. By contrast Colonel Hamerton, immaculate in a white linen suit, ruffed shirt, scarlet cummerbund and bow-tie, was relaxed and poised.

'There is much I wish to say, Your Excellency,' Khalil said.

'Summarize the main points in three sentences. If what you say seems of interest I shall allow you more time. If not, you'll be thrown out.'

Khalil took a deep breath and with only a moment's thought launched into his answer. 'A valley has been discovered deep in the interior. I am being sent to capture it for the sultan. I can deliver the valley to you instead of him. It could be the beginning of the British African Empire.'

A mosquito whined at his ear, otherwise the world was silent. Three sentences, the colonel had said; Khalil surprised himself in managing to tell the story in four. The Resident's expression did not change, he kept his eyes fixed on Khalil's face.

'You are at greater risk than I imagined, Captain,' he said coldly. 'You come to the Residency, where you have no right to be, and put forward a scheme which, merely by describing it to me, makes you a traitor to your country. If his highness hears of it you will suffer a most unpleasant death.'

'I am aware of that, Your Excellency. But as a true Muslim I am opposed to slavery. My faith is more important to me than my country. Or my loyalty to the sultan.'

'These are noble sentiments, Captain, but I find it difficult to believe they describe your sole interest in this matter.'

Khalil hesitated before replying; the Resident would not want to hear about his private vendetta against Tippu. 'I thought you would wish to know of the sultan's plans, Your Excellency. The slave master told me the valley will become a new centre for the slave trade. I have no wish to play a part in such a thing. With respect, it is common knowledge the British hope to rule Africa as they do India. Since your government is now opposed to slavery you will not wish to see new areas subjected to large raiding parties. That is why I have come to you.'

'Really?' The Resident's tone was dry and cynical. Khalil's heart sank. 'I cannot believe that is your only reason for coming to see me. To be frank, I wish to know what you hope to gain. Is it money? Perhaps an intercession by me on your behalf in a dispute?'

Khalil hesitated; Haleema's death was too recent, the pain too great, to describe to a stranger. 'The chief minister has forced me to undertake the mission, Excellency. He made it plain that my wives and children, one of them an infant only a few weeks old, are under threat of torture and death if I do not obey. Such a man deserves to die. As a Muslim it is against God's law for me to kill him. But if this mission fails, and the responsibility for that can be shown to rest on Chief Minister Tippu, the sultan will strip him of his power. That is my hope.'

Perhaps the Resident guessed there was a deeper reason for him to hate Tippu but when he finally spoke he made no mention of it. 'And how do you propose to cause the failure of the mission? Before you reply, let me give you a word of warning: I shall treat whatever you say in the strictest confidence, but I promise nothing more. Do not assume that in listening to your plan I shall give it my support.'

'I understand, Excellency. In brief, I propose to lead the expedition as I have been ordered. I shall find and attack the valley, and seize it. I shall tell the local chief that he and his people are now under external rule. I shall then return to Zanzibar and inform you of the success of the mission. The matter will thereafter be out of my hands. Without mentioning my own part in the plot, you will inform the sultan the valley has become British territory, not his as he had hoped. He will be enraged, and turn on Tippu. He will blame him for the loss of his dream of expansion to the west. That is my plan, sir. May I venture to ask what you think of it?'

Khalil felt strangely detached, as if he was a third person in the room, standing in the shadows listening to himself speaking. And, sadly, he found his performance disappointing. The voice he had heard was low and flat, hesitant, the voice of a man without hope. There was no inspiration, nothing to instil confidence in the listener, nothing that said: 'I am a man who knows what needs to be done. Here is how I shall do it'.

I've failed. The colonel will turn me out. Haleema's death will go unavenged. I've destroyed the valley people instead of saving them....

The Resident sat with arms folded; it was impossible to judge his thoughts.

'I am a diplomat, Captain Khalil,' he said, after a long pause. 'And diplomats are by nature cautious animals. However I can tell you I am already aware of your coming expedition to the interior.'

Khalil could only gape. 'You know about it, Excellency? That I'm being sent to capture the valley? That I've been ordered to bring females for the sultan's harem? Kill elephants for ivory for Tippu?'

'Yes, Captain. It is in my government's interest that I know everything that occurs on this island.'

'But how can you know, Excellency? It's a state secret! I was only told of it myself a few days ago.'

Colonel Hamerton smiled, giving Khalil an impression that these remarks pleased him. 'That I cannot tell you. But little happens on Zanzibar without my knowledge. However, I confess your visit this evening has come as a complete surprise. I understood you were a most loyal and trustworthy subject of his highness. Your clumsy arrival tonight proves the contrary.'

The Resident must have spies and informers, just as Tippu has. That servant of his must be one of them. He heard Tippu putting me in command of expedition and somehow passed the news to the colonel....

Khalil cleared his throat, it felt very dry. 'What do you think of my plan, Excellency?' he asked again.

The Resident pursed his lips. 'It has merit, Captain. But it is far from complete. Let us assume you are successful and return to Zanzibar. Have you considered the endgame? The sultan will demand to know the result of the expedition. He will want to see the women you have brought for him. Tippu will be keen to inspect his ivory. What will you say to them?'

Khalil ignored the chess metaphor, the colonel may have been hinting that he knew details of his personal background. 'I've not given those things much thought, Your Excellency,' he admitted. 'Things often work themselves out in unexpected ways. I was trusting Allah to help me.'

'You must help Allah to help you. You say you wish to hand over control of the valley to me, on behalf of my government. Very well. That is a matter of great international importance. It is not merely an opportunist attack, like the boarding of your dhow by a gang of cut-throat Somali pirates. It concerns the defeat of an independent people, an act with far-reaching significance. Verbal statements are not sufficient, there must be recognition of the situation by formal treaty. To secure my government's support, you must bring back a document acknowledging the acceptance of British rule by the present chief. If I am able to present a signed statement of that nature to the sultan, I shall be in a position of strength. Without it I will be helpless to negotiate.'

'A signed statement, Excellency?' Khalil could hardly believe what he had just heard. 'The chief will most likely be a brutal tribesman, a pagan, cut off from civilization. It will be surprising if he has ever heard of paper! He will certainly not be able to write.'

'I am aware of that, Captain. I have the misfortune of seeing many slaves brought to Zanzibar from the deep interior. Almost all are indeed primitive. But from what little is known of these valley people, it seems they may have benefited from contact with more advanced tribes. Their village is reported to be well organized, they grow crops and have domesticated cattle. But, I must stress to you, whatever their condition, it is essential that you get their chief to make a mark of some sort on a document which confirms the surrender to you.'

Khalil sat silent. This was yet another problem facing him, and he still needed answers to those already in his mind. 'You spoke of questions that will be put to me on my return, Excellency. For instance, the sultan will ask questions about the valley. He will demand to see the women I was ordered to bring him. Tippu will want his ivory. How do you suggest I reply?'

'Once I have possession of the treaty, I shall act at once. I shall be able to deal, officially and legally, with whatever issues then arise. But I am afraid I cannot advise you further at this moment as there are innumerable possible outcomes. You must act as you see fit as they present themselves.'

Khalil nodded. 'You are a good man, Colonel Hamerton. Everyone says so. I have placed my life in your hands yet I feel very safe.'

The Resident shook his head. 'You are far from safe, Captain. On the contrary you are in the gravest danger. You are about to leave on a most hazardous mission into the unknown. You are planning a treasonable act, however principled the reasons behind it. If that is discovered your death will be prolonged, horrific and certain. Amongst the men you are taking with you there will almost certainly be one of Tippu's men, watching and listening to your every move. All that you do or say will be reported on your return. Trust no one, confide in no one. Be especially careful in your dealings with those whom you feel inclined to believe are least capable of treachery.'

Khalil nodded. 'It is said that every ship carries a company's man, Colonel. I know how to watch my tongue.'

'Remember, if you are arrested at any time, I shall deny all knowledge of your visit this evening. Nor shall I be able to intervene on your behalf.'

'I understand.'

'I wish you God speed, Khalil. I shall hear of your return to Zanzibar within hours of your arrival. There will be no need for you to come to the Residency again. I shall send someone trustworthy to you. His password shall be "Boleyn" which is the name of a former Queen of England. Give him the signed treaty and wait until you hear further from me.'

The Resident rang a bell and a British soldier entered. 'Corporal, this gentleman is to be safely escorted under cover away from the

Residency. Under no circumstances is anyone from outside to be told he was here.'

Khalil reached home following his outward route in reverse, again slipping from shadow to shadow to avoid being seen. Umma was waiting for him in the courtyard. 'I saw you leaving and guessed you were going to see the colonel. Were you successful?'

He told her the events of the evening. When he described the pistol discharging and the scare it created she laughed and clapped her hands.

'What did he think of the plan?' she asked.

'That it had merit, but he didn't commit himself. There was nothing he could do except give me advice. He insists I bring back a document signed by the chief surrendering the valley. And he made arrangements for this treaty to be collected from me when I get back. He also warned me I am in danger and to beware of a Tippu spy who would watch my every move.'

Umma nodded. 'He's no fool, the colonel. Why not name your plan after him? It may bring you luck.'

'The Hamerton Plan. It sounds important!'

Umma nodded. 'It's very important, Khalil. Your life depends on it. And on the colonel. And Allah.'

'I am not sure that I can rely on Him, Umma. Why did He allow Haleema to die? Why am I being forced to go on this expedition which is against all I believe? Would a fair and just God allow such situations?'

'Only when it is over, and we look back, shall we know.'

She sat, her eyes fixed on him. *What a wonderful wife she is. With her beside me there is nothing I cannot do. No task is beyond me.*

She placed her hand over his. 'My dearest,' she said softly, 'it's only a short time since you lost Haleema, but I wondered, as you are going away from us for months, whether ...'

'Not yet, Umma,' he said softly. 'Not yet. But I promise, before I leave ...' He reached out and gently stroked her face.

Chapter Five

As the time for Khalil's departure grew near, Umma and the Jewels devoted their entire days to pampering him. It was not cloying concern, he suspected Umma sensed his varying moods, recognizing when he needed company or wished to be left alone, and had instructed Haboosh and Khadija accordingly.

He was, therefore, in a relaxed, almost happy, condition one morning, sitting in the courtyard with baby Ali on his knee, when the outer door burst open and Abdul stepped across the threshold. Khalil's first reaction was dismay at the interruption, swiftly followed by a sense of great unease. *Has my visit to the Residency been discovered? Has Abdul come to question me about my visit, or perhaps to warn me of impending arrest?* It was an immense relief when the slave master came towards him, arms held wide.

'Khalil, my dear old friend!' he cried. 'I've come by sedan chair. Tell your servant to give water to the men who carried me, will you? Now, how are you? That fine young man on your knee must be Ali! How handsome he is. Just like his father of course!'

Khalil remembered his cruel words about the baby's possible fate and involuntarily held him closer. Haboosh must have heard the booming voice and dashed out of the house. She swept Ali into her arms whereupon he burst into tears.

Abdul showed great concern. 'There, little one,' he exclaimed, seeming much concerned. 'I'm your favourite uncle, come to see your daddy!' Turning to Haboosh he said in a brusque voice, 'Take him indoors. Your husband and I have important matters to discuss.'

Haboosh glanced at Khalil for confirmation of this abrupt instruction. He nodded and she quickly went back to the house. Abdul's eyes followed her, fixed on the back of her well-filled *sari*. 'You're a very lucky man, Khalil,' he murmured. 'I can understand your reluctance to being sent off so soon after getting home.'

Khalil ignored the comment . 'I hope you've come to tell me Tippu has found someone else to lead the expedition,' he said coldly.

Abdul shook his head. 'Sadly, no. Almost everything is ready, but you still have a few more days. But first, may I offer my sincere condolences on the sad news concerning Haleema? I was devastated, truly devastated.'

'Thank you, Abdul.' Khalil's reply was cool and distant. 'I can't come to terms with losing her. And having to leave the family so soon afterwards is making it even worse.'

'That was the first thing that came to mind. But I believe going on the expedition is Allah's way of helping you.'

What's he talking about? How can I find comfort in taking charge of a slaving expedition? Especially at this time?

He shook his head. 'Impossible, Abdul. Allah would not consider such a thing.'

'I understand how you feel. But soon you'll be facing the responsibilities of command. Twenty armed men will be relying on you every minute of the day. From the moment you leave, their lives will be in your hands. You'll have no time to mope or mourn. Of course Haleema will be in your thoughts, that's inevitable. But she'll be urging you on, willing you to succeed, telling you to fulfil your orders and hurry back to the family.'

He thinks he understands, but he doesn't. He's not gone through my agony; his words are meaningless.

'You have a goal, Khalil, something to aim for. Let capturing the valley become the whole purpose of your life, the sole reason for your existence.'

'Haleema was my life, Abdul. Without her I am nothing.'

Abdul leaned across the table and grasped his arm. 'No, my friend. She's in Paradise, out of reach until you join her. Your concern now must be for the three wives who remain, for little Ali and the rest of your children. They are your earthly future. Haleema will understand.'

Khalil sat silent. Perhaps there was logic in Abdul's reasoning. 'What has this to do with the expedition?' he asked.

59

'Everything, my friend. I spoke the truth when we met at the market. To ensure your family is safe, you must succeed. Think of that as a harbour light, drawing you on. Your harbour light is to capture the valley! Concentrate on that above all else.'

'And when I have taken the valley?'

'Then a new light will beckon you back to Zanzibar!'

'You make it sound so easy, Abdul.'

'I've never been on an expedition that didn't have problems. When I lost my arm the pain was so great it made me wish for death. But Allah told me I was too young to die, that other, better things lay ahead of me. I never thought I'd rise as high as Slave Master. All I could hope for was to become something more than a common slaver. That made me determined to reach home. It was my harbour light, Khalil. Make the valley yours.'

'I might feel better if I knew more of the background. How was the valley found? How did the sultan and Tippu get to hear of it? I can't sleep at night because questions like these torment me.'

Abdul nodded. 'I can help. But what I am about to say must not be repeated.' He lowered his voice. 'Tell no one, not even your wives. You know how women love to gossip. They're worse than the eunuchs.'

'I'll be as silent as an undiscovered tomb.'

Abdul looked at him steadily. 'I need a solemn promise from you, Khalil. If a whisper of the discovery of this valley gets out, there'll be a rush of slavers trying to be first to reach it. They'd clean the place out, leave not a living soul. Men, women, children, they'd take the lot! They've stripped the country bare for hundreds of miles inland. I tried to warn them. Leave some to breed, I used to say. Ensure there'll be enough for future years. But I was wasting my breath. They are like locusts, devouring everything in their path, moving on only when there is nothing left. Merchandise of the quality reported to be living in this valley is worth its weight in gold today.'

Khalil nodded. 'I swear I'll tell no one.'

'If news does get out, Tippu will make whoever is responsible curse his mother for giving him birth. He has the power to do that, I've seen it.'

'You have my word, Abdul.'

'Very well. This is what happened, so far as anyone knows. Do you remember Muammar, that old rogue of a trader who lived in Medina Street? Yes? Earlier this year he was coming back to the coast with about four hundred slaves carrying a good haul of ivory. He'd done well, but his luck didn't last. There'd been heavy rain for weeks and when he reached the Mutumwa it was more like a huge lake than a river. It had flooded the plain for two miles on either side. It was impossible for anyone to cross, let alone four hundred captives carrying ivory. He turned north, taking the column upstream in the hope of finding a shallow stretch where they could wade over. After a long march he came to a gorge with another river running through it, also in flood. It was a tributary of the Mutumwa, which it joined a couple of miles downstream. He and his four hundred prisoners were trapped in the angle between the two.'

'That must have been a shock,' Khalil remarked.

'A shock indeed, even for an old campaigner like Muammar. He'd already lost more than half his guards through death and desertion. There were less than twenty left. He was terrified his slaves would break free and kill him. All he could do was keep them securely shackled and sit it out until the flood subsided. It must have been very scary.'

'I can imagine. How long was he there?'

'No one knows. Eventually the rain stopped and the river level began to fall so he became hopeful of getting moving again. Then one morning he saw smoke rising from a range of hills far off to the west. Smoke meant people and to Muammar that meant slaves. He went off alone to investigate. He had a difficult job reaching the place, it was so well hidden. Luckily the smoke was in sight all day and served as a beacon. Finally he came to a crest and could look down at the source of the fire through his telescope.'

Abdul leaned across the table until his face was inches from Khalil's. 'What he saw was amazing,' he whispered. 'The smoke came from a smouldering fire of old maize stalks. There was a big village with large huts, well built and arranged around a sort of compound. There were crops, and fat cattle grazing! And plenty of folk about too, men, women and children. Muammar managed to work his way down until he was only a hundred yards from the village, hidden in tall grass. Through his glass he saw the folk were all very tall, and very black. He'd never seen anything like them. And the women! Every one was beautiful, healthy and clean. Absolutely lovely. That's why the sultan is convinced they're descended from Sheba.'

'But is this true, Abdul? Muammar may have been making it up! He could have been dreaming.'

'Bear with me, Khalil. I believe he saw these things. The valley, the village, the people, I am sure they all exist.'

'If that's so, why weren't they discovered years ago? Why hasn't the valley been raided by slavers?'

'Because it's so well hidden.'

'Why didn't Muammar go back, collect his men from the camp and attack the place there and then?'

'I've told you. It was impossible. He'd already got as many slaves as he could manage. He had less than twenty guards to keep control of the four hundred he'd already taken.'

Abdul's answers came quickly, too quickly for them to be of his own making. Khalil guessed that he had put the same questions to Tippu and received these same plausible replies in return.

'So what did he do?'

'He went back to his camp, saying nothing to the guards of what he'd seen. He got the column across the Mutumwa and eventually reached home with most of his slaves and ivory. The old devil made more than ten thousand thaler profit even after expenses and paying the sultan's tax.'

'And then?'

'Well, he'd intended to re-equip at once and go back to raid the valley. Slaves like those would sell for a fortune. He reckoned one of the young girls would bring at least two hundred thaler, if not three, or perhaps even four. He'd make his fortune. Sadly, Allah had other plans for him.'

'What happened?'

'He caught a fever before he got his men organized, became seriously ill and realized he was dying. The night before Allah took him he told his son the story and drew a map showing the valley. But the idiot son couldn't keep his mouth shut and boasted to a little tart in the Shenzi brothel that his father had found a new source of slaves that would make him very rich. The tart reported this to her keeper who, unfortunately for her, was one of Tippu's men. When Tippu heard the story he had the tart strangled in case she told anyone else. He then had the son arrested and the map was found on him. Tippu realized he had stumbled on something very important and needed a witness. As there was a slave connection, he sent for me and we went to the prison together for the interrogation.'

'I'm beginning to see where this business started, Abdul. Please go on.'

'Our chief minister doesn't waste time when he wants something. His bully boys dragged the lad in and shoved his head into a barrel of water. They kept it under so long I was sure he'd drowned. Then they let him up, only for a couple of breaths, and shoved him under again. After that he couldn't wait to gabble out all his father had told him. Tippu wrote it all down and made the lad sign it. After we left, the bullies must have killed him and dumped his body in the harbour. One of my men saw a fisherman looking at it on his canoe next morning before a shark took it.'

'My God, Abdul,' Khalil gasped. 'The lad hadn't committed a crime, yet Tippu did that to him?'

Abdul nodded and smiled without warmth. 'You can see why I warned you not to cross his path.'

'This whole business worries me, Abdul. The people sound happy and peaceful in their remote valley. What right do I have, or the sultan for that matter, to attack them? Then there's the job of driving fifty wretched women back to the coast. And killing elephants. Every part involves violence.'

'Slaving is a violent trade,' Khalil heard Abdul say; it sounded as if he was speaking from a great distance. 'But it's a job you must do. Harden your heart and do it.'

'I'm still not sure I'll be able to cope,' Khalil muttered; his teeth were clenched, his breathing laboured. 'I've always hated slavery.'

'You'll cope,' Abdul said sternly. 'You will and you must. You'll see things differently when you're deep in the wilderness. The discomfort of a few miserable slaves won't worry you.'

Khalil stared across the table. 'By God, Abdul, you're a wicked man. We're both Muslims yet you're such a hypocrite! Our Prophet, May Peace Be Upon Him, said all slaves should be set free.'

Abdul smiled, again without warmth. 'The old, old question, Khalil! It's all a matter of how you interpret His words and personally I have no problem. Firstly, we do not take Muslims into slavery, only the non-enlightened; that's what the Holy Qur'an tells us, there can be no argument about that. And secondly yes, the Prophet did indeed say slaves should be released. But, don't you see, that is precisely what we do when we remove them from their stinking, disease-ridden villages? They're not like us, Khalil. We are highly civilized, they are savages. They're already held in slavery by their own chiefs, as you'll discover for yourself. In taking them prisoner we therefore obey the Prophet and set them free! They are far better off with us.'

'They pay a terrible price for what you call their freedom.'

'Slaving is a violent trade, as I have just said.'

'And a cruel one, Abdul.'

'It depends on your point of view. Anyway, let me continue. Once you take the valley, don't waste time. Pick the fifty most attractive women, rope them together and hustle them away quickly, that will confuse them. Follow the same route you took on the inland march. When you reach the Mutumwa river the *askaris* will have to drag the women across with ropes.' Abdul shrugged and sighed. 'I'm afraid there are always a few who fall and drown. It may be as well to set out with more than fifty, to absorb the losses. Once across the river keep heading east until you reach the elephants your men killed on the inward march. I should have mentioned them earlier. I'll write some notes about their slaughter, it's a messy business. You'll have to make a separate map and mark where they were shot so you can find them again. The carcasses will have rotted by the time you get back to them, a couple of blows with a *panga* will split the tusks from the bone. The women will carry them back to the coast. Slaves and tusks, eh, Khalil? Black ivory and white ivory! Two valuable commodities provided by Allah. And for nothing. All you have to do is go and collect them.'

Khalil pushed heavily against the table and stood up. His whole body was shaking, his hands trembled and his tongue seemed to have swollen to fill his mouth. The words, when at last they came, seemed to be spoken by someone else.

'It's a filthy business, Abdul!' he snarled. 'Roping women together! Dragging them through rivers! Forcing them to carry stinking tusks! I won't personally do these terrible things, but they'll be done under my command. I'll be as guilty as the most brutal *askari*. I hope Allah sees my family are under threat and that I have no choice.'

Abdul's face was pitiless, mocking. 'Haleema's death has made you sensitive, Khalil. That will pass. You'll soon become hardened to the life, once the march is under way.'

After Abdul left, Khalil sat brooding in his chair. The earlier happiness he had enjoyed was utterly destroyed. Haboosh brought Ali back to him but he waved them away. His thoughts were shrouded by evil; he was an unfit guardian for a baby. Until this morning details of what he was about to face had been distant and vague. Only now had Abdul revealed their true horror.

And he had been so matter-of-fact about it! Such things are familiar to him; he's long since become inured to cruelty and suffering. What wicked acts had he done? What things of which he dare not speak?

The one thing that separates me from Abdul is the Hamerton Plan. I see now it was the work of Allah. He spoke to Umma, telling her to involve the colonel in what I am being sent to do. Perhaps it explains Haleema's death too. Not its cause, that was Tippu's doing, but the reason for Him taking her from me. When she died I was left with only Umma in whom I could confide. Allah gave her the plan. Everything is clear. The valley people will be saved. The sultan's rule will never extend beyond Zanzibar. Tippu will be destroyed! Only Allah could envisage such a wonderful scheme. He spoke to me through Abdul too. 'Think of the valley as your harbour light.'

The new realization swept through him like a tidal wave. The expedition was Allah's work, not the sultan's. For the first time since Tippu stepped in front of him the morning he went to pay *Salwa's* dues at the villa he felt elated. He called for Haboosh to bring Ali back to him.

*

Two days later a note from Abdul arrived telling Khalil to meet him on the quay, ready to sail, early the following morning. Later that day he walked up to the cemetery to say goodbye to Haleema. He did not tell her about the Hamerton Plan; not to be outshone, she would undoubtedly have insisted she had thought of it long before Umma suggested it to him.

After supper he asked the Jewels to sit at the table with him; Umma discreetly left the three of them alone. 'You know it is not my wish to leave you, my darlings,' he said gently. 'But life is not like that. It's a struggle, and it pleases Allah to try each of us in different ways.' Umma was well aware of his scepticism regarding the existence of the Almighty but these words were for Haboosh and Khadija who clung to a child-like belief in Him. 'I know you will be good, and look after each other. It is my wish that you obey Umma, just as you did Haleema. I shall leave ample money for your needs whilst I am away. Whatever you require, do not be afraid to ask her. Abdul will visit every week to ensure all is well. I am sure he will make you laugh!' He paused. *Abdul will act the buffoon whilst he looks at them with his lascivious eyes, thinking wicked things. But he won't harm them physically, of that I'm certain.* 'In the last few days I have shown both of you how much I love you,' he went on. 'In return, you have shown how much you love me, and I shall remember that during my long journey. I have decided to spend my last evening with Umma. It is right that I should as she is my senior wife now. There are matters to discuss with her regarding the running of the household during my absence. So, come and kiss me, then go to bed. I shall see you both in the morning to say goodbye.'

Not long after sunrise, with his spare clothes in one bag, and notebooks, compass, sextant and telescope in another, he walked out into the courtyard with Umma at his side. The tearful Jewels were waiting for him; he kissed them both lovingly in turn. Taking Ali from Haboosh he lifted him high above his head; the baby laughed and squirmed, he was growing bigger and more lusty every day. Next he hugged his pretty little twin daughters. Earlier Khadija had helped

Umma dress them identically in their finest *saris* and dainty golden slippers. Lastly he embraced Umma, folding his arms round her slender body, kissing her hair as he held her close. He stifled back the tears welling in his eyes; he had not yet cried for Haleema and now was not the moment.

He reached the gate and turned to look back for the last time. The three women and two little girls all raised their right hands and waved him goodbye. He stepped over the threshold. An old servant closed the heavy door to the courtyard and, carrying the two bags, followed him at a respectful distance down to the port.

The sultan's two-masted schooner *Arafat* lay alongside the quay. Abdul bustled up and greeted Khalil enthusiastically. He was wearing the full dress naval uniform of a British admiral, complete with cocked hat and sword. The empty sleeve of the jacket was pinned across his chest amid a welter of decorations and loops of gold braid.

'All's going well,' he announced, swaggering like an old seadog. 'The stores were loaded last night. The *askaris* will be here shortly and then we can put to sea.'

'You're suitably dressed for the occasion, Abdul,' Khalil remarked, nodding at the handsome uniform. 'You look quite spectacular.'

'Yes, it suits me, don't you think?' Abdul replied, ignoring the cynicism. He struck a dramatic pose, resting his one hand on the hilt of the sword and tilting his big nose at the sky. 'I'm determined to give you a proper send-off.'

'I'd imagined you'd want the departure kept secret,' Khalil said drily.

'I do, I assure you. The uniform is a disguise. No one seeing me in it could guess there is anything underhand going on.'

'There may be logic in what you say, but it's well hidden. How did you come into possession of such finery?'

'By sheer good fortune, my dear friend! Thanks to the intervention of Allah, a British frigate went aground in a gale in North Bay during the southern monsoon last year. You'd have been in Musqat at the time and wouldn't have heard of it. The ship was called the *Eternity*, an unlucky name for her as it turned out; she was on her maiden voyage. Bound for Calcutta and loaded with essential supplies for the

British Army. Cigars, gin, rum, whisky, everything you could think of. The weapons, powder, shot and rope you are taking all came from her. She was also carrying new uniforms for the army and navy. This was one of them.' He took off the hat with a flourish. 'It even has its own tin box!'

'Surely the ship and everything in it still belonged to the British!'

Abdul shook his head. 'Not at all. The sultan ordered the crew's arrest for incompetence in running their ship aground. The sea was breaking her up so he ordered her unloaded and the entire cargo and stores taken up to the palace. When British Resident Hamerton got to hear about it he kicked up an enormous fuss but his highness told him it was none of his business. He pointed out that when the ship grounded on Zanzibar she become part of the island. And, since he owned the island, he also now owned the ship and everything in her. We all had a good laugh, except poor old Hamerton, of course. He has no sense of humour, a typical Englander. He persuaded the sultan to release the crew from prison, and the captain got his parrot back. But the sultan kept everything else.'

At the mention of the colonel, Khalil watched Abdul closely. *Is he hinting that he knows about my visit to the Residency? I could be arrested in the next few minutes, Umma and the Jewels may have already been seized!* A cold panic seized him and he was almost physically sick.

'There's a café over there,' he heard Abdul say. 'Let's go and have a coffee before your *askaris* arrive.'

The place was just opening, a waiter was still arranging the chairs and tables outside and he greeted Abdul effusively then took their orders. As he walked away Khalil noticed he had a pronounced limp.

'He's an old wounded slaver, like me,' Abdul explained, noting Khalil's interest. 'He had half a leg bitten off by a crocodile.'

'Did he survive?' Khalil asked, forcing himself to make the old joke.

'Yes. But the crocodile died,' Abdul said, giving the standard answer with a grin.

'Here come your gallant troops!' he exclaimed a few minutes later.

A column of eighteen African askaris, two abreast with a sergeant in front and another at the rear, came marching along the quay. Every man carried a musket at the slope and had a canvas knapsack on his back. They wore new leather boots, yellow trousers and scarlet short-tailed coats with the coloured lapel facings of a British cavalry regiment.

'More captured booty from the good ship *Eternity*,' Abdul remarked, nodding at the equipment and bright uniforms.

On command the squad came smartly to a halt and turned to face the *Arafat*. The sergeants held a roll-call; as each man's name was called he answered, stepped forward and marched smartly up the gangplank onto the ship. Khalil was impressed; these were the actions of well-trained men, not the rabble he had feared.

'They're the elite of the sultan's bodyguard,' Abdul declared as if guessing his thoughts. 'Let's go on board. I'll introduce you to them.'

They finished their coffee, walked together across the quay and up the gangplank. The men stood at attention in two orderly lines across the main deck. Abdul swaggered to the front; their expressions showed they were much impressed by his uniform which even out-dazzled their own.

'Men,' he called, drawing his sword and waving it above his head, 'today you leave on a historic expedition to the interior. On behalf of our beloved master, his highness the sultan, you will seize a valley which will become part of a greater and mightier kingdom of Zanzibar. You go with his blessing and ...'

Khalil looked about anxiously as Abdul continued speaking. He had stressed the need for secrecy yet he was now shouting the expedition's true purpose for anyone to hear. The waiter stood watching the proceedings from the café door which made Khalil wonder if he was one of Colonel Hamerton's agents, well placed to pick up harbour gossip. He quickly stepped forward and whispered in Abdul's ear that the tide was about to turn; if they didn't get under way soon *Arafat* wouldn't be able to sail for another twelve hours. Abdul promptly ended his speech and introduced him as their commander. Khalil's mother tongue was Arabic but he also spoke fluent ki-Swahili. Originally the language of the coastal African tribe of the same name, the growth of the slave trade over the centuries had made it the *lingua franca* of East Africa.

'*Hamjambo, askari,*' he said in a commanding voice. 'We will get to know each other well over the next few months. I have two intentions. The first is to make this mission a success. The honourable Abdul has reminded you that we go with the blessing of his highness the sultan, so we cannot fail. My second intention is to see you all return to Zanzibar alive and well. I am sure both can be achieved if we work together as a team. Good luck to you all.'

He turned to the two sergeants standing to attention in front of their men. They were both tall, powerfully built men who bore themselves well. The senior of the pair, Juma, had rows of tribal scars cut into the skin of his brow and cheeks giving his face a threatening, mask-like expression. By contrast, Oriedo had smooth aquiline features showing his Nilotic ancestry; he had a noble, dignified appearance.

'Sergeants Juma and Oriedo, I have heard good things from the honourable Abdul about both of you,' Khalil said in a voice loud enough for the *askaris* to hear. 'You heard what I said about working together to make this expedition a success. Welfare of the men is our most important concern and we shall have regular meetings to discuss progress and all matters relating to the *askaris*. You are also free at any time to raise with me any concerns you have. I hope we shall always settle them amicably.'

'Thank you, *mzee,*' Oriedo said with a smile; Juma merely nodded. Khalil was pleased to be addressed as *mzee*, a courteous ki-Swahili word meaning Old Man and conveying a sense of respect. He preferred it to the alternative, *bwana*, meaning master, a term with implications of servility.

It was past noon as *Arafat* closed on the African shore. Along the port rail the *askaris* chattered excitedly as they picked out the line of white sandy beach backed by a line of tall palm trees. For some it was their first close view of the mainland. The name of the bay they were entering was Bagamoyo, the traditional starting and finishing place for slaving expeditions to the interior. Captives arrived from the interior beaten, starved and exhausted to see before them an apparently limitless lake and an armada of dhows, the like of which they had never seen, waiting for them. Millions of captives had arrived here to

70

be shipped by Arab raiders to Zanzibar for auction. *Bagamoyo* in ki-Swahili means *Lay down your heart*, a fitting epitaph for those about to leave their final footprints on Africa.

The light wind scarcely ruffled the surface as the schooner slipped through the narrow passage in the reef at the entrance to the bay. Khalil stood with Abdul beside the master at the wheel as one of the sailors leaned over the rail, swinging a lead and chanting the depth of water. At four fathoms the master ordered the sails taken in. As the ship lost way, the bow cable roared through the hawse-hole and the anchor plunged into the clear water, throwing up a dazzling rainbow spray at the sight of which the *askaris* gave a rousing cheer. The longboat was lowered and, for the next hour, manned by the ship's crew, it ferried the *askaris*, their equipment and supplies ashore.

As expedition commander Khalil had remained on board the ship until the *askaris* were all ashore. As the boat approached to collect him Abdul took his arm and they crossed the deck to the starboard rail. From the admiral's uniform jacket he furtively produced a small bundle of rolled-up cloth.

'Take this, Khalil,' he murmured, looking about anxiously in case anyone saw or overheard. 'It's a prayer mat, a *safari* present from me. It was made especially for you by one of my wives. As you can feel, it's padded. Inside is a canvas packet and inside that you'll find Muammar's original map of the route to the valley. No one apart from his highness, Tippu and myself knows you have it. Don't let anyone know of its existence. Tippu orders that you keep it hidden until you've crossed the Mutumwa river and turned north. That's where the map starts so you won't need it before then. Use it in the normal way' – at this point he gave a nervous snigger – 'no one will suspect you're kneeling on the sultan's big secret five times a day!'

Khalil tucked the package inside his shirt. Abdul handed him a small journal. 'This contains no secrets, merely the notes I promised you. They will take you as far as the Mutumwa.'

He held out his arm and they embraced, kissing cheeks. He took Khalil's hand and held it in a firm grip. 'I will do whatever I can for your family while you are away. Rest assured no harm will come to them.'

Khalil paused at this, wondering if Abdul had sensed his concern in this regard. There was nothing he could do but accept the assurance offered.

'Goodbye, Abdul. Thank you for everything you've done for me.'

'Goodbye, Khalil. May Allah bless you.'

As he spoke these last words Khalil thought he heard a break in Abdul's voice. The idea was quite ridiculous, of course. Abdul, the slave master, the heartless brute, shedding a tear? Never! It must have been a freak of the wind, or an item of gear creaking in the rigging. He climbed down the side ladder and took his seat in the boat. He glanced back at the ship as the sailors began to row towards the shore; Abdul was leaning over the stern rail, waving his admiral's cocked hat.

The surf carried the boat well up onto the beach. Khalil clambered out and walked up to the impressive mound of equipment and stores the *askaris* had brought ashore and stacked on the sand. He turned and watched the boat being hoisted back on board the *Arafat*. She spread her sails and, heeling in the gentle breeze, sailed out of the bay, firing a cannon in a farewell salute. It was, as Abdul had intended, a proper send-off.

Chapter Six

The beach at Bagamoyo that morning was a dazzling white strand, washed by a gentle surf. On the landward side, steep ranks of sun-baked dunes were topped by lofty palms, their fronds rustling gently in the on-shore breeze. To the south, high on a headland and stark against the cloudless sky, stood the ruins of an ancient coral mosque. Khalil strode across the firm sand to where the *askaris* had assembled in a line. On a barked order from one of the sergeants they came smartly to attention as he approached.

'Thank you,' he said, embarrassed at this unexpected show of army pomp. 'Let's get started. Sergeant Juma, what do you advise regarding guard duties?'

'Nine men with muskets and ammunition to patrol the perimeter of the baggage area. Three will patrol the beach as far as the dunes. We are unlikely to be attacked here but we cannot be too careful.'

'Very good. Pick your men. Sergeant Oriedo, the stores and equipment need sorting and distributing. Will you deal with that?'

'I'll take the other nine *askaris* and have them repack our stores, *mzee*. Every man will have a musket, pistol, *panga* and knapsack.'

'Thank you. The rest of the supplies need to be made up into loads capable of being carried by pack animals. They'll arrive shortly.'

The sergeants allocated the men their duties and work began.

It was well into the afternoon when one of the sentries higher up the beach was heard to shout, 'Halt! Put up your hands!'

Khalil saw an *askari* levelling his musket at an old Arab, pathetically holding his skinny arms above his head. A camel and six donkeys stood in a line behind him.

'Let him pass,' Sergeant Juma called to the sentry. 'Shoot him if he causes trouble. But take care not to injure the animals, we need them.'

'*Aleikum-o-assalam, effendi*,' the old man said as Khalil approached. 'I am no danger to you. My name is Omah. The Honourable Abdul sent a man in a canoe yesterday, with a message telling me to meet you here today.'

'*Assalam-o-alaikum*, Omah. You may lower your hands.'

'Thank you, *effendi*.'

Omah was short and wizened, with only one eye and a severe limp. Following Arab custom, he and Khalil began a conversation which totally ignored the true purpose of their encounter. Firstly, formal greetings were exchanged, and solicitous enquiries made as to the health and welfare of each other's extended families. Secondly the state of their animals and crops was described, and finally they declared their mutual thanks to Allah for his beneficence in maintaining the eternal cycle of monsoons.

It was only when these courtesies were complete that Khalil, with a gesture of sudden surprise, appeared to notice the camel and donkeys for the first time. Were these fine beasts for sale by any chance, he asked? If so, he might be interested in buying them. Omah nodded sagely and, with a solemn bow, invited Khalil to step forward and examine them. He patted the neck of the camel who had settled in a kneeling position on the sand and was looking about with a characteristically lofty expression.

'This is Kirru, *effendi*.' Omah said. 'He arrived back from a long *safari* to the north only yesterday. He is in robust health, most biddable and very strong. He is ideally suited to carry you swiftly on your mission. Please, *effendi*, examine him. Sit in the saddle, feel his power!'

The *askaris*, mostly young and all very fit, could march with a heavy pack for ten miles day after day in the blazing sun. Abdul, with his organizing skill, had decided Khalil needed a camel to carry him, and a team of donkeys was required to bear the supplies and equipment.

The owners of the *Salwa*, the Wafulu brothers, kept a string of racing camels in Muscat and, whilst in port waiting for the monsoon to turn, Khalil had passed many a pleasant day exercising the pampered specimens on the training course attached to the stables on the fringe of the desert. He was therefore undaunted by the prospect of spending many hours in a wooden saddle. Kirru was no gelded racing specimen but an entire working animal. His dull brown coat was scarred in places and a thick tuft of ginger hair stuck up between his ears.

Khalil settled himself in the saddle and took up the rein. Kirru, possibly still tired from his recent long trek, showed his reluctance by noisily spitting and snarling. It was only after Omah had spoken sharply to him, and applied two brisk strokes of a bamboo cane to his rump, that he lurched to his feet and with much snorting, plodded a circuit round the camp.

'I shall give you ten thaler for him,' Khalil said to Omah.

The old man's face split in a toothless grin. 'Ten thaler, *effendi*? Only ten, for such a fine beast as Kirru?'

'Let me examine the donkeys,' Khalil said. 'Then we can discuss a combined price for them and the camel.'

His immediate impression was that the six donkeys were, without exception, poor specimens. They stood in a pathetic line, thin and tired-looking; none looked capable of carrying a decent load. Appearing to sense his doubts, Omah launched into a litany extolling the great strength of each animal and the improbable distance it could travel in a day.

'I'll pay one thaler a head,' Khalil offered.

'*Effendi* is jesting again,' Omah said with a sad smile. 'Fine beasts such as these are worth at least ten thaler each. But you can have them for nine.'

'That is a ridiculous price. One thaler is all I am prepared to pay.'

'Please, *effendi*, let us talk like businessmen. I cannot sell for less than eight. There are no more animals to be had for miles along this coast and without them you cannot proceed. I shall accept no less than seven.'

'As you can see, I have plenty of men,' Khalil countered, waving his arm in the direction of the *askaris*. 'They can carry all my supplies.'

'They cannot transport heavy loads like these animals, *effendi*. Or carry comrades who fall sick and are unable to walk.'

75

The bargaining continued for a further ten minutes; a deal was finally struck at five thaler a head for the donkeys, including their pack harnesses. The haggling over Kirru lasted even longer; in the end Khalil was obliged to pay twelve thaler for him. He gave Omah a promissory note for forty-two thaler to present at the tax office in Zanzibar for payment.

Five of the *askaris* were, like Khalil, devout Muslims. Later, as the light began to fade, he led them a short distance off from the rest of the party. They placed their prayer mats in a line on the sand and, turning towards Mecca, knelt in their fifth and final devotions of the day. Religion was as much a part of Khalil's life as breathing and, whilst he gave it little thought most of the time, there were moments when it loomed large. This was such a moment. He tried to ask for a blessing on his endeavours but somehow the words would not come. This, he felt, was a bad omen, as if Allah had turned His back on him for the transgressions he had committed. Despairingly he tried to excuse his sins. *I am leading this expedition to capture slaves, Lord, but what else could I do? I was given orders that had to be obeyed. Refusal would have brought horror to my family. I have vowed vengeance against Tippu although I know I should forgive him. But that I cannot do. Surely You can see that?*

In a final desperate plea he offered up a prayer that he be given the chance to do good, to overcome the evil that hung like a dark cloud over the mission. Perhaps, he thought, Allah may prefer that approach.

Darkness came quickly, the sun sinking behind the dunes to leave a vivid orange sky speckled with a myriad tiny flecks of luminescent cloud. Cicadas began their nightly chorus and fireflies danced, bright blue spots in the warm evening air. A fire had been lit on the beach where the two cooks had prepared an evening meal of rice and fish caught that afternoon in the bay. The *askaris* were in a lively mood. Their black faces were lit by the fire, the whites of their eyes startlingly clear. They ate voraciously, mouths open, scooping up food from the communal bowls with a wedge of *posho*, a maize-meal porridge, gripped between their fingers.

At Khalil's invitation, Omah had stayed to join him for supper. After the meal they sat beside the crackling fire as sparks whirled up into the blackness of the African night. Omah smoked his *hookah* and spoke with nostalgia of his slaving adventures long ago when he had served on expeditions led by the great Tippu himself. They had carried out attacks that emptied whole valleys of every last man, woman and child who had then been driven back to Zanzibar carrying ivory. He described encounters with charging buffaloes and how he had twice been mauled by lions. One of these had almost severed his leg right which accounted for his permanent limp. He had suffered in other ways too.

'One afternoon I was lying in the grass, peacefully spying on slaves in a village below,' he explained, after drawing deeply on the *hookah*. 'We were planning a raid on their village the following morning. Suddenly a cobra reared up close to me and spat venom on the side of my face. Perhaps he had been sunning himself on a rock and I had disturbed him. That was how I lost my eye.' He swept a hand across his brow and spoke without rancour. 'It was very painful. Cobras try to spit their stream of poison onto the bridge of the nose so that it splashes into both eyes. But Allah was kind and I was not totally blinded.'

Omah puffed again at his *hookah* and grew philosophical. 'They were exciting days for a young man,' he said with a sigh. 'But I did not make my fortune. Money is made from selling slaves, not capturing them. Tippu soon realized that but kept the information to himself. He sent me and many others on expeditions whilst he stayed behind arranging rich contracts for sales. He spoke to us of great wealth. Indeed it came, but he kept it all for himself. And now he is the sultan's chief minister.'

'It is the will of Allah,' murmured Khalil, mouthing words he could no longer believe. *How can Allah allow men and women to be traded like carpets, or cloves? Why does He permit Tippu and Abdul, even this garrulous old man sitting beside me, to prosper? Why did He watch me becoming involved in this expedition when its purpose is to perpetrate such evils? Worst of all, why did He let Haleema die? Does He truly exist, or is He merely a mythical figure? Like Sheba, a legend surviving since the beginning of recorded time?*

77

'Yes, indeed,' Omah murmured. 'It is part of His great plan that I am but a dealer in animals, not in men. But, although I am poor, I thank Him. I have a modest house and four obedient wives. I have children, concubines and slaves. What more does a man need?' He spat into the embers of the fire.

Khalil left the old man to his thoughts and walked alone along the beach. In the pitch darkness of the bay, the surf crashed endlessly against the reef. The past two weeks had been hellish. He had lost Haleema, become involved in slavery, placed Umma and the Jewels and Ali in great danger. His belief in the Almighty was crumbling. He yearned to have Umma beside him. She understood, she could unravel the tortuous threads that enveloped him. He cursed Muammar for discovering the valley, and his stupid son for bragging about it. He damned the sultan for his lusts, and Tippu for his guile and the murder of Haleema. Standing on the beach he gazed up at the familiar stars thrown across the sky. Why has all this happened to me? No answer came from Allah. There was only the rumble of breaking surf and the soft rhythmic beat of the askaris' drums in the now chill air.

Next morning he again joined the Muslims for prayers at first light, by tradition the moment when it first became possible to distinguish a white thread from a black. The sergeants ordered the *askaris* to parade. Each carried a musket and a knapsack containing biscuit, a piece of dried fish, a water flask and a supply of powder and shot. In his belt were a pistol and a *panga*, a flat-sided chopping tool with a wooden handle and sharpened metal blade. The muskets and pistols were closely examined by the sergeants. It was essential they were properly cleaned, oiled and primed, the flint correctly positioned and the wad and ball rammed home. These inspections were not mere parade ground posturings; the hundred mile wide coastal strip they were about to cross was roamed by gangs of vicious renegades, many of them escaped slaves, armed with spears and clubs. Desperate for food, guns and equipment, they would attack any expedition without mercy. The *askaris* had to be ready to fight at an instant; a misfiring pistol or musket could lead to disaster.

The six donkeys were loaded with sacks of food, bundles of spare weapons, barrels of gunpowder and lead shot, coils of rope, shovels, the medicine chest, kegs of water, cooking pots and the rest of the equipment and supplies. One of the *askaris*, Tembe by name, was appointed groom by Sergeant Juma and he saddled Kirru. The column formed up with Khalil astride Kirru at its head. Behind him was an advance guard of three men led by Sergeant Juma; the donkeys followed, each led on a short rope by an *askari*. Three *askaris* took up position on either flank, bringing up the rear were the last three men with Sergeant Oriedo. When Juma confirmed all was ready, Khalil gave the order to start the trek.

An indistinct path meandered through the dunes up to a grove of palm trees on top of the ridge. On the crest Khalil held up his hand to signal a halt. It was still early in the day but the land in front was already shimmering in the heat. Grey-green at first, the vast plain before them changed to a muted misty blue in the far distance, melting softly into a haze where the earth met the sky. Khalil was not alone in regarding this dramatic view with awe. The *askaris'* chatter gave way to silence as they looked out to where their journey, and their fates, lay. The few Arab traders who had ventured into the far interior, and lived to return to civilization, spoke of lakes the size of seas and lofty white-capped mountains. There were vast herds of elephants, rich in ivory, roaming the vast plains. Great tribes of tall warriors and infinitely desirable women lived in a paradise of plenty. This was the land into which Khalil was about to lead his twenty men.

He took a final look back at the white beach of Bagamoyo Bay. Beyond it, across the sparkling blue waters of the Zanzibar Channel, lay all that he loved. Haleema, asleep in her grave; Umma and his Jewels, his children, his home, and *Salwa*. Whether or not he ever saw them again was from now in the hands of Allah, if He existed. If not, then his fate, as well as that of the expedition, lay in his own hands. Perhaps that was a better, surer way to be. He looked back along the column of *askaris* and wondered if, as Colonel Hamerton had warned, Tippu had placed a spy in their ranks. *Beware of those you least suspect*, he had advised. Khalil sighed for the innocence of his lost life as master of the *Salwa*. Sailors were more honest, better men than soldiers. He gave a final sigh, and squared his shoulders. Return in four months, Tippu had ordered. Impossible, Abdul had declared. What was the truth? One month had already passed; Abdul had said it would take three just to reach the Mutumwa river! Khalil smiled to himself, wondering how Allah would solve that problem. He turned his back on the sea and nodded to Juma. The march to the valley, to Abdul's distant harbour light, began.

At the bottom of the landward side of the dunes all traces of the path had disappeared. The *askaris*, wielding their *pangas*, began hacking a passage through a trackless ocean of tough thorny bushes. Progress was slow; by late afternoon they had travelled no more than six miles inland. Khalil, after a first day in Kirru's wooden saddle, had blisters on his backside that burned like fire whilst his spine ached as if beaten from neck to waist with a heavy stick. The *askaris* too were tired. Confined to barracks since selection for the mission, they were out of condition. It had been an exhausting eight hours for them, endlessly slashing at tough springy branches under a blazing sun. There was great relief when a clearing suitable for a night camp was reached. Four men were posted on guard, the donkeys unloaded and, with Kirru, staked out to graze the surrounding bush. A fire was started and the cooks set about preparing the evening meal. An antelope shot during the afternoon march was skinned and gutted, the carcass chopped into joints and placed on the fire. The smell of roasting meat filled the evening air.

In the days that followed the expedition settled into an organized routine. Each morning the camp was astir before first light. The Muslims said their prayers, firearms were inspected, the donkeys were loaded and the march began with Khalil at the head astride Kirru. Soon after dawn, under a clear sky, it was pleasantly cool but within an hour the sun was almost overhead and the heat became debilitating. The thorn bushes encountered on the first day gave way to dry, lifeless scrub extending in all directions where only an occasional clump of trees gave the landscape a sense of perspective.

The few villages the column came to consisted of a few circular mud huts topped with rough turf, surrounded by pitiful patches of straggling maize and cassava. Chickens pecked in the dust; skinny cows and goats grazed what they could find, watched over by naked pot-bellied children with large sad eyes and stick-like arms and legs. The adults stood by their huts in silence, watching the sweating *askaris* with their heavy loads pass by. Nothing was to be gained by exchanging pleasantries. The sole advantage these people derived from living in this barren coastal strip was that, as subjects of the sultan, they were exempted from capture as slaves.

Four hours after the march began a halt was made and the first meal of the day prepared by the cooks. This was followed by a lengthy break whilst the heat of the day was at its greatest. Two *askaris*, under the directions of one of the sergeants, rigged a simple shelter for Khalil. It was merely a length of bright barter cloth, spread across the tops of a couple of bushes, but it gave welcome shade. The *askaris* disregarded the heat and were content to lie snoozing in their uniforms in the full blaze of the sun with muskets close at hand. When in the late afternoon the temperature became more bearable, the march was resumed. An hour before sunset the night's camp was set up. The evening meal was cooked and eaten after which final prayers were said. As the velvet darkness fell, the drummers began to play, soft and soporific, a sound that continued until the musicians themselves fell asleep.

Towards mid-morning on the third day Khalil, riding out in front, heard shouts coming from the column. He pulled Kirru's head round and they trotted back. One of the *askaris*, Khalil did not yet know them all by name, lay shivering violently on the ground. He was delirious and had thrown off his uniform jacket and knapsack; under the blazing sun his near-naked body was drenched in sweat yet he shivered and moaned repeatedly he was cold.

'He has malaria, *mzee*,' Sergeant Oriedo announced as the man vomited violently into the dust. 'At this morning's parade two other men complained of having severe headaches. I fear they too will also become ill. And it's likely there will be more.'

Khalil turned to the other sergeant who stood by silently. 'What can we do, Juma?' he asked.

The sergeant merely shrugged. 'We cannot stop. If we do, and

81

more men become sick, we will become bogged down. Every man must keep up with the march, however ill he feels.'

Khalil looked hard at Juma who met his eye unflinchingly. 'That seems very harsh,' he said.

'You asked me what we can do. The answer is nothing. The march must proceed. They are soldiers, and know what to expect. There is quinine in the medicine chest. Give it to the sick men if you wish, but it is of little use.'

He turned away. *He's a callous brute*, Khalil thought. *Surly too, the opposite of Oriedo. But he's right, I suppose. We must keep moving.*

The *askari's* name was Sabuni; he died that night and was buried before the column set off next morning. The *askaris* were dispirited at the early loss of a comrade and it was suppertime before the first laugh of the day was heard. In the following week four more men developed malaria, but the pace of the march, set by Sergeant Oriedo striding out at the front of the column, did not slacken. The equipment of the sickest men was carried by the *askaris* in the column. Those who were ill formed a wretched group at the rear, staggering along and continually harangued by Juma. He carried a thin switch cut from a shrub which he continually flourished; Khalil suspected that when he was not watching, the sergeant used it to whip any man failing to keep pace with the remainder.

Khalil was thankful he was riding Kirru as he could never have kept up with the *askaris* on foot. Being mounted had other advantages. From the saddle he had a wide view across the surrounding scrub, something denied to the marching men as the parched growth was well above head height. And riding out in front of the column gave him time to think and make plans. He read Abdul's cryptic notes every morning, but they gave only basic information. Ahead lay an escarpment rising to the central African plain where conditions would be better. It was something to look forward to, an early marker on the long march to Abdul's harbour light.

On the fifth day of the march there was a second death. As the column breasted a long rise through a particularly dense stretch of thorn bushes, an *askari* named Likilo suddenly collapsed and lay twisting and screaming, clutching at a wound on his left leg. Within seconds it was bleeding profusely; the *askaris* quickly recognized the signs and news passed down the column.

'Viper! Viper! Likilo's been bitten by a viper!'

No one saw the snake; it must have slithered quickly into the scrub after its attack. The men dropped their loads and rushed to offer what little help they could. Likilo screamed in agony; his strength became superhuman and he wrenched himself free as *askaris* tried to restrain him and prop his head on his knapsack. His leg below the knee was rapidly distorted by a grotesque purple swelling from which thick dark blood flowed in a constant stream, forming a pool in the dust around which a dense cloud of flies swarmed. His cries turned to a choked gasping rattle as the toxins spread through his body, paralysing his throat and diaphragm. Less than ten minutes after the snake had bitten him he was dead.

Khalil read a simple prayer over his shallow grave as the *askaris* stood in silence. As they turned away to form into line once more he stood reflecting on the loss of yet another man. *How many more times am I going to do this? It's only a week since we left Zanzibar and already two men have died. I could be next, if it is Allah's will. Perhaps he sees the evil in this mission and has decided none of us shall reach the valley alive.*

The march resumed. The usual chatter and cheery laughter among the *askaris* had again ceased. Only the swish of trudging feet in the hot sandy earth, and the occasional clink of equipment, could be heard. Likilo had been a popular man, a natural comedian who could raise a laugh in any situation, however grim. His sudden loss, made worse by the ugly way in which his life ended, cast a sombre shadow over the expedition. *Whose corpse will be the next be shovelled into the ground,* Khalil wondered? *Left to rot out on this dreadful plain. Every man must be thinking, will it be mine?*

In the days that followed it seemed the days grew hotter and the bush thicker. The *askaris* complained volubly their loads felt heavier, that every mile they trudged took longer than the last. Their anticipation of adventure, high in the days that had followed departure, faded to nothing as the grim reality of life in the African wilderness became apparent. Thanks to Kirru, Khalil was spared the physical effort demanded of the *askaris*, but he had his own problems. They rose and swirled about him like dank mists in a mangrove swamp, disjointed, rambling, persistent. Progress was much too slow; they'd be fortunate to get back to the coast in eight months, not the four Tippu had ordered. *I'll be punished, and probably lose more than the villa. And when, or if, we reach the valley, will the chief co-operate? What can I do if he refuses? What about the tusks Tippu is expecting? When we meet elephants, do I order them to be killed, or rely on the Hamerton Plan working, in which case the ivory will not be needed? Even if all goes well, and I return to Zanzibar with a document signed by the chief, how will the colonel deal with the sultan and Tippu, without letting them know of my involvement? What about the women I'm supposed to bring back for the sultan?*

He was unable to think about home, incapable of visualizing the family, or imagining what the house must be like without Haleema. At times he even forgot that she had died, that she would never again greet him when he walked in the door after a voyage. He worried how Umma was coping in her new position as senior wife. The Jewels, the twins, and little Ali; were they all well? How they must miss him! He thought of Abdul paying his promised weekly visit. They must all dread him coming, although they were in no physical danger. Haleema would have stood no nonsense but, unless Umma did the same, he would be free to cast his lascivious eye over them ...

Khalil knew he was torturing himself to no avail. *I must banish all thoughts of home. My life and the family's depend upon me giving this mission my full attention. I must remember Abdul's shining harbour light.*

Three days later Khalil was again recalled from the lead by urgent shouts. He rode Kirru back to the column to find that Ombalo, one of the men thought to be suffering from malaria, had suddenly collapsed. He lay writhing on the ground, clutching his belly. His face was a ghastly sulphurous colour, he suddenly vomited a copious amount of foul-smelling black fluid.

'That is the yellow fever,' Juma said, turning to Khalil and confidently making a diagnosis on the spot. He dropped his voice. 'He will not live long. Quinine does not cure this disease even though like malaria it is spread by bad air. We must hope no more *askaris* become ill with it; we cannot afford to lose too many.'

'If it is yellow fever there is nothing we can do for him,' Khalil agreed in a whisper. He had seen cases on ships; those who caught it invariably died. As Juma said, it was a disease known to be spread by bad air arising from swamps although it remained a mystery how it could develop far out at sea where the air was always so fresh and clean. A British naval surgeon in Mombasa had recently suggested the infection was somehow caused by bites from mosquitoes which bred in the freshwater barrels on the decks of ships. He had been scorned by his superiors as being either drunk or mad.

'We cannot leave him in such a state, Juma,' Khalil said.

'We must; he has not long to live. It would tire the men too much to carry him for his last few hours. They need all their strength for the march.'

They looked at each other; abandoning a man here in the wilderness was equivalent to a death sentence.

'There is nothing else to be done,' the sergeant urged in an impatient voice. 'He is beyond help. Proceed with the march. I will stay behind to make him comfortable, then follow.'

Khalil looked down at Ombalo. The infection was overwhelming him, he lay drenched in black vomit and bloody diarrhoea; it seemed his innards were dissolving in a putrefying mess. The stench was unbearable.

'Very well, Juma,' he said, reluctantly. 'Do what you can for him. Catch us up as quickly as you can.'

Khalil remounted Kirru and called to Oriedo to get the men back into line. They were visibly downcast at the abandonment of a comrade.

Should I speak to them, explain the futility of the situation? Rally them to hasten the march across the plain? But the misery on their faces showed it was the wrong moment for empty exhortations. Nodding to Oriedo to give the order to march off, he wheeled Kirru in a half circle to take up his position at the front.

It was then, over the heads of the *askaris*, and some twenty yards behind the column, that he caught sight of Juma chopping and scraping at the sandy earth with his *panga*, close by the recumbent figure of Ombalo. Khalil suddenly realized the charade in which he had unwittingly played a part; Juma was not abandoning Ombalo alive. Not, as he had claimed, 'making him comfortable' in the accepted sense of the phrase. He was digging his grave. Once the column was out of earshot, he would shoot him and bury his body. It would be a sort of comfort, a quick end to his misery, but it would also be murder. That was something Khalil felt, as expedition leader, he could not allow without prior discussion. He drew Kirru aside and waved to Oriedo to march the column past. He dismounted and walked back to where Juma was digging.

'What are you doing, Sergeant?' he asked.

Juma did not look up. 'You can see for yourself. I'm digging Ombalo's grave. Do you wish to help?'

'Help you to kill him, you mean?'

'Do you want him left to be eaten by a hyena while he is still alive? Is that the end you prefer for him?'

'Killing him would be murder. That is a crime.'

'A crime!' Juma spat contemptuously. 'There is no law out here! He will be grateful to me for putting a ball through his brain. And so would you in his condition. If you do not wish to help, get back on your camel and ride on.'

Khalil was startled. At sea, as captain, he was accustomed to being treated with respect. Now he was momentarily speechless at the impudence of this mere sergeant.

'I am your commanding officer,' he said, rapidly assembling his thoughts. 'Have a care what you say.'

Juma stood up slowly and stared insolently. 'You are just a sailor,' he sneered. 'What do you know of soldiering? You spend your life on your pretty little ship, going where the wind blows you. And now a camel carries you while I march with my men! I should be in command of this expedition, not you!'

Khalil smiled, Juma had played into his hands. 'Ha-ha, Sergeant. You are jealous of me!' he said mockingly. 'You are unhappy because the sultan knows you are incapable of leading this mission to its destination. You cannot navigate, you cannot read or write. You are merely a bully, a surly brute who beats sick men with a stick.'

Juma glowered at him ferociously but said nothing as Khalil pushed home his advantage. 'You may frighten the men, but you do not scare me. You rule by fear, but that is something I can bring to an end. At present the men think you have my support. I have only to show that is not the case and they will turn against you.'

'I have been commended by the sultan,' Juma said sulkily.

'That I can believe. This is an important mission. You could gain promotion, possibly to sergeant-major, on my recommendation when we return to Zanzibar. But only if you act in full accordance with the rules.'

Juma resumed digging with his *panga* but Khalil knew his words were making an impression. 'You will begin by calling me *mzee*, as Oriedo does. You will cease bullying the men. And you will do nothing like this again' – he paused and gestured towards Ombalo – 'without my specific agreement. Do you understand?'

There was a pause, not too long, before Juma stood, drew himself up to attention. 'Yes, *mzee*!' he barked, staring straight ahead.

'Very well. I understand your predicament regarding Ombalo. Deal with the situation as you think fit on this occasion. But in future all matters of such importance must first be discussed with me. Carry on.'

'Yes, *mzee*! Thank you!'

Khalil walked back to Kirru, mounted him and rode after the column. He sensed, with some self-congratulation, that he had handled a difficult situation well. But Juma would have to be carefully watched. He was both truculent and aggressive and likely to be vindictive. A dangerous man to cross. It would be interesting to see how long he stuck to his new, respectful attitude towards authority. And there was every chance he was Tippu's man. Perhaps Colonel Hamerton had been right and there was a spy in the ranks.

Chapter Seven

The renegades' attack, on the eighth day of the march, was sudden and vicious. They had chosen their moment well. The *askaris*, exhausted from toiling up a long slope through dense bush in intense heat, had eaten their midday meal and settled down to snooze with full bellies. Khalil had retired for the afternoon to his shelter on the edge of the clearing. He too had dined well and his eyelids felt heavy. His bed, a thick mattress of leafy branches covered by a folded blanket, was comfortable. He lay on his back, hands behind his head. As he drifted into sleep he allowed his thoughts to linger on the three men already lost. *What will happen to their families? Another six months at least will pass before we return to Zanzibar and they receive the news that their husband or father or son has died. They'll only receive his pay up to the day of his death. I'll try to persuade Tippu to pay those who depended on them up to the date of our return. If it's been successful, he might agree....*

A silent shadow slid across the thin cloth of the shelter, only inches above his face. He was instantly alert, a sea captain instinctively expects the unexpected, regardless of his situation. The shape continued moving noiselessly until it stopped at the mid-point of the shelter. Stealthily, Khalil reached for the pistol he had laid beside the mattress before lying down. His fingers closed round the butt; his thumb pulled back the hammer with only a faint click. He trained the muzzle on the shape as it began moving again, sliding lower and lower. A wild-looking, unknown face, surrounded by a mass of unkempt hair, ducked below the bottom edge of the drape and peered in at him. The range was little more than a yard; Khalil squeezed the trigger. There was a soft *pop*! a puff of smoke and the face dissolved in a bloody mask. As the body toppled backwards Khalil leapt to his feet. At that same moment pandemonium broke out in the clearing. Juma was barking orders; an irregular staccato of shots erupted then screams, yells, more orders, more shots. Khalil flung himself out of the shelter. Kirru, nostrils flaring and eyes staring wide in alarm, rapidly cantered past and disappeared into the surrounding scrub.

In the clearing a grim fight was in progress. The salvoes of gunfire had ceased; with no time to prime and reload, the action was now hand to hand. Juma was in the forefront with his men ranged on either side, hacking with *pangas* at a knot of dishevelled screaming figures dressed in rags and wielding an assortment of clubs and crude spears. Oriedo appeared at one side with three *askaris*, each armed with several pistols. They fired at close range into the mass of renegades and the leader threw up his arms and collapsed in a heap. On the far side another screamed and tumbled into the surrounding scrub, yet another buckled at the knees and lurched off into the bushes. As the last of the attackers turned and fled, an *askari* swung a musket to his shoulder and shot him in the back as he leapt into the scrub. The smell of burnt gunpowder hung in the hot air and blue smoke drifted lazily across the clearing. After a momentary silence the *askaris* began cheering wildly.

'Silence!' thundered Juma. 'Silence, I say! Reload, but hold your fire. And stop behaving like idiots. Anyone'd think you'd won a war, not scared off a few oafs armed with sticks.'

'In the name of Allah what happened, Sergeant?' Khalil demanded. 'Who were these animals? Was a watch set? Where were the guards? It's broad daylight yet one of the attackers almost got into my shelter! I could have been speared as I slept! Our entire force might have been butchered!'

'Renegades, *mzee*. Escaped slaves, outlaws, deserters. Gangs of them roam this plain. As for the guard, Otapu and Blasio were ordered to patrol the perimeter. I will find out why they failed in their duty.'

'See that you do. Give me a report without delay. Were any of our men hurt, Oriedo?'

'One *askari*, Wanjala, was killed, *mzee*. His head was crushed by a blow from a club when the attack began. A few men have cuts and bruises, nothing serious. Your camel bolted but I do not think he was injured. The donkeys have come to no harm.'

'Just before the attack, the sentries were seen standing together, gossiping like a pair of women,' Juma reported a few minutes later. 'I will punish them for wilful neglect of their duties. With your permission,' he added.

Khalil noted he had dropped the courtesy title of *mzee* but remained respectful otherwise. 'As you wish, Sergeant. But not too harsh, I suggest. With the loss of Wanjala and the other three *askaris* we can't afford to have men unable to march as a result of a too severe a flogging.'

'Watching a good whipping will make the rest take more care in future,' Juma growled. 'Neglecting guard duty is a serious offence. You would be justified in ordering them hanged. But, you are right, we need them.'

'I will leave you to do as you see fit. But bear in mind what I have said. Arrange a decent burial for Wanjala. Can you spare an *askari* to act as my bodyguard while I find Kirru and bring him back? Some of the villains escaped into the bush. They're probably far away now, but there's always a chance some may still be hiding close by.'

Khalil pushed his way through the bushes at the side of the clearing with an *askari* close behind. Near the side of the shelter the attacker he had shot from his bed lay sprawled in the scrub. Most of his face had been blown away; white fragments of bone mixed with brains and blood spattered the green leaves of the bushes around him. Khalil looked down at him without remorse. Had it not been for his quick action, it would be his corpse lying with the same flies buzzing round. For a moment he wondered how Haleema would feel if he told her he had blown a man's head off. Then he remembered she was dead, and turned away from his victim. Nearby was a second dead man; a ball had entered his left eye leaving his face otherwise unmarked; on exit it had carried away the back of his skull. Further into the bushes lay a third renegade, still alive. A *panga* slash had ripped his belly open and coils of bloodstained guts were spilling out. As Khalil stepped over his legs the man smiled up at him in a friendly way. He moved on, moments later a pistol shot rang out. Khalil whipped round, the bodyguard was standing astride the dead man, grinning cheerfully. He waved his pistol in the air. 'It's what we always do, *mzee*,' he called. 'The hyenas can't eat him alive now.'

Kirru was grazing quietly in a patch of thorns; he raised his head as Khalil approached and took the rein to lead him back to camp. As they reached the clearing the repeated crack of lashes being administered by the sergeants, and the sharp cries of pain from the two guards, could be heard. Juma's concept of justice was swift and, despite Khalil's request for leniency, if the accompanying sounds were a guide, severe.

Twice a day in his journal Khalil noted the weather, listed details of significant events and described any topographical feature worthy of mention. He took regular compass bearings and estimated the distance travelled during the morning and afternoon marches. In the evening he plotted on a fresh page the approximate course the expedition had followed throughout the day. And every fourth night, with the aid of his sextant and mariner's knowledge of the brilliant stars in the blackness of the sky, he calculated the latitude of their position. Matching this with his earlier dead reckonings, he knew within a mile or so, the point in the unmapped wilderness of East Africa where the expedition was about to lie down to sleep.

Following the renegade attack the number of guards at the overnight camps was increased from two men to four. A strong sense of nervousness pervaded the ranks. On the march the *askaris* were constantly looking about, frequently turning to glance behind, edgy at the possibility of another attack sweeping down on them. Khalil too was vigilant. From his lofty seat he had a good view all around and continually scanned the surrounding bush through his telescope.

When camp was made on the late afternoon of the tenth day of the march Khalil's latest calculations showed the expedition had marched 110 miles since leaving Bagamoyo. As the sun began to sink in the western sky, the heat rapidly diminished and the watery mirages obscuring the way ahead since early morning evaporated. A welcome cool breeze wafted across the plain, rustling the dry leaves of the acacia trees casting their shadows over the surrounding bush. Standing on a slight rise adjoining the camp, Khalil caught sight through his glass of a faint blue line along the still illuminated western horizon. It could only be the escarpment marking the inland boundary of the coastal plain, the first important waypoint of the march. The next stage of the route, after a steep climb, would lead on to the high central African plain which according to Abdul's notes, heralded much better marching conditions in the days to come.

Late in the morning of the following day, the column reached the base of the escarpment. A copse of shady trees nestled at the base of the first slope where a sparkling stream cascaded down from a rocky outcrop. After a meal and a short rest the ascent of the escarpment began.

Khalil was soon reminded of Abdul's warning in the notes that it was a tough climb. The path was faint, very steep for the most part and in places difficult to follow. Where stretches were visible ahead, the rising route zig-zagged across the slope, reversing direction every few hundred yards. There was a precipitous length where the sharp corner of a bluff had to be negotiated. The path was only three feet wide with a vertical rock face forming one side, on the other was a drop of hundreds of feet. Khalil dismounted and walked along this section of the track leading Kirru by the rein. The camel showed no fear, following quietly and placing his big feet carefully at every step. The loaded donkeys were much more nervous, shying away in terror at the narrow way along the very edge of the cliff. Each had to be blindfolded and their heavy bundles removed while *askaris* led them, one by one, to the safety of the far side. Juma's advice to the first man, not the brightest in the party, to remember to let go of his donkey's bridle if it was about to topple over the edge, was met with laughter from the rest of the column. The animals' loads were manhandled along the track by men working in pairs. It was hot, hard and dangerous work and darkness was approaching as the last donkey scrambled up onto the plateau.

When Khalil settled down to sleep that night he was plagued with thoughts of Colonel Hamerton's warning of the possibility of a Tippu spy in the ranks. '*Beware of those you least suspect,*' he had said. Who was better placed for the role than one of the sergeants? Was it Juma? He had shown himself to be brutal and disrespectful. But would a spy be so foolish as to act in such a conspicuous manner? Was it not more likely to be Oriedo, well-liked by the men, who never failed to use the courteous *mzee*? Perhaps they were both were spies! Working together to an agreed plan, each in his own way finding faults to report back to Tippu? The colonel could be wrong, of course, and there wasn't a spy in the ranks after all. Juma may be nothing more than a bully, Oriedo merely a conscientious, trust-worthy assistant, doing his best despite the overbearing attitude of his companion.

Khalil groaned and turned over. Umma and the Jewels now slipped uninvited into his thoughts. How were they coping on their own? He tried hard to think of Haleema, but she was somehow shielded from him. A misty barrier swirled about her tall graceful figure, preventing him from reaching her. Umma was more real and his thoughts lingered on their joyous last hours together. It was late before he drifted off into a restless sleep.

The difficult ascent of the escarpment brought the expedition a just reward. The dreary coastal plain, with the uncompromising harsh-ness of its sun-baked scrub, was left behind. For as far ahead as could be seen were vistas of green savannah, rolling forest-clad hills and valleys and, in the far distance, a snow-capped mountain. The relent-less heat had gone; at more than 5000 feet above sea level the air was fresh and cool. Spirits rose among the men and a new urgency became apparent in their step. There was the prospect of fresh meat every day, vast herds of antelope roamed the land they were about to cross.

Camp was pitched late the following afternoon on a pleasant grassy slope. Preparations for the evening meal were well advanced when the sound of singing was heard. Moments later, surrounded by a chanting bodyguard of spear-carrying warriors, the local chief was carried into the clearing on a litter. It was carefully lowered to the ground and he rose to his feet. He was an impressive sight, jet-black, well over six feet tall with a big head and large round face. He was enormously fat. The skin of a large leopard was slung over one shoulder and another tied round his immense waist like a skirt. Coiled about his wrists and ankles were strips of copper wire, a row of crocodile teeth hung from a length of string round his neck.

'*Hamjambo,* Chief,' Khalil said. 'I was about to come to greet you in your village.' Turning to Juma he ordered, 'Bring a seat for our guest.'

A water keg was brought and placed beside the chief who ignored it. He stood looking about with a contemptuous expression on his huge black face.

'I trust you will join me for supper?' enquired Khalil, struggling to maintain the courtesies.

'Where is my *hongo?*' the chief demanded haughtily. *Hongo* was the ki-Swahili word for the payment traditionally demanded of an expedition. It was supposed to pay for unhindered passage through a territory but was usually merely the first of many bribes extracted from travellers.

'Your *hongo,* Chief? Of course,' Khalil replied with mock enthusiasm. 'We are happy to pay for your protection. It's a matter we can settle quickly. Are you sure you won't eat with us? No? Well, please take a seat, sir. Let us discuss the settlement whilst my men and I dine.'

'Muskets. I want muskets,' the chief said.

'I am afraid I have no muskets to spare, Chief. But I have some trade goods of the best quality which I am sure you will like....'

After half an hour the amount of *hongo* to be paid was still in dispute although the initial tension had relaxed. The chief changed his mind about taking dinner and a large platter of hot roast antelope meat was brought for him. He ate using his fingers to stuff food into his mouth, belching noisily whilst continuing to haggle with Khalil. More warriors and local villagers filtered into the camp to stand in respectful silence behind their chief, listening to the protracted negotiations. Agreement was finally reached. Juma, on Khalil's orders, unfastened one of the bundles of trade goods and took from it three yards of brightly printed barter cloth, a bag of salt, a fistful of coloured beads and half-a-dozen small mirrors. These were handed over with solemn ceremony as the chief's bodyguard chanted a celebratory song. Minutes later pairs of men staggered into the camp carrying on their shoulders poles from which were slung gourds of *pombe*, the potent native beer. Khalil, a Muslim, did not drink alcohol. He sat beside the pagan chief who did.

'How many wives have you got?' the chief asked in an amiable tone.

'Three,' replied Khalil.

The chief snorted. 'I have dozens. Too many to count. And children. Hundreds of them.' His hand made a broad sweep. 'All the women here are my wives,' he said. 'Every one. Would you like some? Choose any you want. Take them with you. I can get plenty more.'

Khalil shook his head. 'Thank you, Chief. But I am on an important mission for my sultan. I dare not allow myself to be distracted by the charms of your beautiful young ladies.'

The chief gave him a withering stare, turned his back and gave full attention to the *pombe* which was being passed freely among the crowd. The off-duty *askaris* joined in. There was a moon, and after a while dancing began with men and women gathered in separate groups, stamping their feet and chanting in unison. The chief's men had brought their drums and the two *askari* players joined in with their instruments. *Banghi*, the local narcotic made from the sun-dried leaves of the *phalli* tree, was produced and smoked in crude smouldering pipes passed between men and women. Excitement increased as the drumming became more frenzied; the chanting was replaced by a cacophony of yells and screeches. Figures darted in and out of the darkness beyond the fire and general mayhem took over. The chief smoked *banghi* furiously and drank a prodigious quantity of *pombe* before slumping forward onto the fire in a stupor. His bodyguards dragged him clear, heaved him onto the litter and carried him off with his *hongo* piled beside him.

Oriedo had earlier placed the five Muslim askaris on guard for the night. They had been hand-picked for their abstinence from alcohol, a sober watch was essential to protect the expedition's equipment and supplies from pilfering during the distraction of the festivities. Later Khalil went round and checked all were present and alert. He bade them good night and returned to his shelter. He lay down, wrapped in his blanket against the cold night air. Sleep did not come easily as he was again worrying how Umma and the Jewels were managing without him. Was Abdul keeping his word, and protecting them properly? What new measures could Tippu have introduced that may affect their well-being? In the darkness of his shelter he heard the festivities continue late into the night. When the noise of the revellers finally died away, it was replaced by a chorus of screaming hyenas and baboons, growling leopards and cheetahs, and the majestic, dominating roar of lions.

Chapter Eight

The slave girl left the procession and came to stand beside him. 'I know your wife, Haleema,' she said, speaking in Arabic. 'She is a stupid, selfish woman. Fortunately she has not long to live. Let me take her place. You will no longer want the Jewels.'

Khalil sat upright, suddenly, almost violently. The girl had been a dream, but there had been a shout, and the dull thump of a musket shot. He grabbed his pistol and, stark naked, dashed outside. The *askaris* were assembling, others came running as Juma barked out orders. Oriedo and two men were throwing fresh wood onto the glowing embers of the fire which blazed up quickly, lighting the surrounding area.

'What in God's name happened?' Khalil demanded.

'Askari Tembe has been speared to death.' In the flames the tribal scars across Juma's snarling face were terrifying to see. 'His musket and ammunition have been taken. Men from the village have done this.'

'The chief saw where our guards were posted. Perhaps he only pretended to be drunk when he fell down,' Oriedo said. 'When he got back to his village he decided to attack us, hoping our men would be distracted by the women and the *pombe*.'

'We'll burn his village to the ground,' Juma snapped. 'Kill him and his warriors. Leave the rest to starve.'

Khalil shook his head. He was still shocked, but able to think rationally. 'The loss of a single musket is nothing, Juma. Even if they have more powder and shot, which I doubt, they're incapable of priming or loading. It's likely they think you simply point the weapon and pull the trigger for your enemy to fall dead. No, we've learnt a lesson and will be more vigilant in future.'

'No,' Juma shouted. 'I insist on vengeance. You don't see the danger, or have my experience. These people must be severely punished.'

He stood belligerently, hands on hips. The *askaris* clustered at the opposite side of the clearing, listening and watching the drama unfold.

'I fully understand your anger, Sergeant Juma,' Khalil said calmly. 'I, too, am grieved at the death of Tembe. He was a fellow Muslim, we prayed together daily and he was Kirru's groom. But his death was due to two men, the chief who gave the order and whoever speared him.'

'The chief ordered it, that is certain. But the whole village must be punished!' Spittle flew from Juma's lips as he snarled the words.

'It would be wrong to destroy the village for the wickedness of two. To turn the women, old people and children out into the wilderness would be unnecessarily cruel. It would mean fighting and we could lose more men, killed or wounded, something we cannot afford to let happen. We have a mission to complete. That is of prime importance. We have gained a lesson from this sad business and, as a result, can save lives, not lose more.'

Juma stood glowering, eyes ablaze. He stood his ground for several seconds then turned away, muttering angrily to himself, and strode off. Khalil glanced up at the moon.

'It will be sunrise in less than an hour,' he said calmly to Oriedo who had stood by silently. 'We'll move on at dawn.'

'*Mzee*, take care,' Oriedo whispered. 'You have enraged Juma and he is a man who bears a grudge openly. He never forgets a slight. There will be trouble from now on.'

Khalil nodded. 'I realize that, Oriedo. This is not the first time he has defied me. But I am leader of this expedition and I make the rules. Juma resents that. He must obey my orders, whether he likes it or not.'

'You now have a dangerous enemy in the expedition, *mzee*. And some of the *askaris* will listen to him. Not all, but the bullies and those who live in fear of him will do so. There is little I can do to help.'

These are not the words of a Tippu spy, Khalil thought. *Juma must be the man to watch after all*. 'Thank you for the warning, Oriedo,' he said quietly. 'You are in a difficult position, I know that. This situation is something I must and shall resolve alone.'

Not long afterwards a long red and yellow streamer lit the eastern horizon; within a few minutes the top edge of the sun was visible and details of the camp began to emerge from the shadowy darkness. The two sergeants were supervising the loading of the donkeys. Juma's continuing anger was plain to see. He twice used his fists on men slow to respond to his orders. He then swaggered across to Khalil and spoke without looking him in the eye.

'We will not bury our comrade here, in land belonging to our enemy,' he said sullenly. 'We will carry his body on a donkey and find a spot elsewhere.'

'I agree, Juma. Here is not appropriate. I shall decide on a suitable place for Tembe's grave. As a Muslim he is entitled to a religious burial which I shall conduct.'

The sergeant nodded curtly and turned away. Khalil hoped his reply would begin the process of healing the rift between them. But his expectation was not encouraged when he heard Juma's order for the column to move on.

'Company will retreat!' he barked, clearly indicating that in his view Khalil was guilty of the most heinous of military actions.

The day's march began with the *askaris* especially vigilant. It was impossible to guess what the chief might be planning, or of telling how much he knew about firearms. He might own an arsenal of weapons bought, or more likely stolen, from previous expeditions. But it was most likely that the musket taken was the only one he possessed. Whatever the situation, it was advisable to take precautions. Khalil reviewed the arrangements with the two sergeants although Juma merely sulked, adding nothing to the discussion.

The column moved off with two armed scouts ranging ahead whilst others spread out on either side in case of ambush. Khalil, sitting high on Kirru, continuously surveyed the surrounding scrub through his telescope. Nothing was seen and as the morning wore on, confidence grew that the column had crossed the unmarked border and was now into the next chief's territory.

Late in the afternoon they came to a small wooded glade, dappled with shadows. It was here that the body of Tembe was laid to rest. Khalil read an extract from the Qur'an at the graveside, flanked by the sergeants. When the short ceremony ended he turned and offered his hand to them. Oriedo shook it solemnly, but Juma hesitated before doing so and there was no strength in his grip. To Khalil it was a signal their argument was not forgotten. If, as seemed increasingly likely, he was Tippu's spy, the incident would only serve to make him all the more treacherous.

The land through which they were now travelling was ruled by a series of feudal overlords amongst whom uneasy and irregular truces existed. Tribal warfare, with savage retribution in blood and fire, regularly erupted without warning. Invariably the causes of conflict were trivial; hundreds of deaths resulted from disputes over frivolous matters such as the ownership of a particular goat or woman, or from minor territorial intrusions, real or imagined. In the course of the march in the following weeks the expedition entered and left numerous separate demesnes. The borders between them were never apparent and the first indication that a boundary had been crossed was the arrival of the local chief demanding his *hongo*. Invariably muskets were first demanded, in hope rather than expectation, and a lengthy bargaining session ensued. When agreement was finally reached, Khalil simply handed over the agreed goods, explaining to the chief that his men were not permitted to take part in celebratory dancing or drinking. A party of sorts was nevertheless often held in the nearby village and the tempting sounds of revelry reached the *askaris* who were strictly confined to camp. To ensure none slipped away, the sergeants carried out head counts at irregular intervals throughout the night. Any *askari* found absent was soundly thrashed on his return. Khalil was relieved that Juma, despite his continued hostility, was still paying attention to his regimental duties.

As the camp was stirring a few mornings later, Oriedo reported to Khalil that one of the donkeys had died during the night. She had been a friendly old character, her grey muzzle showing her advanced age. Although never strong-looking she had, without demur, carried two full water kegs and a bundle of spare muskets ever since leaving Bagamoyo. She had been a particular favourite of Likilo, the snakebite victim, and every evening he had fed her out of sight of the rest of the animals with scraps left over from the men's meal. Two *askaris* buried her on the campsite and laid a flat stone on the grave to prevent hyenas digging up and eating her remains.

The following evening, as the time to make camp approached, two of the remaining five donkeys suddenly went lame. They were barely able to walk and there was no prospect of recovery. It was clear they could go no further. Khalil was heartened by the fact that Juma, albeit grudgingly, asked permission to shoot them before doing so. He led them into the scrub and shot them with pistols.

'We could have a change of diet for supper tonight,' Khalil said to Oriedo. 'I have eaten horse-meat often in Muscat.'

A look of horror came over the sergeant's face. 'Eat our donkeys, *mzee*? The *askaris* would be horrified! Cow or goat meat, yes. But not the donkeys. They were our friends. We are not cannibals!'

Khalil was taken aback; the thought that the men nursed affection for pack animals had not entered his mind.

'If Kirru died, would you dine on him?' Oriedo asked. 'I think not.'

Khalil shook his head. 'I merely thought it would be a welcome change of diet for them.'

'They enjoy bush meat, *mzee*. It is what they are used to and there have been no complaints. We shall bury the donkeys as we did their old companion yesterday, with protection of their graves against hyenas.'

'Very well, Oriedo. I rely on your judgement in this matter.'

The deaths of the three pack animals did not cause a serious problem. Three of the four sacks of maize provided by Abdul at the start of the journey to feed the *askaris* during the crossing of the coastal plain had now been eaten. This reduced the amount of heavy stores to be carried; the supplies were distributed evenly between the three remaining donkeys.

In the days that followed, Khalil's hopes of a change in Juma's attitude failed to materialize. His resentment continued to smoulder and, when it was necessary for him to speak, he was invariably churlish. Khalil was not the only one against whom the sergeant directed his aggression. The orders he gave to the men were delivered in a truculent manner; and he used his great strength at the slightest provocation. During one afternoon march an inquisitive antelope, grazing in bushes fifty yards off to the left, raised its head to peer at the passing column. An *askari*, not one of Juma's favourites, swung up his musket and fired and the animal dropped like a stone with a ball through its brain. It was an impressive shot, although luck had played a part in the outcome. The *askaris* cheered wildly, but Juma was enraged at the man for firing without orders. A severe reprimand, accompanied by a cuff about the head, would have been adequate punishment. But it was not to be. Khalil, who had swung round on hearing the shot, watched as Juma barged his way through the column, seized the man by the shoulders and head-butted him, breaking his nose and cutting his lip badly. The *askari*, blood pouring down his face, accepted the punishment stoically whilst his comrades, familiar with Juma's outbursts of ill-temper, ignored the incident. Khalil knew he could not intervene since discipline in the ranks was the sole responsibility of the two sergeants. From the saddle he glanced down at Oriedo and saw his face was set like a mask, devoid of emotion. The march was halted briefly whilst the buck's throat was cut and his legs lashed to a pair of spare muskets. Until the night camp was reached, he was carried on the shoulders of two pairs of *askaris* to the accompaniment of rousing marching songs. Khalil was relieved to see the injured *askari* join in with the singing, a sign that no offence had been taken.

Juma's brutish attitude was not the only cause of concern to Khalil. One evening he was unable to find his sextant. He had kept it wrapped in a cloth in the bottom of one of Kirru's leather saddle-bags. He had a clear recollection of returning it to the usual place three nights earlier, the last time he had used it. His possessions were few, so it did not take him long to carry out a thorough search. But there was no doubt, his sextant had gone. It had been given to him by his uncle on the occasion of his appointment as master of *Salwa* and had been with him on every voyage since. Its loss to the expedition was not yet grievous, its main use had been to fix the latitude of their position. This had remained almost constant since leaving Bagamoyo as the march had been approximately due west and it had changed little. But, after crossing the Mutumwa river, they would be turning north in accordance with Abdul's instructions. Their latitude would then change hourly and without the sextant the daily positional fix could be ascertained only by dead reckoning. The most important section of the new map, showing the route from the Mutumwa to the hidden valley, would therefore be only approximate.

Khalil sat pondering the problem. He was certain Juma had stolen the sextant. He had had ample opportunities to do so and he would have known it was kept in one of the saddle-bags. It would have been easy for him to slip into the shelter during the course of the evening meal and take it. The instrument was of no value to him, his only motive could have been mischief. He had probably thrown it into the bush. Khalil tried to swallow his vexation but with only partial success. He did not mention the loss to Oriedo.

A more serious problem came to light a few days later. Tembe, who had been speared in the recent attack, had been Kirru's groom. Following his death, Khalil had assumed the responsibility himself. As he was saddling him one morning the camel was restless, turning and snorting in an unusual manner.

'What's wrong, old friend?' Khalil enquired. 'Not wanting to go walking today?' He checked the saddle belly-band since it was easy to cinch it too tightly and cause discomfort. But it was comfortable. As he straightened up he noticed Juma staring across the clearing at them; there was something oddly sinister about his expression. Khalil felt uneasy, and sensed a premonition of danger. Had he caused Kirru harm, given him poison perhaps? He knew which plants were harmful, even fatal. If anything happened to Kirru, Khalil would be forced to continue the journey on foot and it would be impossible for him to keep up with the *askaris*. Perhaps abandoning him in the wilderness was Juma's intention. The sergeant was as yet unaware of the expedition's true objective, but once he knew it, Khalil knew his life would be in danger.

He turned back to Kirru, ran his hands over his back and sides, below his guts, feeling for any areas of tenderness. The camel stood still, staring ahead. Next he slid his hand down each of the camel's forelegs, picking up each foot in turn and examining the broad pads. All was well. He moved to the rear and as he felt the left hind leg, Kirru suddenly delivered a backwards kick that hurled him to the ground. For some moments he lay motionless on his back, the sky above was spinning. Two *askaris* ran forward and helped him slowly to his feet.

'Thank you,' he gasped. He was breathless and badly shaken, his shoulder throbbed with pain. 'Kirru appears to have an injured leg. Take his saddle off, I must examine him.'

When the saddle was removed, Khalil tugged on the rein and ordered Kirru down. The camel hesitated, then gingerly lowered himself to the ground. Instead of tucking in his legs below his body in the usual manner, he lay sprawled, lying on his side. His left leg above the hoof was swollen. At first it was impossible to examine it closely in view of his tendency to kick and it was several minutes before a team of men, supervised by Oriedo, managed to immobilize all four of his limbs with ropes. Juma, Khalil noted grimly, kept away from these activities, occupying himself with directing the men packing the donkeys' loads. Khalil knelt in the dust beside Kirru's injured leg. In the centre of the swelling was an unnatural groove from which the ends of a string were visible. Khalil gently drew them together and with his knife cut the loop between the knot and the skin. He pulled the thread away and held it up. It was the remains of a ligature, cutting off the blood supply to the foot and making it impossible for Kirru to walk any distance.

Khalil gave orders to delay the march until Kirru was sufficiently recovered to continue. It would take several days for the swelling to subside, extending the length of the journey and finally extinguishing all hope of a return to Zanzibar within the four months stipulated by Tippu. The decision to halt was popular. Both sergeants welcomed the chance to carry out extra training, and the men enjoyed the change of routine. The incident, although distressing, was therefore of benefit to the general morale of the expedition.

Khalil made a conscious effort to dismiss his near certainty that

Juma was responsible for the ligature; but the thought persisted, assailing him with further worries. Juma could not have acted alone; he may not have been personally involved in causing the injury. Whether or not he had tied the ligature, Kirru would not have stood meekly allowing it to be done. There must have been accomplices among the *askaris* to secure him, and others serving as lookouts. Who could they have been? Khalil had noticed certain men were allocated the easier jobs, given the better cuts of meat, and issued with the best muskets. Which of them were likely to be involved in harming Kirru? Older men, held indebted to Juma for past favours? Or younger, overawed, or more likely frightened, by his brute strength and supposed mystical powers?

A further thought came to mind. Had Juma also been responsible for the sudden and unexpected lameness in the three donkeys he later shot? Khalil cursed his own failure to inspect the animals more closely; he had accepted the reports and approved the sergeant's suggestion that they were no longer able to carry loads and should be killed. Why had Oriedo raised no objection? Had he too taken Juma's word, or had there been some complicity between them. Was Oriedo one of Tippu's men after all? Khalil dismissed the thought. But he knew he could not allow the matter to pass unremarked. He must get Juma on his own and make a forthright declaration of his suspicions. Despite the sergeant's preferred weapon of persuasion being his fists, Khalil felt a surge of relief as a decision crystallized in his mind.

Chapter Nine

That evening Khalil waited until the sergeants dismissed their squads after the day's training. 'Sergeant Juma!' he called in a friendly tone, as the *askaris* went to supper. 'Will you come over here a moment? There's something I'd like you to see.' Juma sauntered over with exaggerated nonchalance.

'Follow me,' Khalil said quietly, as if about to share a confidence. He led the way into the surrounding scrub. Twenty yards from the camp, as the sergeant came up behind him, Khalil quickly turned, whipped up an arm and, with the edge of his hand, struck the sergeant a hard blow across his throat. It was an action he had seen used by a Chinese mate, scarcely more than five feet tall, to subdue a giant drunken seaman on the quay at Musqat. The man had fallen like a toppled tree, and Juma's collapse was equally dramatic. He made a loud choking noise and dropped to his knees. Khalil, in a rush of triumph, swung back his foot and kicked him full in the face as he knelt before him. There was a satisfying crunch of bone, the sergeant rolled onto his side and lay still.

Khalil stood panting with excitement. Blood-lust, dormant since he had repelled the Somali pirates from his dhow years before, now flooded his mind. Had there been a stone to hand he would not have hesitated to smash Juma's skull to a bloody pulp. His pent-up rage – against Tippu, the loss of four men, the problems yet to be faced – found expression in the two blows he had already struck. A third would have avenged him even more. But the moment passed. Juma twitched and stirred as consciousness returned, groaning and moaning as he became aware of the pain of his injuries. He sat up, still groggy and looked about. Khalil stepped forward, Juma cringed away from him.

'You have been repeatedly insolent to me,' Khalil said coldly, staring down into the sergeant's face, now smothered in blood and swelling rapidly. 'You stole my sextant and injured my camel and perhaps one or more of the donkeys. I am your superior in rank, and I have now proved I am also your superior in strength. This is a warning. If you ever again question my orders, or speak, or do anything against me' – he changed his voice to a slow menacing hiss – 'I shall kill you.'

He stood back and Juma slowly got to his feet. Perhaps he sensed another attack was imminent and feebly raised a hand as if to protect himself. It was a sign of abject surrender, a plea for mercy, a recognition of defeat.

'I'll tell the men you had an accident,' Khalil snapped. 'I don't want them to think I'm another brute, like you.'

Juma was absent from supper that night. Normally he had a prodigious appetite and invariably seized more food than anyone else. The atmosphere among the *askaris* was notably light-hearted, altogether much more pleasant than usual. The sergeant's non-appearance was discussed openly and the conclusion reached that he must be busy communing with the spirits. Some of the *askaris* believed he had the power to turn himself into a hyena during the hours of darkness and prowled about, alert for conversations that were critical of him. One daring wit suggested throwing supper into the bush for him.

When he appeared the following morning the *askaris* were obviously shocked at his injuries. Both eyes were closed by massive contusions, his nose was huge and flattened. His throat was bruised and so swollen he was unable to speak.

'The sergeant suffered an accident before supper last night,' Khalil announced. 'He was kicked in the face by one of the donkeys.'

Many *askaris* plainly had difficulty in restraining their laughter. Juma, looking bewildered, gazed blankly round and slowly nodded his head to confirm Khalil's explanation. Oriedo stemmed the outburst of chatter that followed.

'Sergeant Oriedo, take charge of all training today,' Khalil ordered briskly. 'Sergeant Juma is excused duty until further notice.'

*

It was three days before Kirru, with Khalil leading him, recovered sufficiently to walk a couple of miles before beginning to hobble. A steady improvement followed, although it was over a week before the march returned to its normal daily stretch.

Juma's recovery was also slow. The swellings took a week even to subside to the stage where his eyes were no longer mere slits. The new broad, probably permanent, bullish shape of his nose added to his already fearsome appearance. His usual barrage of barked and shouted orders was reduced to short painful croaks. Khalil found it difficult to believe he could be responsible for such severe injuries. The success of his blow to the sergeant's throat was pure luck, far exceeding his expectations, and the kick in the face that followed had been equally effective. Juma was a fighter with an awesome reputation throughout the army and Khalil knew the outcome would have been very different if his attack had not come as a complete surprise to him.

Gratifyingly, the result he had hoped for had been achieved. The sergeant was no longer the proud and fierce man from whom the *askaris* shrank in fear. He was subdued beyond recognition, allowing Oriedo to make all the decisions and issue the necessary commands. He acted like the most junior lance-corporal; firmly yet gently easing men into line on the morning parade, helping with menial tasks around the camp and even, at times, helping the cooks prepare meals. A few mornings later he came across to Khalil, grinning broadly despite his misshapen features. '*Mzee,*' he croaked, '*Askari* Kiogi is suffering from diarrhoea and shat himself on parade!'

Khalil recognized this as a pathetic attempt at humour to bridge the gap between them. 'I am sure you know of a plant to cure his condition, Juma,' he replied coldly. 'You have my permission to search for it and prepare the necessary medicine.'

A week later, without warning, the column reached what seemed to be the edge of the world. As they came out of a mile-long stretch of pleasant woodland, a narrow band of scrub ended abruptly at the rim of a vast chasm extending as far to the north and south as could be seen. The eastern wall of the Great Rift Valley tumbled a thousand feet in a chaos of near-vertical rock faces divided by sharp ridges and deep ravines clothed in dense vegetation. Far below, the floor of the valley was a sombre plain stretching away to dissolve in a distant misty blue haze. Although it was early in the afternoon Khalil ordered the night's camp to be made a few hundred yards back from the dramatic edge. The perilous descent to the valley floor would take most of the next day and an early start would be necessary.

Inevitably, events failed to follow expectations. In the morning, as the *askaris* formed into their column, Juma hurried across to Khalil.

'Elephants, *mzee*! Lots of them!' he reported excitedly in his still croaky voice. 'I gave *Askari* Kiogi medicine as you ordered, but he still has the diarrhoea. He was relieving himself in the rocks up there when he saw the tuskers.'

Khalil dismounted and walked rapidly with Oriedo and Juma up the rise on the north side of the camp. They each carried telescopes. On reaching a small stony gully, they lay flat and crawled forward to look over the crest. In front was a bushy scree-covered slope plunging down to a narrow stream bed. On the far side, a similar bank rose sharply to a high rocky ridge. In the bottom of the gorge were the elephants. Some were grazing, tearing at the lower branches of the trees; others stood contentedly in the lush grass. More were gathered around a muddy pool, all that remained of what would be a sizeable stream in the rainy season, flowing along the valley to discharge as a waterfall over the precipice into the valley far below. Khalil counted at least thirty elephants, ranging in size and age from an enormous bull to six young tuskless calves. The remainder of the herd was made up of cows and young bulls and heifers of various ages, many bearing ivory.

'They make easy targets,' Juma whispered, but Oriedo shook his head. 'They're too far away. We may wound a few, but most will escape.'

Khalil lay only half-listening. *What am I to do? This is possibly one of the best chances of killing elephants we shall ever get. If I let it pass, and Juma or one of the* askaris *is a spy, Tippu will hear I disobeyed his order to bring him ivory. But if the Hamerton Plan goes ahead, we'll be returning without captives. And without captives the tusks can't be carried back to the coast! And, if the plan is successful, the ivory won't matter....*

He plunged into a torment of indecision. Kill the elephants, perhaps for no purpose? Or leave them grazing, and risk being tortured by Tippu? The two sergeants stood staring at him, waiting for his orders. He desperately needed more time to think. But that was impossible; he had to decide now. He trained his telescope on the bull standing alone behind the herd. The younger males grazed on the outer fringes, the females and calves clustered in the centre. Abdul's brief notes on killing elephants screamed in his head.

'*It's a messy job, tuskers' skulls are so thick. The* askaris *must get close, no more than forty yards away, then fire at their legs to bring them down. Once they are helpless, the men gather round and fire shots into the tuskers' ear openings to mince their brains.*'

He also remembered Abdul staring across the table at him and saying, '*Could you bear to see these horrible things being done to those you love most dearly for the sake of a few dumb elephants?*'

'Let's get back out of sight,' Khalil whispered. They slid back, keeping their heads down until the ridge hid them from the herd. A childish expression of anticipation was fixed on Juma's battered face whilst Oriedo remained calm, ready to comply with whatever order was given. Khalil already knew in his heart that the herd was doomed. The Hamerton Plan might fail, so he had no alternative but to order the slaughter. *All I can do is make their deaths quick, causing as little suffering as is possible.*

'This is what we shall do,' he said to the two sergeants. It was an effort to keep his voice cold and uncompromising. 'Two teams will take up position on either side of the herd. Oriedo, you will be in charge of five men over on the far side of the stream. You and I, Juma, will be with four others on this side. When I blow my whistle, every *askari* will fire at the bull's rear legs. Our shots will only be effective from that range, and only if we all aim at the same target. There's no point in shooting at his head; the shots would bounce off his thick skull. The combined volley into his legs will bring him down.'

'You mention only nine men, *mzee*,' queried Oriedo. 'What of the other four?'

'Three of those will form a third team. They will carry tinderboxes and be in the trees behind the herd. On hearing my whistle for the *askaris* to open fire, the three-man team will start blazes in the forest. The elephants will be alarmed at the sudden sound of firing. When they see the bull fall they will be leaderless, and the fires will add to their confusion. The steep sides of the gorge will block their escape, driving them even more frantic. The only way left open to them will be down the gorge. They will flee from the flames and at the far end tumble to their deaths over the cliff into the valley below.'

Oriedo and Juma stood looking at him with their arms folded. Khalil's mind was in turmoil as he stared back at them. *Are they thinking I've gone mad? Have I missed an obvious flaw?* The pair turned to look at each other, then back at him, before their faces split into broad grins.

'*Mzee*, that is an excellent plan,' Juma croaked. 'Forcing tuskers to charge over a cliff! You speak like an expert hunter!'

'One man will remain in camp to guard our animals and stores,' Khalil added. He turned to Oriedo. 'Which *askaris* will form the fire-raising party, and who will remain in camp?'

'I'll put Banjo in charge of lighting the fires,' the sergeant replied. 'He is very reliable. One of his assistants will be old Ngali, the cook. His eyesight is bad now and he was never a good shot, even when he could see properly. He will do exactly as Banjo tells him. The other will be Kimilili. He's young, and will be very disappointed not to be chosen as a shooter. But this is his first expedition and he has had little experience with a musket. Kaliwa will be the camp guard. He is suffering from an infected arm and unfit to be a marksman.'

'Very well. Give Banjo and his two men a tinderbox each. Tell them they are not to set the trees ablaze until they hear the first round of musket fire.'

'Sergeant Juma and I shall give them full orders, *mzee*.'

'Thank you, Oriedo. We'll mount the attack as quickly as possible. The bull could lead the herd out of the gorge at any time and we cannot afford to lose this opportunity.'

The nine armed *askaris* and three fire-raisers set off in a single file led by Khalil and Juma whilst Oriedo brought up the rear. Half a mile from the escarpment Banjo and his two men carried on into the forest whilst Khalil and Juma, with four shooters, turned left and crept through the trees into the gorge. Oriedo continued with his five *askaris* across the stream to climb the slope on the opposite side. The scrub gave adequate cover, and the sound of trumpeting and noise of branches being torn down confirmed the elephants were still feeding below.

In a thicket directly opposite and above the herd Khalil raised his hand to halt his team. The range was nearer fifty rather than Abdul's suggested forty yards but it was as near as they could get without risk of the bull detecting their presence. He stood flapping his great ears, occasionally trumpeting and tossing his trunk in the air. Khalil wondered if this was a sign of agitation, a suspicion that all was not well. He was standing side-on, exactly the right position for musket shots from both sides to inflict the maximum damage. Juma and the four *askaris* poked the barrels of their muskets through the bushes and took careful aim at his mud-caked hind legs, Juma signalled silently to them to cock their hammers.

Through his telescope Khalil scanned the far slope opposite in the hope of seeing Oriedo and his men in place, but there was no sign of them. He hoped this meant they were well concealed, not that some unforeseen situation had delayed them. He cursed his failure to arrange a silent signal from Oriedo. Elephants had poor eyesight and a piece of cloth cautiously hoisted on a pole would have confirmed the sergeant's team was in position. But it was too late to think of that now. He slipped the whistle between his lips and gripped it with his teeth. Sweat ran down his brow. If he whistled to open fire before Oriedo's men were settled in place, the opportunity of simultaneous shots at the bull from both sides would be lost. On the other hand, if he delayed too long, the likelihood increased of a clumsy *askari* firing prematurely and warning the herd of danger. Banjo and his two fire-raising assistants were waiting in the forest further up the gorge, tinderboxes at the ready, listening for the first shots.

Khalil counted slowly up to ten, then backwards down to one; agonizing moments of indecision passed. The bull continued tossing his head, curling his great trunk and sniffing the air. Did he suspect danger? Was he about to round up his herd and hurry them back into the trees to safety? *He's a harmless, peaceful great beast. What right do I have to come here and slaughter him and his family? Damn Tippu to hell! Damn his greed for ivory! But the deed has to be done.* He slammed a mental door on his feelings and blew the whistle.

There was a ragged succession of bangs from the muskets beside him. The effect was instantly dramatic. The bull screeched loudly; perhaps as planned the volley from the men on the far side had struck him at the same moment. He lurched to the left, staggered a few steps then sank to his haunches, head down. One of the cows rushed up and nuzzled his rear with the base of her trunk, trying to push him to his feet. His great body swayed before he slowly rolled over onto his side and lay still. Juma's men were already reloading their muskets, ramming fresh charges down the barrels.

'Tell them to aim for the cow this time,' Khalil snapped harshly at Juma. 'The bull isn't going to get up again.'

Through his telescope he watched the beginnings of panic develop in the leaderless herd. The men fired again, the cow screamed and staggered backwards before her legs, too, buckled. Her calf milled about, weakly trumpeting. Two more cows rushed up and nudged at her and the bull, still lying where he had fallen. Khalil looked to his right and saw the first blue wisps of smoke from the fire rising above the trees. Moments later tongues of orange and yellow flame flickered, a breath of wind brought the homely smell of wood-smoke. Suddenly, explosively, the whole band of sun-baked forest bordering the end of the gorge erupted in a blaze, crackling and spitting. Burning fragments shot up like rockets then arched downwards, trailing smoke as the conflagration swept on before the wind. Foliage was licked by the flames and vanished in an instant. The fire swept on, leaving blackened trees standing like martyrs at the stake, burnt branches out-stretched like arms in an execution pyre. The air danced and shimmered.

High up on the rocky slopes bordering the gorge, Banjo and his assistants emerged, throwing burning brands down into the scrub. Fiery pockets erupted and spread like liquid, tumbling down the bushy slope. The elephants dashed helplessly from side to side, trumpeting screeches as the flames swept closer. Juma and his men fired freely now. A shot hit the nearest young bull who swung his head round at his flank as a thick stream of dark blood spouted from a gaping wound in his groin. The flames reached the lower slopes and the elephants recoiled before the searing heat, circling and shrieking as their fear mounted.

'Run!' Khalil snarled desperately at them between his teeth. 'Run, you stupid beasts, run! There's nothing else you can do!'

Juma leapt to his feet, shouting and pointing across to the far side of the gorge. Khalil swung his telescope round. Kimilili, the young *askari* from the fire-raising team, had left the other two and was running alone down the side of the gorge towards the herd, waving his arms wildly; the faint sound of his shouts reached Khalil.

'He's never seen elephants before!' Juma croaked, excitement and shouting had aggravated the damage to his throat. 'The fool thinks he can drive them like cattle! He's crazy!'

It was craziness indeed. An enraged cow, a calf at her heel, wheeled and, with her trunk held out in front, ran at the boy. He saw her coming and tried to swerve out of her path but stumbled. Before he could recover, the cow was on him. She stamped on him with her fore feet then picked up his crushed body in her trunk and tossed it sideways like a rag. Juma snatched a musket from an *askari* and fired a shot at her. Perhaps the ball struck her as she seemed to loose her balance on the scree and slid backwards in an avalanche of dust and stones.

A young bull was first to take flight. Khalil watched him stumble in panic across the rocky bed of the stream only to turn back at the foot of the slope. He was trapped in a funnel, steep sides to the left and right, and behind a fiercely burning fire. There was now no escape other than down the gorge. He stood for a few moments before trumpeting a long wailing, despairing call then spread his ears and began the fatal charge towards the far end where the rim of the cliff lay silhouetted against the morning sky. Two younger bulls followed, then two more. The rest of the herd milled and rotated in a wild screeching circle, a sentient wheel of despair. One by one they peeled off at a tangent to join the dark stream, growing as it thundered down the gorge.

Khalil kept his telescope trained on the leading young bull. He was almost at the precipice when he faltered, perhaps realizing the folly of his action. But it was too late, the followers engulfed him and in a mass the charge swept on to the final contour and plunged over the edge. Khalil tore his gaze away, sick in heart, unable to watch the final horror. Juma and his men stood watching.

A minute later, out of the entire herd, only a single cow and her calf lingered on the edge of the cliff. Perhaps it was she who had killed the young *askari*. She may have been at the rear of the charge and was able to turn aside at the last moment, her calf following. By chance she stood facing in Khalil's direction. It seemed to him she was staring directly at him, the architect of the disaster. She raised her trunk and trumpeted eerily, a mournful cry which struck him like a curse.

'Call the men together, Juma,' Khalil said wearily. 'Let's get out of this place.'

Words from the Holy Qur'an came to him: *There is no beast upon the earth but is not like unto mankind. And to the Lord shall they return.*

Wearily he walked back up the slope alone and returned to camp. Later, in the privacy of his shelter, he wept in shame at what he had done.

Despite the loss of young Kimilili, trampled by the cow elephant, the *askaris* were elated by their success. There was constant chatter and larking in the ranks as they headed back to camp. The sergeants were equally excited. Oriedo did nothing to subdue the men's high spirits, a broad grin remained spread across Juma's battered face. It was all too good, too joyful to last.

When the roll call was taken Banjo and Ngali, the cook, were missing. A search party was sent to find them in the smouldering remains of the forest. They returned carrying three barely recognizable bodies on makeshift stretchers. Two were badly charred and the third, young Kimilili, had been smashed to a bloody mass by the cow elephant. It seemed Banjo, over-conscientious in carrying out his orders, and old Ngali, had both been trapped by the flames perhaps whilst trying to save Kimilili from his foolish escapade. The three bodies were buried side by side in a common grave on a grassy slope above the Rift Valley. Banjo had been a Muslim so Khalil said an extra prayer for him, ending with words of the Prophet: *The faithful do not die but are translated from this perishable world to the Kingdom of Eternal Existences.*

Juma led a party down the face of the precipice to inspect the carcasses. He returned after an hour and reported to Khalil.

'A few elephants were still alive after their fall, *mzee*, but badly injured. The *askaris* killed them by shooting volleys into their ears. Some dead bodies are lying on ledges part-way down and we managed to lever two of them off using poles so that they fell to the bottom. It will be easier to take their ivory when we return. Two calves had survived, they may have fallen on top of other tuskers instead of onto the rocks. They were wandering in the bush, trumpeting for their mothers. We tried to shoot them but they ran off. They will not survive long on their own. Lions or leopards, or perhaps a family of jackals, will soon take them.'

Oriedo had taken two men down into the gorge. 'The fires are still burning but almost out,' he reported. 'The ivory of the bull and cow is scorched, *mzee*, but still fit for sale. The bull's tusks are exceptionally fine,' he enthused.

Chapter Ten

Next morning, as the expedition moved off, vultures were already wheeling overhead in anticipation of a day-long gorge on the fresh carcasses. Khalil led the column along the edge of the rift, searching for a way down to the valley floor. It was several miles before the beginning of a stony gully, running diagonally across the face of the precipitous cliff, offered a possible way down to the plain far below. The gully was littered with enormous boulders buried in dense scrub. The donkeys stubbornly refused to tackle some of the steeper slopes and had to be unloaded then dragged, one by one, by teams of cursing *askaris* heaving on ropes from the front whilst others behind flogged them with sticks. Their loads were brought down by teams of men working in relays.

The problems of the descent took Khalil's mind off the tragedy of the previous day, for which he was thankful. As the column neared the bottom there came a moment of light relief. A family of wild goats, the only other sign of life, had accompanied them, scampering down the rocks on a parallel route whilst keeping level with them. As the *askaris* reached the bottom the big male stood alone on a high inaccessible ledge like a victorious general reviewing his troops. At the foot of the precipice Oriedo ordered his men to line up with their muskets at the slope then present arms to him in true military fashion.

It had taken most of the day to make the descent. The sun, like a huge orange, sank towards the distant serrated edge of the valley's distant western wall. Against the bright lemon and gold of the evening sky, the long wisps of high cloud turned into vivid, blood-red streamers proclaiming to the world, at least in Khalil's mind, his part in the elephants' slaughter.

It was Oriedo, whilst supervising the unloading of the donkeys for the night, who saw the tiny flashes of white up on the eastern skyline. He hurried over to Khalil.

'*Mzee*, there are two Arabs at the top of the gully we have just come down. I think they were trying to keep out of sight but I caught a glimpse of them. I think they may be following us.'

Khalil examined the crest quickly through his telescope; although he saw no movement he was sure Oriedo was correct. It was not uncommon for Arab traders to send men to spy on other expeditions to discover their destinations.

'Thank you, Oriedo. Don't tell the *askaris* or they'll be continually looking back and the men, whoever they are, will realize they've been seen. We'll set a trap for them in the morning.'

Camp was struck as usual soon after dawn and, in case the strangers on the ridge were already watching, Khalil resisted the temptation to sweep the valley side with his telescope. The column formed up as normal with Khalil astride Kirru leading and the *askaris* with the three donkeys.

After an hour's march they came to a small plantation of trees bordering a stream tumbling over a rocky shelf. A litter of boulders lay on either bank making it an ideal place for an ambush. Khalil was tempted to lead the party himself but reluctant to leave Juma in charge of the askaris for what may be an absence of some hours.

'Pick two men you can trust,' he told Oriedo. 'We will continue as normal; with luck the men following us won't notice our numbers are reduced. They've probably been trailing us for days and becoming careless. Take them prisoner if you can and catch us up. Kill them only if it becomes necessary.'

'When they've talked I'll shoot them,' Juma muttered. It was a sudden change; after yesterday's slaughter of the elephants when he had been elated, today he was scowling and brooding. *Is he reverting to his old attitudes*, Khalil wondered. *Are the effects of his injuries wearing off? Or did I damage his brain with my kick, causing him to change his mood from day to day? It's yet another worry. Will they never end?*

The march continued. The midday rest passed without incident; the evening campsite was reached and the evening meal ready when the ambush party at last appeared. Their two prisoners were dishevelled, arms tied behind their backs and ankles hobbled by lengths of rope. The *askaris* jeered at them. Arabs in distress were not a common sight and provided a welcome distraction. When the two captives saw Khalil they fell grovelling at his feet, invoking the blessings of Allah and the Prophet upon him and begged for mercy.

'Take them away,' Khalil ordered abruptly, ignoring their pleas. 'Let me have your report, Oriedo.'

'We hid in the rocks beside the stream, *mzee*, the two men on this side, I remained on the far bank. Two hours after you left us we heard voices and they appeared, chattering like women, and started to cross the stream. I waited until they were halfway then stood up holding a pistol in each hand and called on them to surrender. One of the *askaris* moved down the other bank and stood with his musket aimed at them. The other waded into the stream and took their guns and fancy daggers. They said they were harmless merchants who had lost their way, but I called them liars. They got on their knees and wailed that their leader had ordered them to follow our column and report back to him from time to time.'

'Thank you, Oriedo. That's a very good report.'

Khalil sat eating his evening meal, glancing across the fire now and again at the two prisoners. They sat tied back to back, guarded by an armed *askari*. *What should I do with them? If they'd put up a fight it would have given Oriedo and his men an excuse to shoot them. To order their deaths now, in cold blood, would be murder and I'll have the blood of fellow Muslims on my hands even though Juma would do the shooting. Keeping them as prisoners means feeding and guarding them, day and night. Allah, what a predicament! They could jeopardize the mission. It's too late to decide their fate now; I'll put it off until morning....*

He did his round of the night watch, speaking a friendly word to each *askari*. He ignored the prisoners who sat too frightened to speak, appealing to him with their eyes. The looks on their faces brought back memories of the slave girl in the parade in Hunain

Square; she too had pleaded silently to him, staring at him and begging for her life. How long ago that seemed, how carefree life was that morning. It was later that same day Tippu had spoken to him at the villa about the expedition and this nightmare began.

As he lay in his shelter wrapped in his blanket against the chill of the night his thoughts drifted back to the slave girl. *What has become of her? I told the servant I sent to buy her from the old Arab trader to say nothing. Does she know the man she appealed to in the square that morning had become her benefactor? It's unlikely. Did Tippu taken her into his harem? She may be a servant, an ayah to some of his numerous children.* He sighed. He would never know her fate. He fell into a dreamless asleep.

'What about the prisoners?' Juma grunted, as the column prepared to leave next morning. 'Shall I take them into the bushes and shoot them?'

Khalil had been hoping a night's sleep would bring about the return of his docile attitude but it seemed not. He shook his head. 'We are short of men,' he replied. 'Those two can be made to serve us.'

'That is both dangerous and foolish. They are our enemies. If I'd been in charge of the ambush I'd have shot them like vermin.'

'They'll be useful to us. I'll speak to them.'

Juma snarled in exasperation. 'They'll cause us trouble,' he growled.

'If they do so then they'll be punished, Sergeant,' Khalil said evenly.

He walked over to where the two Arabs stood tied together. 'My sergeant says you both should die,' he said. 'You were spying on us and that is what you deserve.'

The men sank to their knees, clasping their hands and babbling for forgiveness in Arabic. 'We were forced to do it, *effendi*,' the elder of the two wailed.

'By our master,' sobbed the younger.

'Stop that,' Khalil snapped. 'Stand up.'

They got to their feet, visibly pale and trembling. Khalil felt shame at bullying helpless prisoners but he had to be careful not to show a soft attitude in front of the men. 'There is only one way you can save your lives,' he said in ki-Swahili loud enough for the *askaris* to hear.

'Anything, *effendi*. We will do anything,' the older of the two men moaned.

'You will act as slaves on this expedition. You will do whatever you are ordered by myself or either of my two sergeants. You will make no attempt at escape. If either one of you misbehaves, you will both be shot. Each of your miserable lives is now in the other's hands as well as in mine. The choice is yours. Accept my conditions and live. If you are still alive when we get back to Zanzibar, I shall release you. Refuse and you will be shot here and now. What is your answer?'

'We will serve you, *effendi*,' the elder said without hesitation.

'With our lives,' added the younger one.

'That is exactly what you will be doing,' Khalil snapped. 'Your lives are now in my hands. I swear on the name of the Prophet I'll blow your heads off if you give trouble. Remember, if one disobeys an order, you both die.'

He turned to Juma. 'Sergeant, I think our donkeys have been working too hard lately. Give these prisoners some of their load to carry.'

The *askaris* grinned their approval. Even Juma stopped scowling.

The floor of the rift valley was a pleasant rolling savannah. Although the wet season had ended two months previously, the landscape was still verdant. Great herds of antelopes, wildebeests and zebras roamed the open plain. Buffaloes, giraffes and solitary rhinos with white egrets perched on their backs picking off ticks, were a common sight. Rocky outcrops were often inhabited by families of baboons who shrieked defiance at the passing column. Late one morning when they halted for the midday meal close to a spreading acacia a drowsing leopard lay along one of the branches watching them through half-closed eyes. Lions were a common sight. One afternoon they passed within a dozen yards of a pride feasting on a freshly killed wildebeest. Cubs, their faces bloodied from feeding, romped playfully among their elders whilst vultures circled slowly overhead. Jackals and hyenas skulked in the undergrowth, waiting for the big cats to have their fill and move off into the shade to sleep with full bellies so they could scavenge the flesh that remained. With the memory of Likilo still fresh in their minds the *askaris* kept a watch for snakes and all that were seen were chased and killed whenever possible.

Despite Abdul's assurance to Khalil that the valley floor was the place to find elephants, they saw few. One morning a solitary cow was sighted walking beside a stream with her young calf. And the next day a bad-tempered rogue bull trumpeted loudly at them. Old and lame, he had probably been ousted from his herd by a younger and more virile upstart. He would soon fall prey to hunting lionesses. Oriedo, knowing how Khalil had been sickened by the elephant slaughter, tactfully refrained from drawing his attention to the bull but Juma announced loudly he was pleased so many tuskers had been killed when the opportunity had presented itself.

After a further week's march, the expedition came to a stretch of land that showed obvious signs of heavy flooding. Long black dunes of silt lay in ranks, deposited when the waters had receded. Somewhere upstream an entire forest had been swept away and carried to this spot by the torrent; hundreds of uprooted trees littered the ground. Scrubby thorn bushes, normally brown and withered, thrived in the unusually rich wet ground, bearing fresh leaves whilst rare flowers and tufts of bright green grass sprouted from the alluvium.

Camp was set up on a small grassy knoll and Khalil rode forward alone. For almost a mile Kirru picked his way gingerly through the debris and mud banks until they reached the edge of a broad river. It was at least 300 yards wide, flowing swiftly, south, between low muddy banks. There was no doubt in Khalil's mind that they had at last reached the Mutumwa river. Somewhere on the far side Muammar, the discoverer of the valley, had been stopped by the flood which had deposited the debris he had just ridden through. Abdul's notes said: *Now the rainy season is over the water level will be low so you won't have any difficulty getting across.*

Despite this confident assurance Khalil was soon aware that reaching the far bank would be no simple task. On the far side five huge crocodiles, mouths agape, lay basking on a muddy promontory. Abdul had failed, whether intentionally or not it was impossible to know, to mention these fearsome obstacles. They were not alone. A short distance upstream a family of hippos, including a vast bull weighing two tons, heaved themselves out of the flowing brown water onto a sandbank. Khalil pondered the problem at length before nudging Kirru's with his heels and riding back to camp.

Next morning, leaving two men to guard the camp and animals, Khalil led the rest of the *askaris* to the river. They clustered along the bank, staring across the muddy water. 'There's a croc!' an *askari* exclaimed, pointing a finger.

'And another!'

'Two there, against the bank!'

'There's one swimming. He's huge! And look at those hippos! They're as big as elephants!'

'We can't run crocodiles over a cliff, *mzee*,' Oriedo said sorrowfully.

'No. I wish we could,' Khalil replied with a smile. 'I hated killing the elephants, but I wouldn't hesitate to exterminate those creatures. I've always hated crocs.'

'I hope you have a plan,' Juma said abruptly. 'They don't make friends easily.'

'Yes, Juma. I have. We can't wade or swim the river. Allah forgot to give us wings so we can't fly over. A bridge would take weeks to build and a tunnel is out of the question. Only one solution remains. Build a raft and pull it across with ropes.'

To a sailor the answer was obvious, but it surprised the two sergeants and he was pleased to see the amazed looks on their faces. 'It must be small enough to handle yet big enough to get the men, stores and equipment over to the far side in four or, at the most, five trips.' He tried to give the impression of still working out the details although he had lain awake for hours mentally jiggling with weights and volumes.

'What about Kirru, and the donkeys, *mzee*?' Oriedo asked.

'They will also be got across,' Khalil replied. How that was to be done he had not yet decided but was reluctant to admit it. 'Let's get the raft built first. Then I'll explain about the animals.'

The *askaris* set to work. On Khalil's directions, twelve of the washed-up trees with straight trunks of roughly the same diameter were

123

selected. The roots and side branches were chopped off with *pangas* and the trunks trimmed with axes to suitable lengths and carried down to the water's edge. Three were laid parallel, four feet apart; the remaining nine, notched to fit snugly over the first three, were placed on top at right angles. The whole assembly was tied together with lengths of stout rope; wooden wedges were driven in to tighten the lashings. The finished raft was twelve feet long, tapered at either end, and ten feet wide. The work took all day and it was a weary party that trudged back to camp where the cooks had prepared a special meal for their return.

The following morning camp was struck and the expedition, including the two prisoners and the four animals, moved down to the river-bank. Every man was needed to drag the raft over the mud and into the water where it floated evenly with sufficient freeboard. The *askaris* celebrated the launch by lining the bank and having a communal pee over the logs. They christened the raft *Likilo* in memory of their comrade killed by the snake. Lines were attached to the bow and stern to haul it back and forth across the river.

'First we have to get a rope across to the far bank,' Khalil announced. 'Cut some long poles. On the first trip the men on board will use them to push against the current whilst punting the raft forward. To prevent it being carried downstream the *askaris* on this bank will hold the stern line taut, paying it out only slowly.'

'I'll go first with four men,' Juma said shortly. 'They can work the poles, two on each side, while I keep guard against the crocs and hippos.'

Khalil looked across at the far bank. *The first journey will be particularly risky since it's impossible to guess how the crocodiles will react. The nearest pair have lain motionless all morning, not paying any heed; there's been no sign they've been watching us. Perhaps Juma's relying on his magical powers scaring them off! The men he takes will be his cronies. Allah may help by overturning the raft midstream and wiping out five of my enemies at a stroke.* But there was only one possible reply he could make.

'Take whatever arms you need to fight off an attack.'

Juma selected his men and they clambered on board the *Likilo*. She sank a little under their combined weight but they showed no concern as the *askaris* pushed the raft out into the river. She at once began to swing downstream and the men had to dig their poles deep into the bottom mud, pushing hard back against the current. The *askaris* held onto the stern line, letting it out slowly as the raft edged away from the bank. Despite their efforts the *Likilo* could only inch crab-wise against the current, bobbing and jerking erratically in the flow. Before reaching halfway she was already a hundred yards downstream from the starting point.

In view of the presence of the crocodiles less than a hundred yards upstream Juma's courage over the next few minutes was outstanding. Khalil had a momentary glimpse of him standing naked on the side of the raft, poised with his arms up ready to dive; the next moment he had plunged into the swirling stream. His black head dipped below the surface, reappeared, then dipped again and he was swept out of sight. A full minute passed before Khalil next caught sight of him, far downstream and wading through the shallows with the end of the bowline tied round his waist.

Clambering onto the bank he hauled on the rope whilst the men on the raft renewed their efforts with the poles. They reached the bank and scrambled ashore, seized the line and together with Juma dragged the raft back upstream until she was directly opposite the starting point. Juma gave a casual wave to signal a successful first crossing. As the empty raft was pulled back with the stern rope, the *askaris* chanted a Swahili shanty to keep their efforts in unison. On the far side Juma let out the bowline, keeping it sufficiently taut to prevent *Likilo* swinging with the current.

With Juma on the far bank, his malign presence evaporated like morning mist. Khalil was able to have a reasoned discussion with Oriedo, free from the need to consider his words with care lest he gave unintentional offence. Their conversation was considered and practical and it was a most pleasant interlude. With five men safely across Khalil and Oriedo, seven *askaris*, the two prisoners, the expedition's supplies and equipment, Kirru and three donkeys remained on the east bank. The men and the supplies were no problem to Khalil, an expert in cargo-handling.

'Divide the stores and equipment into two equal batches,' he told Oriedo. 'Mix the supplies evenly so if we lose one load, it won't be a total disaster.'

With two *askaris* and the first batch of the stores on board, *Likilo* floated comfortably again with ample freeboard. Juma and his men on the opposite bank heaved hand over hand on the bow rope as Oriedo and an *askari* paid out the stern line. On reaching the far side the *askaris* disembarked, the stores were lifted ashore and the empty *Likilo* was quickly pulled back by those still waiting to cross. The crocodiles continued to bask on the mudbank, motionless yet menacing although they had shown no interest in the raft. But it was impossible to tell if they had been watching.

By noon the *Likilo* had crossed and returned twice. All the stores, Juma and nine *askaris* were now on the far bank. Only Khalil, Oriedo, *Askari* Teso, the two Arab prisoners, Kirru and the three donkeys were still to cross.

'Kirru goes on his own next, Oriedo,' Khalil said. 'I'll tether him to the stern and he'll swim across behind the raft.'

'He may excite the attention of the crocodiles, *mzee*,' Oriedo warned. 'They have been patient so far but a camel in the water will be a temptation to them.'

'Perhaps we could shoot one of those hippos,' Khalil suggested, nodding upstream at the group lying like stranded whales on the sandbank. 'The blood in the water would attract the crocodiles, diverting their attention while Kirru, and on the next trip the three donkeys, swim across.'

'I doubt it, *mzee*,' Oriedo said, stroking his chin pensively and staring at the river. 'Hippos are like elephants, very difficult to shoot dead. And when injured they become very aggressive. Their blood will spread in the water but it would send the crocs into a frenzy. I once saw six of them fighting each other over a goat that had fallen into a river. They were like a pack of mad dogs.'

'So what do you suggest instead?'

Oriedo pursed his lips. 'Why not send the two spies across with Kirru? They can sit on the raft and speak Arabic words of comfort and assurance to him. He would be happier with their company I think.'

Khalil looked at the two Arabs standing meekly on the bank. For some days he had been postponing a decision on their fate. *Is this an opportunity to settle the matter? An important route change is imminent. Once across the river the expedition turns north, putting the two Arab spies in possession of vital information on its direction. Also, they cannot be taken on the raid on the valley when the time comes. They'll have to be left behind under guard, reducing the number of askaris available to mount the attack. But Oriedo has presented the perfect answer! When they cross the river their lives will be in the hands of Allah. Whether they live or die will be His decision. They came as spies and according to the Prophet, May Peace Be Upon Him, all actions are judged by the motives prompting them. Who is better than Allah to decide theirs?*

He turned to Oriedo with a smile. 'Sending the prisoners across with Kirru is an excellent idea. I wish I had thought of it myself!'

He called the two Arabs over. 'You will cross the river now,' he said, 'taking my camel across with you, swimming behind the raft. Offer him encouraging words in our Arabic language which he understands. He will be frightened and in need of your reassurance.'

The men looked at each other before the eldest spoke. '*Effendi*, your camel is not alone in being frightened. We are also. You must give us guns for protection. Or men to guard us from crocodiles and hippos.'

Khalil shook his head. 'I cannot trust you with guns. You are spies and meant to do us harm. And there are no men to spare. As you can see they are all now on the far side. But the raft has been going back and forward all morning and has not been attacked. There is no reason why it should be this occasion.'

'Have mercy on us, *effendi*,' the younger one pleaded.

'You are in the hands of Allah,' Khalil said grimly. 'He'll watch over you.'

Oriedo tied a rope to Kirru's bridle and fastened the other end to the stern of the *Likilo*. Teso forced the two Arabs forward. They continued to protest volubly; he waded into the river, pushing the raft clear of the bank. Khalil stroked Kirru's nose and spoke softly to him as Oriedo signalled to Juma to start hauling. As the slack of the tether was taken up, Khalil gave Kirru's rump a smack to urge him forward.

He gave a baleful glare but walked out from the bank with only token reluctance. Within a minute he was swimming strongly, only his hump and neck showing above the water. He acted as a sheet anchor in unison with the rope held by Oriedo, steadying the stern of the raft across the current.

'A ship of the desert swimming a river,' Teso remarked, smiling at his own wit.

Khalil ignored the comment and kept his glass fixed on the raft. The Arabs were kneeling on the logs chanting a continuous prayer, begging Allah's protection; the sound of their voices drifted across the water. They paid no attention to Kirru who continued swimming strongly. A curious hippo floated upstream of the raft watching with hooded eyes as the raft reached the far side. Juma's men hauled it in to the bank and the two Arabs scrambled ashore. Kirru walked up out of the water and shook himself vigorously, showering the assembled *askaris* and causing great hilarity. Relief flooded through Khalil, but, as he turned to speak to Oriedo, he heard angry shouts. He swung back and through his glass saw the two Arabs on the bank surrounded by the *askaris* who were gesticulating wildly.

'The Arabs are refusing to get back on the raft,' he said to Oriedo.

Juma had guessed, correctly, that they were to make a second crossing with the donkeys and must therefore make the return journey. The elder of the pair was on his knees, clutching an *askari*'s legs; the other held up his arms, wailing a prayer heavenwards. Juma was holding a pistol to the head of the kneeling man; Khalil steeled himself for the sound of a fatal shot. But two *askaris* dragged the Arab away and shoved him and his companion back on board the *Likilo*. Oriedo and Teso took up the rope and began to haul. The raft jerked away from the far side and began its return crossing. On board the prisoners knelt side by side, again wailing pitifully. The journey was quick and without incident; minutes later *Likilo* glided into the bank. The two men desperately tried to climb ashore but Oriedo and Teso pushed them back. Khalil stood above them with a pistol in either hand.

'Stay where you are,' he called down in Arabic. 'Remember, the penalty for refusing to obey my orders is death. You will make a final crossing, this time with the donkeys. When you reach the far side this time you can remain.'

'*Effendi*, in the name of Allah, do not make us cross again without weapons. Crocodiles were swimming close to the raft, getting ready to attack us!'

'Cross the river, or I will shoot you both now,' Khalil ordered, keeping his two pistols trained on them. 'Oriedo, tie the donkeys to the raft.'

A tether was attached to each of the three bridles and the free ends lashed to the stern. Teso pushed the raft out into the stream while Oriedo gathered the tethers and led the animals forward. At the water's edge they dug their hoofs firmly into the mud, jerking back against the rope and braying loudly but the pulling power of the raft as it was caught in the current overcame their resistance. They were dragged forward and plunged into the river in a great cascade of foaming brown water. The Arabs, cowering in the centre of the raft, renewed their wailing with their arms raised. The donkeys surfaced and they began swimming. On the far side Juma and his men hauled on the bow rope and the perilous journey began.

Khalil kept his glass on the raft. Horror struck a hundred yards out from the bank when the fearsome scaly head and front legs of a large crocodile suddenly reared vertically out of the water and crashed down onto the raft, its wide mouth snapping hungrily towards the two Arabs. They screamed briefly as they tried to cling to the sharply tilted timbers before sliding helplessly into the water. For an instant their white gowns floated on the surface then the crocodile's grey-green belly showed as it rotated, coming in to attack from below. A moment later the gowns disappeared in a lather of red swirling foam. The donkeys, still attached by their tethers, bucked and thrashed as the raft rocked violently. 'Let the stern rope run free!' Khalil yelled to Oriedo and Teso.

Likilo, no longer restrained at the stern, was swept rapidly downstream. On the far side Juma and his men clung to the bow rope, allowing her to swing pendulum-like in a wide arc towards their bank. The bobbing heads of the three donkeys were visible above the churning water for a few moments before a crocodile surfaced and snatched one of them by its muzzle and dragged it down. The other two swam free of *Likilo*, the crocodile having bitten through their tethers. Frantically they paddled for the bank, their ears folded back and eyes big and staring with fear. Miraculously they reached the shallows and clawed with their hoofs at the thick grey mud, struggling to reach safety.

Juma's men ran along the bank, screaming encouragement at them. A young crocodile appeared, scuttling across the mud on its ungainly legs, mouth agape. Two *askaris* knelt with their muskets and shot at it but the creature gave no sign of being wounded. It reached the nearest donkey, seized her rear legs and pulled her down. She screamed as the crocodile dragged her over the mud and into the river. The brown water closed over them, drowning the screams and hiding the horror from view. An *askari* fearlessly waded through the mud towards the last donkey and grabbed the remains of her tether. The glutinous mud gripped his legs; a chain of his comrades quickly linked arms and reaching out, hauled him and the terrified beast to the safety of the bank.

Khalil, Oriedo and Teso hauled the *Likilo* back in silence. *No words can ever describe that*, Khalil thought. *It was so bloody and brutal, foul and violent, I'll never be able to speak of it.* He stared across the Mutumwa; it slid past at his feet, quiet now, with no sign of crocodiles.

'That leaves us with only one donkey, Oriedo,' he said. 'There are kegs of gunpowder, ammunition, spare weapons, shot and the medicine chest to carry.'

'Yes, *mzee*. The Arab slaves were like donkeys, carrying stores.'

'Yes. It's strange they came as spies yet now we desperately need them. It will be an even tougher march from now on. Will the men be able to carry on?'

'They are *askaris, mzee*, and very proud. They will do their duty.'

Not long afterwards they were ready to cast off for the final time. The three men bristled with an array of muskets and pistols, each carefully primed and loaded. Khalil offered a short prayer to Allah, beseeching His protection in their coming peril before Oriedo and Teso pushed the *Likilo* into the river with a pole. Viewed from the bank the water had appeared smooth but from the raft, with the tops of the logs only inches above the surface, it was greatly disturbed by eddies and swirls. Floating debris, sunken trees and submerged mudbanks caused opposing currents; brown water slopped continuously across the raft. The bow rope, hauled by Juma's men on the far bank, drew it slowly out into the river. The end of the stern rope was tied to a tree on the receding bank and paid out slowly by Teso at the stern to keep the raft on as straight a course as possible as it was towed through the churning water. Khalil knelt on the starboard side, facing upstream and Oriedo at the bow, both holding cocked muskets to their shoulders; their belts bristled with loaded pistols.

As the raft reached mid-point Teso suddenly shouted and dropped the rope. He swung his musket down and fired from the hip; throwing the weapon down he snatched a pistol and fired again, all in the space of a few seconds. One of the shots had scored a hit, Khalil caught a glimpse of a huge crocodile, its head streaming dark blood, roll over and sink into the brown water. Another dived in the wake of its wounded companion, attracted by the blood.

A scaly head with massive jaws agape reared out of the water only a yard in front of Khalil. The rows of teeth were large, unevenly spaced and sharp-pointed; the inside of the mouth was slimy and dark red, unblinking yellow barred eyes stared up at him. It was a loathsome evil thing, intent on killing him. He swung his musket down and pulled the trigger, the ball smashed into the terrible mouth. The crocodile groaned and rolled away in a satisfyingly red turbulent froth. Khalil threw the musket aside and grabbed a pistol as a broad scaly back glided past, a yard off to his left. The pistol misfired, he dropped it, dragged another from his belt and pulled the trigger without pausing to aim. A neat round hole appeared on the line of the crocodile's spine. Its head came up and turned, jaws snapping at its own injury as the current swept it past.

He suddenly became aware of shouts and cheers and looking up, was amazed to see the *Likilo* had almost reached the bank. The nightmare of the Mutumwa was over. *Askaris* waded fearlessly out into the stream to draw the raft in. The three men scrambled ashore; Khalil knelt in the mud and offered a prayer of thanks for the safe crossing, adding a supplication for the souls of the two Arabs.

A major obstacle had been overcome; all that remained was a straightforward march north to the valley in the footsteps of Muammar. But on the return march the river would have to be crossed again. And the crocodiles would be waiting.

Chapter Eleven

The land beside the river was swarming with biting flies and Khalil ordered the stores moved to higher ground where camp was set up. Over supper he told the two sergeants there would be no marching the following day. With the loss of the two Arabs, and now only one donkey remaining, the supplies and equipment would have to be redistributed. When that had been done the *askaris* could rest, apart from guard duties, and recover from the ordeal of the Mutumwa.

Next morning the camp was busy with the job of sorting and repacking. With the river now close by there was no longer a need to carry water so the cooks' remaining supplies of salt, sugar and flour were packed in the dried-out barrels. One of the gunpowder kegs was half-empty; the remainder was shared out between the men to carry in their back packs. The second keg was full and formed part of the one remaining donkey's load, together with the medicine chest. For the first time on the march, Kirru would be carrying supplies. Until now his only burdens had been Khalil and his personal possessions in the two saddle-bags. In future a bundle of spare muskets, cooking pots and utensils and coils of rope would be strapped behind his saddle. The *askaris* would carry the remaining items of equipment, in addition to their weapons.

With the sergeants and the men fully occupied, Khalil retired to his shelter. With the Mutumwa crossed in accordance with Abdul's instructions the column must now march north. The time had come to look at Muammar's map. He picked up the prayer mat Abdul had given him before the *Arafat* left. He had knelt on it five times every day since leaving Bagamoyo but only now was it to reveal its secret, the final route to the valley. For a full minute he turned the mat over and over, musing on what mysteries it might contain. He still retained a healthy scepticism regarding the whole story. The existence of the valley, its attractive inhabitants and, especially, the supposed Solomon and Sheba connection, combined to make a tale seeming too fantastic to be true. Perhaps the map would answer his doubts. With the point of his knife he carefully cut each of the tiny threads along the side of the mat. A slim canvas package, folded once and neatly stitched along the other three edges, slipped out. It appeared to be padding, the sort of thing a loving wife would insert to cushion her husband's knees during prolonged prayers. He slit the package open, it contained a single scrap of paper. With a feeling akin to awe he smoothed it out on his thigh and stared with dismay at Muammar's sketch.

To describe it as a map was a gross distortion. It was merely a pair of scrawled lines forming the western alphabetic letter 'T' and two crudely drawn circles. There was no scale of distance or compass rose, nothing to show which edge of the paper was the top. Khalil's dismay turned to fury. This meaningless scrap had been the cause of Haleema's death! Because of it he had been sent on this wretched journey in which nine *askaris* and two pitiful Arabs had already died, and a herd of peaceful elephants butchered. All for nothing.

Everything is clear! There never was a secret valley; the handsome black people don't exist! Tippu invented the story to amuse the sultan, a mere mention of the Queen of Sheba would excite his interest. To add credence to the tale, Tippu drew this sketch himself. The sultan, swept away with enthusiasm, ordered him to organize this mission and he had no option but to obey. He expects me to fail, and everyone to die, leaving no trace of the expedition. That's why he agreed to give me the villa, he thought I'd never return....

As the day wore on the camp fell silent. While the *askaris* were enjoying their rest day, Khalil lay brooding in his shelter. Yesterday evening all had been clear. Abdul's notes had ended; they had served their purpose well. With the *askaris* safely across the Mutumwa, Muammar's map would show the final miles of the route north to the valley. *But there is no map, only this useless sketch. The whole, sick-*

ening journey has to be done in reverse, back to Zanzibar with nothing to show for all the blood and sweat it has cost us. Tomorrow we have to re-cross the Mutumwa and fight the crocodiles again. They must be instruments of divine retribution, sent by Allah to destroy the mission for the evil of its intentions....

He did not leave the shelter all day except to relieve himself. When evening came, and Oriedo called that supper was ready, he replied he was ill and would not be joining the men. Fearful of the night and the thoughts it would bring, he took the bottle of laudanum from the medicine chest and gulped a mouthful. His head was reeling even as he recorked the bottle. Suicide was one of the greatest crimes a Muslim can commit yet, for a fleeting moment, he hoped the laudanum would allow him to die in his sleep and end this torment.

The sun was up when he woke; he had slept soundly. For a while he continued lying on his back, gazing up at the soft light coming through the cloth roof of his shelter. Today he must tell Juma and Oriedo the expedition was going no further and to order the *askaris* to prepare for the return march to Zanzibar.

He sat up. The lingering effect of the laudanum made him giddy, yet his mind was strangely lucid. The crumpled scrap of paper lay on the ground where he had thrown it the previous night. He picked it up, smoothed the creases and looked at it again. *Why had old Muammar spent his last mortal minutes drawing a fake? Was it even remotely possible the sketch held a secret after all? What if the story Muammar's son had screamed out under torture was true?* The questions whirled like dervishes in his brain. He stared at the paper, narrowing his eyes like a sage trying to decipher the meaning of an ancient manuscript.

The two lines on the map were drawn roughly at right angles, but Muammar would have known only Arabic script so there was no hidden clue there. The two circles were crudely drawn with no suggestion as to their meaning. He lay back again and tried to recall Abdul's account of Muammar's journey. There was no reference to it in the notes, but his verbal description came drifting back, distant whispers that formed a fragmented version of the tale: '...*he reached* the Mutumwa ... it was in flood, two miles wide ... he turned north ... met another river ... became trapped between the two....'

One river flowing into another, according to Abdul. And there, on the sketch, were two lines joining at a right angle! Was it merely a coincidence? Khalil felt a first prickle of excitement. Hurriedly saying prayers, he dressed and went outside. The camp was active; the *askaris* had the donkeys loaded and were preparing for the day's march. Would it be to the east for home, or north to the valley? The next few minutes would surely tell. A short distance from his shelter was a flat bare area several feet across. He picked up a stick and in the sand scratched two lines, joined in the shape of a letter T. He added the two circles in the positions corresponding to those on the map and finally drew a rectangle around the sketch representing the four sides of the scrap of paper.

Muammar's map, in a magnified scale, lay at his feet. *Suppose the pair of lines on the sketch represent the two rivers. Muammar had been travelling east when he had reached the Mutumwa flowing south. It had been in flood so he had been forced to turn north. Some time, days, or even weeks, later, he had come to a second river and could go no further.*

Khalil walked slowly round the sand map, stopping at the mid-point of each side, trying to fit such a journey in place. There was only one viewpoint fitting the old man's route. If the letter T represented the two rivers, the horizontal bar had to be the Mutumwa. Approaching it from the west, Muammar was unable to cross and had left to travel north in search of a shallower stretch. His track now lay below the right-hand side of the bar. He had continued until he had met the tributary river which must be the vertical line of the 'T', and had been trapped in the angle. It was there he had set up his camp and from where he had later seen the smoke rising from the valley! *Yes, it's possible. But where's the proof? What do the two circles mean?*

Khalil stood absorbed in the problem, staring down at the scratched lines for a full minute before his heart suddenly pounded and the blood roared in his ears. *The solution is obvious! The sun had been Muammar's compass, his only means of navigating, so he had drawn it on his sketch, just as a mariner would show a compass*

135

rose with a north point. So the first circle is the sun. Trapped in the angle between the two rivers, he had seen smoke rising in the west, on the far side of the tributary. The second circle marks the position of the hidden valley!

Khalil was stunned by his discovery. Yesterday's anguish, the large dose of laudanum that could have ended his life, had been unnecessary. The map was no proof of the valley's existence, but it made the effort of going on to search for it worth the effort. He scuffed out the sand map with his foot, tore the sketch into small pieces and walked across to the smouldering remains of the camp-fire. He dropped them into the glowing embers. A flame flickered and in a moment they had gone. If the valley existed, its location now lay only in his memory.

The column was ready to move off when he called to the two sergeants and they squatted together near the shelter.

'It's time for you to know more about our destination,' he said. 'On the *Arafat*, before we sailed, the slave master told you we were being sent on a special expedition on behalf of his highness. What he did not tell you was why it was special. It's time you both knew.'

He had captured their attention and they sat forward expectantly, eager to hear the secret. *How different this scene would have been if I was about to tell them they were about to turn round and start marching back to the coast. That their courage in facing the Mutumwa crocodiles had been in vain, the deaths of their comrades worthless....*

'To the north is a valley in which an unusual tribe of people live. Only a slave trader who is now dead has seen this place. From now on our route will be based on information he supplied. We are to attack and capture the valley in the name of the sultan. That is why we have come all this way.'

'Have we your permission to tell the men, *mzee*?' asked Oriedo. 'They have been asking how much further we have to march.'

'Yes, tell them what I have said. But I do not know how far we still have to go. It may take only a few days, perhaps weeks.'

That was all they needed to know for the moment. Oriedo nodded his appreciation, Juma said nothing and his face gave no clue as to his thoughts. Khalil wondered what was going through his mind. *Is he dreaming of taking command of the expedition and become conqueror of the valley? Does he see himself leading his victorious* askaris *and a column of roped slaves through Zanzibar town up to the gates of the palace, to present them to a grateful sultan?* Only time would tell.

Khalil led the column north from the camp. Close by them the Mutumwa flowed quietly south. An arid plain, shimmering and dancing in the heat, stretched to the horizon in all directions, wavering mirages hid the junction between earth and sky. The ground was bare and sun baked for the most part; only here and there had scrub managed to grow. A few clumps of low trees were the sole landmarks. The lack of other indicators of progress created an atmosphere of depression in the ranks; the *askaris'* usual lively chatter and banter were muted as they slogged along with heads held low. Only to the east was there greenery; the land bordering Mutumwa was well watered and there was a profusion of flourishing trees and bushes. Elsewhere the plain was dotted with occasional rocky outcrops, the shattered remains of some ancient geological cataclysm, polished smooth by aeons of wind and sun. Here and there stood termite hills, red fingers of iron-hard murram earth towering twenty and more feet above the ground like the enigmatic sculptures of a long vanished tribe.

Chapter Twelve

Despite the grim conditions, Khalil was, for once, quietly elated as Kirru plodded along under him. *The Mutumwa has been crossed without the loss of a single askari, and I've unlocked the secret of Muammar's map. Perhaps my fortune has changed at last! Surely, the march from now on will be straightforward. How far ahead is the valley? A week, two at the most, and we should arrive. Why didn't Abdul warn me about the crocs? I must remember to ask him ...*

The distant sound of a shot shattered his daydreams. It was followed by shouts and more musket fire. Looking back over his shoulder he saw the centre of the column had broken, flying apart like a tensed chain snapped at its weakest link. The *askaris* were scattering; and the donkey was loose, frantically dashing to and fro, kicking his back legs wildly and scattering his load. Khalil pulled Kirru's head round and headed back.

'Crocodiles,' Juma gasped as he rode up. 'Two of them. One took Teso – he was on the raft with you yesterday. The other got Ngombe, the *askari* with the big nose. The crocs took them back into the water. Both are dead.'

He nodded grimly towards the bank where two muskets lay half-buried in the mud. Leading down to the river were the troughs made by the crocodiles' bellies, rows of clawed feet marks lay on either side. Dark blood smeared the slime, slowly curdling in the lapping brown water. The place was probably a regular watering place for antelopes and zebras; crocodiles would lie in the bushes to snatch animals coming to drink. The *askaris*, trudging along with their spirits at low ebb, had failed to spot them and had paid the penalty for their negligence.

Khalil sat with his head bowed under the weight of his guilt-ridden thoughts. He too had failed to see the danger, being preoccupied with self-congratulation. He was the leader, he had chosen the path to this disaster and the men had followed blindly. *Yesterday on the raft, Teso saved my life; today, on the march, my carelessness killed him. And poor Ngombe, always cheerful, with a big nose showing he may have been part Arab. Allah! Are You there? Do You exist? Are You killing my men to punish me for the evil I have done? How many more do You wish to see die? Is ten not enough? Twelve, with the two Arabs lost yesterday? It was You who willed their fates. You have taken more than half my men and I still have to find and capture the valley. Is it Your plan that none of us survives?*

Order was finally restored. Recapturing the donkey provided much-needed light relief for the *askaris*; freed from his load he brayed and kicked wildly in his efforts to escape further work. It was an hour before he was cornered and finally roped. The loss of Teso and Ngombe required yet another distribution of supplies and rearrangement of the column. Only eight men remained, plus the two sergeants. The march recommenced with Khalil on Kirru, followed by Juma with three men. Behind them came three *askaris* in single file, one of them leading the last donkey; Oriedo and the last two men brought up the rear.

For the next ten days the column continued north, parallel to the Mutumwa River now over a mile off to the right. The land was table flat, devoid of any feature. Grey-green scrub stretched unbroken to the horizon, shimmering in the brassy heat, day after day. It was impossible to march in a straight line. Khalil led the way, steering Kirru along a tortuous path avoiding the denser clumps of scrub. There were wide areas of particularly vicious thorn bushes; their enormous barbs caught clothing and ripped the skin. In the dust and heat, wounds rapidly became septic; every man had one or more suppurating slashes on his body.

There were few signs of human habitation. They came to the ruins of many villages, long abandoned. The predations of slavers – Abdul had accurately described them as being like locusts – over the past two centuries had cleared the populations of vast areas. A great tangible sadness was present, whispers of past terrors and pestilences that had swept over this land. Disease continued to ravage the wretched few not taken by slavers. One morning as Khalil was riding a hundred or so yards out in front of the column he came to an unexpected dip in the land. At the bottom lay a shallow stream, flowing east towards the Mutumwa and for a moment he wondered if this was the tributary marked on Muammar's map before deciding it was too insignificant. He did not notice the men at first and it was not until Kirru began to wade the stream that he looked across to the far bank and saw the line of grotesque figures. They were naked; each held a stick linking him to his neighbour. At the front, leading the line, was a skinny boy perhaps ten years old. Khalil jerked the rein to halt Kirru.

'They have the *craw craw*,' Juma murmured, coming up alongside. 'You Arabs call it river blindness. You need not fear these men, they cannot see.'

'It's not fear I feel, Juma, but pity.'

Their blindness is a blessing, the sight of their own bodies would surely cast them into a pit of self-loathing and madness ... Their eyes were swollen, upturned in the sockets, grey-white and bloody. In places their skin hung in grossly swollen folds; elsewhere it was thick and wrinkled like the hide of an elephant. Juma waded across the stream to the far bank and spoke to the young boy.

'He says these are the only men left alive in his village,' Juma reported on his return. 'They are in a desperate state as they cannot work their fields, their wives and children are starving. This boy is already showing signs of the disease. See how the skin on his legs has pale patches, like those of leopard? That's how this infection starts. Within a year or two he also will be blind and being led by a stick. But who will be left to lead him?'

'Why has he brought the men here?'

'He brings them to bathe every day. He says the coolness of the water takes the pain from their bodies for a short time.'

'Let's leave them in peace,.' Khalil said.

'We should shoot them.'

Khalil stared at him, shocked by the suggestion. 'That would be a kind deed, Juma, but it would be murder. And unlike *Askari* Ombalo, who died of yellow fever, these are not our people. I can't give you permission to kill them. There is the young boy to consider. He still has his sight.'

'For that reason he would have to be the first one shot. But what sort of life has he, leading these blind men? He knows he'll soon be one of them.'

'I agree with all you say, but I refuse to order the execution of innocent men. I cannot allow you to kill every sick person we meet.'

'No, not every sick person, that is true. But this is an isolated group. With the young boy dead these men will be helpless. They will hear a few bangs then their turn will come. Their suffering will be over.'

'What about their starving wives and children?' Khalil asked

'They'll die anyway, whether these things' – Juma gestured contemptuously towards the group –'live or die. The women may stand a chance if they are not yet diseased themselves. This sickness is found near slow-flowing streams and swamps. They could move somewhere else and allow their children to avoid it.'

From the saddle Khalil stared down at Juma. He had remained silent and his face was immobile. *Is he intent on doing good, seeking to shoot these wretches in an act of benevolent kindness? Or is it blood lust, a desire to wield the power of death, an urge to see men die by his hand? He shot Ombalo, watched without emotion the destruction of the elephant herd. He was keen to kill the two Arab prisoners.*

Expressionless, Khalil jerked the rein and Kirru moved forward. Oriedo and the *askaris* followed, passing the diseased men and the boy in silence. Half an hour later when Khalil looked back he saw Juma had rejoined the column. The meeting with the blind men was never mentioned again.

As the days passed Khalil, sitting high on Kirru's saddle, kept a constant watch for evidence that Muammar's column had passed this way but there was nothing to confirm it. Insidiously, his doubts returned. Perhaps Muammar's map was after all nothing but a meaningless scrawl. Or, as he first thought, a fantasy produced by Tippu to amuse the sultan. Even if the sketch was genuine, he may have misinterpreted it. Perhaps Muammar's two lines forming the letter T were meant to be tracks, not rivers. Reading the sketch in the sand had fitted the details together too easily, the answer was too simple. The thought grew, day after day, that he was leading his men to their deaths. It became an obsession, a conviction that his smart solution was nothing more than a fanciful attempt to make sense out of a few random facts, a conjuring trick which had fooled only himself.

He could no longer pray. Although he continued to join the two surviving Muslim *askaris* in their devotions, he remained silent; the sacred words recited five times daily since childhood had lost all meaning for him. At night he lay wide awake as disorganized thoughts tumbled through his mind. The temptation to take laudanum became so great he emptied the contents of the bottle onto the ground. Sleeping little at night, he often dozed off in the saddle, waking just in time to grab the pommel to prevent himself crashing to the ground.

By the afternoon of the twenty-first day of the march north he decided it was impossible to go further into this unknown wilderness. The only question was, when to turn back? Should he press on for one more day? Two at the most? He was unable to decide; always another ridge lay ahead, beckoning him on. Mirages shimmered and danced along the horizon. Through his glass he saw ranges of invitingly green hills, a vast blue lake remained in view for hours. But the visions never drew nearer; instead they constantly changed shape, became more enticing before vanishing completely.

His ability to pray returned. One night, in the darkness of his shelter, he realized he was murmuring pleas for guidance in his awful predicament. How this came to be he could not understand; the day had been like any other, no worse, no better. *Yet here I am praying! Am I going mad? Is Allah telling me He is now willing to listen? Or is belief in Him a form of madness itself?*

On the morning of the twenty-fifth day after crossing the Mutumwa, Allah answered his pleas. Hearing Juma calling, he turned Kirru and wearily rode back to where the *askaris* were clustered. Three skeletons, bleached by the sun with only tattered scraps of shrivelled skin clinging to them, lay scattered in the sand.

'Slaves,' Juma grunted, rolling one of the skulls with his foot. 'The bones have been disturbed by animals. See how the hands and feet are chewed off? Hyenas and jackals did that. They ate the flesh and offal soon after death, if not before. Later, vultures came down to pick the bones clean. Termites will soon finish off what is left.'

'Why do you say they were slaves?' Khalil asked.

'Who else would die together like this?' Juma sneered, as if the question had been put by a fool. The effect of the injuries inflicted by Khalil had all but gone. 'They died here, at this very spot. Maybe they were sick and their owner abandoned them before they died. This one has a rope around his neck; that one's arms are tied together. Only a slaving expedition would come this way. These were not guards: they would be decently buried by their comrades. No one bothers with slaves who die. Their bodies are left to rot in the sun.'

Khalil nodded; the evidence seemed conclusive. 'Tell the *askaris* to bury them, Juma. They've been a good signpost for us.'

He turned Kirru and rode on. *So we are in Muammar's footsteps after all. And how clever of Allah to use dead men to prove it*!

Two days later they came to a wide band of forest. Beyond the trees lay a deep gorge in which a swiftly flowing river swept eastwards. Khalil felt an immense sense of relief; without a doubt they had at last arrived at the tributary, the second river shown on Muammar's map, the vertical leg of the letter T. The old slaver's journey north had ended here; the gorge was too deep, the torrent too strong, to be crossed by roped slaves carrying ivory.

The *askaris* began setting up camp on the river bank under Juma's supervision. Khalil and Oriedo walked together downstream along the edge of the gorge until, after half a mile, they reached an area that had clearly been the site of a large camp in the not too distant past. The detritus of occupation lay strewn everywhere. Heaps of ash and half-burnt trees remained from large fires, bushes had been hacked down and piled along the perimeter to form primitive barricades. Dismembered bones of butchered antelope, broken water gourds and fragments of cloth littered the site. In one corner lay a score or more rectangular mounds of soil. Slaves who died on the march could be left behind to rot in the bush but unburied putrefying corpses would not be tolerated in camp.

Khalil stood looking about. There was no doubt in his mind that the long march from Zanzibar was over. He had brought the expedition to the very spot from which Muammar had first seen the distant smoke. It was here the story of the hidden valley had begun. His horizon suddenly changed. No longer would he wake to face yet another weary ten hours astride Kirru trudging through the bush. On the far side of the gorge lay his final outward destination.

Chapter Thirteen

From dawn the following morning two *askaris* were constantly posted with telescopes in a tall tree at the edge of the camp to scan the distant western hills for signs of smoke. They were changed every hour to ensure a proper watch was maintained. Every man now knew the true purpose of the expedition and there was keen interest in what lay ahead. Despite a careful watch throughout the day nothing was seen.

Khalil chose Juma to go on reconnaissance with him to search for the valley. The sergeant remained unpleasantly obdurate, swaggering about camp with an exaggerated air of self-importance. He seemed proud of his flattened brutish nose and gruff voice, lingering effects from the blows he had received. Orders from Khalil requiring action on his part were met with an insolent stare and when a reply was unavoidable he merely grunted or spoke with a snarl. The situation was wearisome and, as Khalil readied himself for the reconnaissance, he took no pleasure from the prospect of spending a full day with Juma. A single advantage lay in the opportunity to be alone with a man who could be Tippu's spy; there was a chance he may let something slip, giving himself away. And it was safer to have him at his side rather leave him alone with the askaris, free to foment trouble unhindered.

They set off, each armed with pistols and *pangas*, and carrying knapsacks containing ammunition, food and water. Khalil led the way with the compass, heading west along the bank of the tributary. At first the ground was flat and littered with pebbles, the bed of a long-vanished lake. After a couple of miles the land began to rise, green and undulating. A family of giraffes grazed the high branches of a plantation 200 yards off to their left. The bull stared at them in apparent disbelief and Khalil wondered if he and Juma were the first humans he had seen. Further on a quarrelsome family of hyenas, tearing at the stinking remains of a large antelope, slunk away at their approach. A series of steep wooded valleys now ran diagonally across their path and beyond rose a prominent ridge capped by a group of tall trees. It was such an obvious landmark Khalil felt sure Muammar, who must have come this way too, would also have headed for it. Their progress was slow; in the bottom of each valley thick thorn bushes were formidable obstacles through which they had to slash a path using *pangas*. It was tiring work; as the sun climbed higher the temperature rose steadily. It was only when they got clear of the final valley and a short steep climb brought them to the ridge that they found welcome shade under the trees. Juma swung himself up onto a projecting branch; he reached down to take Khalil's raised hand and wordlessly hauled him up alongside. Above them the main trunk divided, offering comfortable forks in which they settled. Hidden from view by foliage they raised their telescopes and inspected what lay before them.

A hundred yards in front, the ground fell away, plunging down to a sharp bend in a rocky canyon through which thundered the waters of the tributary. They smashed against a jumble of enormous boulders before sweeping in a mighty surge to pour over a series of steep cataracts. On the far side rose an almost sheer cliff, the smooth rock face broken by narrow ledges. Above it a steeply pitched scree extended to the edge of a dense wood. To the west, where the trees ended, the land dipped to form a verdant south-facing valley which curved back into blue distant hills. A broad stream meandered along the valley floor to plunge over the rim of the chasm like a silver column into the river far below.

This can only be the valley Muammar found. It's what we have come so far, suffered so much, to reach. Even from here there's a timeless tranquillity about the place, a sense of loveliness and peace. Paradise must look like this.

'There's smoke higher up the valley.' Juma's gruff voice broke the silence. 'Faint, beyond the shoulder of that bluff.'

Khalil shifted his telescope to the point Juma described; after a

146

moment's concentration he picked out a pale column, barely visible against the background of bright sky. 'Yes, I see it. If we cross the river and climb the scree to those woods above the cliff, we can work our away along, hidden by the trees. We'll be able to look down into the valley and see where the smoke is coming from.'

Juma grunted his agreement. 'It may be a village, or just a nomad's fire.'

They slid down the steep slope towards the bottom of the chasm. The great roar of water was deafening, its thunder magnified by the echoes returned from the grim rock face opposite. In contrast to the sunlit plain above, this was a frighteningly cold and lifeless place, visited by neither man nor animal. If the above valley is Paradise, Khalil thought as he glanced about uneasily, this is the dark underworld. Crossing the river was perilous; fierce torrents swept between the boulders with terrifying noise. Juma led the way, leaping from one rock to the next with no sign of fear. Halfway across lay an eight-foot yawning gap; between the two massive stones a cataract of brown water plunged down to a great swirling pool. Even Juma paused before making the leap; the boulder he was standing on only had sufficient room to take a couple of steps. With a mighty yell he launched himself into space, crashing down on all fours on the sloping face of the far stone before scrambling to his feet. Khalil stood on the first rock, facing the gap. *Can I trust him? He could easily give me a shove when I land beside him and I'll plunge into the water and be lost forever. If he wants to assume command, this is a perfect opportunity.* Khalil waved aside the hand Juma held out. He thought of Umma's smiling face, her arms wide, welcoming him to her before flinging himself across the gap. His fingertips clutched a tiny ridge then Juma gripped his shoulder and pulled him up. The deafening noise of the cataract made speech impossible, Khalil merely nodded his thanks. He had been wrong to mistrust him.

The remaining gaps were narrower and easier in comparison but no less dangerous. They finished the crossing with a final leap onto a tiny sandy bank at the base of the cliff. Khalil shut his mind to the prospect of crossing back. He reassumed the lead. With his sailor's skill at climbing, and having a good head for heights, he used the foot and hand holds offered by tiny ledges to haul himself up the vertical cliff face, reaching the top well ahead of Juma. He sat at the lower edge of the scree, nonchalantly waiting for him to arrive. It was a small victory, but Juma could not be allowed to win every stage. From there it was an easy scramble for them both up the scree to the dense trees crowning the crest.

'That was hard work,' Juma panted once they reached the shade. 'It will take the men with their weapons and heavy packs a whole day to reach here from the camp.'

'Yes. We'll haul the muskets and equipment across the river and up the cliff separately. That will leave their hands free to cross the river and make the climb.'

'That's good planning,' Juma grudgingly admitted. 'After a sleep in these woods we will be fresh to attack at dawn the following morning.'

'Kirru will have to be left behind at the camp,' Khalil said.

'I'll pick an *askari* to guard him until we return.'

'That will reduce our total to eleven. Eight *askaris*, you and Oriedo and myself. Only eleven of us to attack an unknown force. What if they put up a fight? They may be fierce warriors and defeat us.'

Juma shrugged and spat derisively. 'We'll have the advantage of surprise when we attack. They're most likely to be just peasants with bows and arrows. We'll smash them.'

Khalil seized the chance to introduce a vital step in the Hamerton Plan. 'Even if we capture the valley without loss, with only eleven men we can't take prisoners and march them all the way back to the coast.' He spoke casually, watching Juma's reaction.

The sergeant shrugged again. 'We'll rope them together on the march and at night tie their ankles. They won't be able to escape.'

'We'd never get them down the cliff and across the torrent below.'

'Lower them on ropes to the bottom and drag them over to the far side. We've come this far to capture them, we won't give up now.'

'Then there's the Mutumwa to cross,' Khalil persisted. 'The crocs will be waiting. We won't be able to use the raft, it would take days to get numbers of prisoners across. We'd lose most, if not all of them.' Khalil shook his head decisively; it was time to show his authority. 'No, Juma. It's impossible. Our most important task is to seize the valley for the sultan. Capturing slaves is not the main purpose of this expedition. We won't be able to carry the ivory back to the coast but that can be collected by a separate party. The sultan will be anxious to hear news of the valley, prisoners will slow us down.'

'We'll force the pace, hurry them along. Leave it to me.'

'No, Juma.' Khalil spoke harshly, indicating discussion was at an end. 'I have made up my mind. We take no slaves. We capture the valley, disarm the inhabitants, tell them they're subjects of his highness, and return to Zanzibar.'

'What if they don't accept? After we leave they'll run away.'

'They have no choice but to accept.' Khalil suddenly felt he was acting like Tippu, forcing an unwelcome order on a reluctant inferior. It was a painful lesson he remembered well. 'I'll tell their chief he is subject to Zanzibar law and must do as I say. If, after we have gone, they leave the valley then it's no loss. The valley is what his highness desires, not a few miserable peasants. No prisoners, Juma. That's my decision.' He stared at the sergeant who eventually turned away. *He's wishing he'd pushed me into the river. That wasn't his only chance, we've still got to cross it on the way back.*

It was obvious the woods were in use; pathways had been chopped through the dense undergrowth and short logs, suitable for fuel, lay cut and stacked in orderly heaps. Khalil and Juma moved stealthily through the trees for almost a mile until daylight began to show through gaps ahead. They dropped to the ground and lay flat, crawled forward until they reached the edge of the forest. In the shade of the overhanging lower branches they took out telescopes and began a careful survey of the land in front of them.

A broad meadow swept down in a gentle slope; cattle were grazing and the distant tinkle of a bell worn by the lead cow could be heard. Beyond the meadow, fenced off against the animals, lay cultivated fields with strips of growing crops of maize, cassava, yams and sweet potatoes. Figures were at work, planting and weeding, sowing and harvesting. Some strips had been cleared of old vegetation and the debris lay in smouldering heaps giving off pillars of smoke. Khalil realized this was the source of the column they had seen from the far side of the chasm; probably the same that had first drawn Muammar's attention.

On the floor of the valley lay a village unlike any settlement Khalil had ever seen. Eight longhouses were neatly arranged around the sides of a rectangle. Clearly the work of master builders, each had a beautifully thatched steep roof with wide overhanging eaves. The walls were smoothly finished in white plaster and decorated with stripes, circles and chevrons in bright reds and blues. They were connected by thick protective fences of branches woven into panels and pinned at intervals by stout wooden stakes to enclose a spacious compound with a surface of beaten earth. On the south side, in place of a section of the fence, was an open gate which Khalil guessed at night would be closed once the livestock had been brought in from the fields.

Two large, open-sided stores with raised floors stood at the top of the compound. A row of open fires, each contained within a circle of stones, burned under clay cooking pots. There were at least two dozen people in view; women knelt in a line grinding grain with stones, others tended the fires and steaming pots. A group of men sat with their backs against one house weaving baskets from rushes. A woman emerged from the hut nearest to Khalil and he watched her through his telescope. She walked gracefully, erect and with purpose; on her head she carried a large water gourd, supporting it with one hand. She turned, distracted by a small child playing in the compound. The evening sun lit her face and he saw she was as black as charcoal.

He lowered the telescope. The sight of this woman was final proof of the story that had brought him here. He had set out from Zanzibar thinking he was chasing a fantasy, yet, little by little, this conviction had been eroded. Deciphering the map gave the first real pointer, the skeletons proved the column was on the right track. The remains of Muammar's camp showed the existence of the valley was possible, but even then his doubts had lingered. It might be uninhabited, or the old man's description of the tribe mere figments of his dying imagination.

But the valley existed, and was lived in by tall, beautiful people. The way the woman he had just seen walked seemed to display a royal ancestry. It was a fabulous discovery, one that would amaze the entire civilized world! Muammar, who found it, had died, so it was he, Khalil, master of the dhow *Salwa*, to whom the honour of announcing it was to fall! It was a marvellous moment, several seconds passed before reality struck him like a mighty physical blow. *I've not come to uncover a historic secret: I was sent to destroy! On my orders this beautiful valley will be laid waste....*

He was too stunned even to pray for deliverance from this fearful situation but at that same moment Allah came to his aid. Or so it seemed. Khalil suddenly saw a way out; Juma was the only other witness of this discovery. He slid his hand down to grip the butt of his pistol and he stared at the back of the sergeant's head with its short black curly hair and strong thick neck. *All I have to do is put a ball in his brain, drag his body through the forest and push it over the cliff. I'll go back to camp and explain that as Juma crossed the stream, he slipped on wet rocks and fell into the raging torrent ...* He heard himself speaking the very words: 'In the icy cold water his hand slipped from my grasp and I had to watch him being swept to his death.'

The expedition, naturally saddened and dispirited, would return to Zanzibar. It meant abandoning the Hamerton Plan, of course. And Tippu would not be destroyed, but this beautiful valley would be saved. It was a fair price to pay. He could say, truthfully, that he had followed Tippu's orders to the letter; interpreted the map and, despite suffering great losses, reached Muammar's old camp. He and Juma had then gone ahead to the valley and carefully examined it. They found it uninhabited, with no sign of anyone ever living there. Sadly the tall black inhabitants had been an invention of Muammar's. Juma drowned on the way back to camp....

Khalil warmed to the idea. Such an account, vividly delivered, would satisfy even the most suspicious interrogator. *It would put me in the best possible light, proving Tippu had chosen the right man for the job. It was not my fault the valley was uninhabited, the blame lay squarely on Muammar. And I would not return empty handed, there's a rich collection of ivory for Tippu waiting to be collected. Unfortunately, there were no slaves to bring it back to Zanzibar but it can easily be found and retrieved. Tippu will have to admit that I have fulfilled my part of the agreement in every respect. He may even be persuaded to relinquish the villa to me after all! The family will move in, I'll take* Salwa *to sea again. The fresh air and blue sea will banish the nightmare memories of the journey. In a few months the valley will, as Abdul had promised, be nothing but a bad dream....*

But, before he finished painting the final details in his mind, Khalil knew the plan was impossible. It was not, as he first imagined, an honourable way out, an escape offered by a loving and caring Allah. It was merely a pathetic scheme of his own making, a sordid, desperate attempt to escape the inevitable. His pistol could misfire and Juma, realizing his intention, would kill him instead. Even if his shot was successful, and Tippu accepted his story, another expedition could be sent to check the truth of his report. Or some other trader could stumble on the valley, as Muammar had done. And the sultan's hope of the valley becoming a stepping stone to the conquest of Africa would remain. Its existence had been proved and being uninhabited it could be occupied without a fight....

One way or another the truth would emerge and he, Khalil, would be exposed as a liar. Tippu would destroy him, Umma, the Jewels and the children. Khalil groaned aloud There was no escape. The words of the Hindu scripture *Bhagavad-Gita* rose frighteningly in his mind: *I am become Death, the destroyer of worlds* ... On his orders this peaceful earthly paradise was to be torn apart when the sun next rose.

'The village will be easy to attack,' Juma said, after they had withdrawn into the shelter of the trees. 'As I thought, it'll be an easy job.'

'Are you are sure?' Khalil asked in a flat despairing voice.

'Certain. The people living there are ignorant fools, with no knowledge of defence. Their huts have thick thatches that will burn easily. The fences are in our favour too. When we break down the gate they'll be trapped behind them.'

'You don't think they'll put up a fight?' He asked the question with a heavy heart, knowing the answer.

'It's obvious! They're just peasants,' Juma said scornfully. 'They might have a few spears, perhaps bows and arrows for defence against wild animals and hunting. But no firearms. We'll defeat them easily.'

Khalil groaned inwardly; attacking defenceless people made the deed all the worse. But perhaps by not fighting their casualties would be light. He shook his head. 'It's a pity we have to attack such a peaceful place.'

Juma shrugged dismissively. 'We have orders from the sultan which must be obeyed. Slaving is a business like any other. Those people are our supplies and we must take them.'

'I have told you, Juma, we are not taking slaves. I was speaking of where they live. It's a paradise on earth. And we are going to destroy it. We are going to destroy paradise. Does that not mean anything to you?'

Juma shook his head. 'You are a Muslim, a religious man who believes in certain things. I am a pagan. We both live in the same world but you see it through mistaken eyes. If I want something, I take it. If the man I take it from is the stronger, he will defeat me and take it back. If I beat him then it is mine.'

Instead of kicking his face I wish I'd smashed his head in with a stone, Khalil thought, as they set off back to camp. I could have told the *askaris* it was due to the donkey's kick. That was an exceptional moment and the chance won't come again. He's brave, diving into the Mutumwa with crocodiles so near proves that. But at heart he's a brute and a bully, cruel and heartless. He'd gouge out my eyes and slit my throat without hesitation. I'm glad I didn't risk trying to kill him; it might have been his turn to have the luck.

In camp the next day was spent sorting the equipment and supplies. Midway through the morning a shot rang out; it sounded like an attack and there was instant alarm. The *askaris* grabbed their muskets and looked anxiously about for the intruders; Juma emerged from the scrub, grinning.

'I've shot the last donkey,' he announced calmly. 'We couldn't take him on the raid, and when we have taken the valley there'll be plenty of slaves to act as porters.'

Khalil recognized the blatant attempt to make the taking of captives a necessity. 'Sergeant Juma,' he thundered, 'you acted without my orders. I told you several times we are not taking prisoners. You've killed our last pack animal so on the return journey his load must be carried by the men. I doubt if they'll thank you for that.'

It was a telling comment. The donkey's load included the medicine chest and the spare gunpowder and shot, unwelcome additional and heavy burdens for the *askaris* and they muttered angrily amongst themselves. Juma glared. Khalil met his eye with a steady gaze until the sergeant looked away.

During the afternoon two small antelopes were caught in a net strung out in the bush. Their throats were cut, the carcasses chopped into joints and placed on the fire to roast. That evening a large stew of meat and wild cassava was prepared and everyone ate their fill. The remaining cooked meat and bags of biscuit were distributed and the water bottles filled. Khalil and the Muslim *askaris* said their final prayers, and he asked Allah for His blessing on their mission.

The *askaris* were drawn up ready for departure an hour after dawn. Every man was heavily loaded with two muskets and a knapsack packed with ammunition, food and full water bottle. In his belt were two pistols and a *panga*, a long length of rope coiled diagonally across his shoulder. Khalil walked down the line; he exchanged words with each man, looking him in the eye. He was proud of them; they had marched over 500 miles through rough country, faced danger and disease, seen the deaths of half of their comrades, come through the horror of the Mutumwa. And yet they were smart, clean, and ready to fight.

'Very good, men,' he said in his most commanding voice. 'An excellent turn-out. Let's hope for a short sharp battle tomorrow with no casualties.'

'Thank you, *mzee*,' Oriedo said, giving a smart salute.

'Askari Chakula, fall out!' Juma ordered. 'You will remain here at camp to look after the camel.'

After Ngombe, the cook, had died in the fire during the elephant stampede, Chakula had become the eldest of the surviving men. Oriedo muttered to Khalil, 'He's an old soldier, been in the army over twenty years. He won't mind missing the attack, he's seen enough fighting. But take care, he's one of Juma's cronies. Don't trust him.'

Khalil nodded. 'Guard him well, Chakula,' he said kindly, handing Kirru's rein to the *askari*. 'Keep him tethered at all times, day and night. Move him from place to place in the clearing so that he doesn't go hungry.'

'We'll be back tomorrow afternoon,' Oriedo added. 'Keep a constant watch for wild animals sniffing about. They won't have tasted camel before and may be tempted to try it.'

'Yes, Sergeant,' Chakula replied. 'I shall do my duty.'

'Remember what I told you,' Juma growled. Khalil wondered what he meant, the words seemed to carry a hidden message.

The *askaris* marched off in single file; for the first time Khalil led them on foot. He followed the track taken the previous day with Juma, the cleared paths made progress easy and after two hours the column reached the ridge above the chasm. Oriedo and the *askaris* spread out along the edge of the gorge and lay flat, peering down at the raging brown water they were about to cross. Juma climbed the big tree and through his telescope carefully examined the valley for signs of activity.

'No smoke visible today,' he reported curtly to Khalil.

'That may mean they have nothing left to burn,' Khalil said to Oriedo as Juma joined them. 'Both of you make sure every man knows from now on they must move quietly and carefully,' he ordered. 'There is to be no talking. Muskets are not to be loaded until the order is given. Nothing must be done to alert the people over there we are closing in on them. Is that understood?'

'Yes, *mzee*,' Oriedo replied; Juma remained silent.

'We'll climb down into the chasm in three teams. Move from cover to cover, keeping low. Juma, you know the route so go first with three men. You follow, Oriedo, with another three. I'll come with the last two *askaris*. Remember, no talking. Voices will echo in the gorge and may be heard at a great distance.'

When the last of Oriedo's group was well ahead, Khalil and his men slid over the edge to begin the descent. It was a difficult task with a heavy load and it was half an hour before the party reassembled on the river-bank. The thundering roar made verbal orders impossible; the sergeants gave instructions using hand signals. The river was crossed by each man leaping from boulder to boulder with a lifeline about his waist; weapons and equipment were hauled across separately in bundles using rope slings to keep them clear of the water. It was another hour before every man and his equipment was safely over the river and gathered on the small beach at the foot of the cliff. A patch of thick grey sticky clay lay at the opening to a spring and Oriedo ordered the *askaris* to smear thick streaks on their faces. The effect was immediately startling, imparting a ferocious warrior-like appearance to even the most docile member of the party. Muskets and back packs were stacked at the base. Khalil led two *askaris* up the cliff face using the hand and foot holds remembered from the previous day. It was a daunting task and his two companions, unused to climbing, took several minutes to recover before dropping two lengths of rope to those waiting below. The equipment was hauled up first, then the men began climbing the ropes. Juma was first to reach the top, then, showing no concern for his own safety, stood on the very edge of the terrifying drop, holding out a hand to help each man over the final edge. Even without equipment the effort took its toll and the *askaris* threw themselves to the ground, gasping for breath. Five had completed the climb; Juma was leaning over to help the next man when he gave a sudden cry and fell back.

'The rope, *mzee*!' he shouted, using Khalil's courtesy title for the first time in weeks. 'The rope snapped! *Askari* Shamba has fallen to his death!' He shook his head as he held up the end of the line. 'It must have been rubbing on a rock,' he called, clearly shaken by the accident.

Khaki was equally shocked, he and the sergeants ought to have ensured the rope was sound. He was relieved when Oriedo scrambled to safety; despite his normal toughness he too looked shaken, his face drawn and tired.

'It was very unpleasant, *mzee*,' he told Khalil. 'Shamba brushed against me as he fell. I will never forget his scream, or the sound of his head smashing on the rocks beside me. He rolled into the river and was swept away.' He moved closer and spoke in a whisper. 'That was no accident, I am sure Juma cut the rope. He and Shamba had an argument.'

He moved away quickly, leaving Khalil dismayed by his assertion. If Juma could kill one of his own men, was there nothing he would not do? He walked across to the edge of the cliff but the rope Juma had claimed was frayed had gone. He must have unfastened it from the tree and dropped it into the gorge to hide the evidence.

The last of the men reached the top using the second rope. The column regrouped, equipment was collected in silence and the *askaris* moved on up the steep scree, slithering and sliding on the loose surface. Stones rattled down the slope, the noise echoing across the chasm; it was with much relief they reached the trees and slid quietly inside. The remainder of the afternoon was spent quietly resting. Juma went to look for signs of activity in the forest but reported there was no one to be seen. It was too dangerous to light a fire to cook an evening meal; they ate the cold meat and biscuit from their haversacks. An hour before sunset Khalil walked to the edge of the wood. The village lay bathed in the light of the evening sun, the thatch of the long buildings gleamed like gold, contrasting the shadows cast across the compound. Villagers gathered round the fires where the last meal of the day was in progress, the occasional murmur of voices drifted up to him in the warm air. Khalil tried not to think of the mayhem and destruction to come; he fought an almost irresistible urge to run down to the village, warn the people of the coming disaster, tell them to flee for their lives. But he did nothing. That night he prayed to Allah to protect his men and himself in the coming raid and to watch over the people of the valley.

Chapter Fourteen

It was shortly before dawn when Khalil led the *askaris* silently through the forest. Emerging from the trees they turned right and moved up the valley side. Just visible below, in the light of a late moon, were the pale roofs of the village; the dark forest background would obscure the column from anyone down there out and about so early. Khalil counted his steps, muttering the number to himself. When he reached one thousand, about half a mile after leaving the shelter of the forest, he whispered to Juma to give the order to halt; it was passed back down the line. Above the trees to the east the first rays of the sun were striking the underside of a long bank of dawn cloud, turning it from dark grey to a delicate pink. From the village came the sound of a rooster crowing. The attack plan, drawn up the night before, was simple. Juma and Oriedo, each with two *askaris*, were to position themselves respectively on the east and west sides of the village. Each man was to carry brands of dry grass and bark that would burn fiercely when lit from a tinderbox. Khalil and the remaining two men would tear down the gate as soon as the fires started; the entire party would then storm into the compound.

'Is everyone ready?' Khalil whispered to Juma.

'Yes, ready. They'll be waking soon. We'll catch them still half-asleep.'

'Pass the order to move quietly down to the village.'

It took only minutes to reach the compound fence. Khalil crept round to the gate with his men and together they crouched and waited, giving Juma and Oriedo and their *askaris* time to get into position. Last night's sight of the village, peaceful in the evening sun, remained stark in Khalil's mind. Yet again he damned Muammar.

And Tippu. And the sultan. *May they rot in hell for sending me here, making me do this thing.* He counted slowly up to ten, offered a prayer for a quick and bloodless raid. Time had run out for paradise; he blew hard on the whistle.

There was an immediate rattle of musket fire in the cold morning air. The first cluster of fiery brands arched like comets through the dawn light, plunging down onto the thatched roofs. The dry reeds crackled as the flames licked upwards hungrily, lighting the thatch with an orange glow. Flying sparks leapt from one roof to the next; the blaze spread at an astonishing speed. There was instant pandemonium amid the smoke and flames; terrified screams from the villagers mixed with the frenzied shouts of the attackers. Khalil and his men wrenched at the gate and the grass ropes securing it broke free as they flung it aside. Juma, Oriedo and their four men joined them and together they charged into the compound. The *askaris*, their clay-painted faces devilish in the flickering light of the fires, barked like savage dogs, adding to the mounting terror of the villagers running to and fro, shrieking in fear. Women clutched babies to their breasts, men cradled screaming infants in their arms. Cattle and goats, penned for safety in the compound overnight, grew frantic with the noise, bellowing and bleating as they charged madly about in the chaos. Some dashed to freedom through the gap where the gate had stood but men and women attempting to follow were turned back by warning shouts from an *askari* stationed there to prevent their escape.

The attack lasted only minutes. The villagers, surrounded by the *askaris* gripping muskets diagonally across their chests, were pushed roughly back into a rectangular space hemmed in on three sides by the walls of two huts and an undamaged length of fence. The faces of those at the front were lit by the flames; men stood dazed and bewildered, women sobbed, children screamed and clung to their parents.

'Did they have firearms, Oriedo?' Khalil demanded.

'No, *mzee*. They made no resistance.'

'Was anyone killed?'

'None. A few of the people were trampled by animals, some received injuries from burning thatch and one or two will have bruises. Nothing serious. None of our men were injured.'

'Thank you, Oriedo. It could have been much worse.'

'It was a good attack,' Juma acknowledged with a grunt. 'We've shown them who is boss. They'll treat us with respect now.'

'I'll have none of that,' Khalil snapped at him.' There will be no beatings, the people are to be treated decently. Women must not be abused.'

'There is one strange thing, *mzee*,' Oriedo said. 'They do not speak ki-Swahili.'

Khalil stared at him in amazement. 'You must be mistaken,' he said. 'Everyone speaks ki-Swahili.'

'I shouted at some of them during the attack, telling them to get back, stop resisting and so forth. They took no notice, didn't seem to understand what I was saying.'

'I'll soon knock the basic commands into them,' Juma said ominously. 'Leave it to me.'

Khalil wheeled on him. 'Are you deaf, Sergeant? Or an idiot? I have given orders regarding treatment of these people. You will obey me or suffer the consequences.'

Khalil heard the *askari* beside him suck his breath noisily at this open rebuke. Juma's scowling face contorted with sudden anger, with his prominent brows and flattened nose he looked like an enraged baboon.

'You are the idiot, Arab.' He spat out the words, gobs of spittle flying from his mouth. He spread his arms wide in a contemptuous gesture at the crowd. 'People? You call these people? They are nothing! Just slaves! Every one! I led my *askaris* here to seize them, all the way from the coast while you sat like a fat old *bwana* on your camel. Every man here would be crocodile meat but for me!'

With a sudden sweeping movement he grabbed a young girl from the front of the crowd and dragged her out, wrapping his thick arm tight about her neck. Her head was bent back and her eyes wide with horror.

'This one is mine,' Juma snarled as she struggled, kicking and shrieking.

The villagers surged forward, calling out in dismay at this outrage. It was a dangerous moment; there was no time to give an order to the *askaris* to contain them. Khalil snatched the pistols from his belt and fired a shot in the air. The shouts from the crowd turned to screams of alarm and they cowered back, terrified by the strange sudden noise. Juma jerked in surprise and swung round, still holding the girl with his arm locked across her throat. He glared at Khalil and dropped his free hand onto the handle of his *panga*.

Perhaps he meant to threaten the girl's life, or launch a murderous attack on Khalil. Whatever his intention it was a fatal mistake. To draw the *panga* from his belt he swung the girl sideways and her body no longer shielded him. Khalil calmly raised his second pistol and fired at him from a range of four yards. The ball smashed into Juma's chest, catapulting him backwards. His mouth gaped open soundlessly and a great gout of bright blood spurted from his front. His arm still gripped the girl and she was dragged down with him to lie screaming across his corpse.

Khalil stood immobile with his arm outstretched and hand still gripping the pistol. The six *askaris* remained rooted like statues until Oriedo roared an order at them to get back into line. The girl, drenched in Juma's blood, crawled free, scrambled to her feet and ran blindly back into the arms of the crowd. Khalil slowly lowered his arm and waved the pistol muzzle at the body. 'Have that thrown over the cliff into the gorge, Sergeant Oriedo,' he ordered.

He felt nothing; no relief at having escaped death by seconds, no concern at what might follow. It was several moments before he wondered what Haleema's reaction would be when he described what had just taken place. A barrage of questions would be followed by her assurance he had acted correctly, that Allah would understand and forgive ... then he remembered she was dead and he would never know what she thought.

Oriedo spoke, breaking into his dream. 'The men will be glad the hyena is dead, *mzee*.'

'Thank you, Sergeant,' he replied. 'Tell them there is to be no more fighting, no talk of taking slaves.'

He turned to face the crowd. A collective moan filled with a tangible dread came from them. They had retreated when he fired the shot in the air, now they stumbled and fell as they shrank further from him. Their fear was understandable. He was the leader of the devilish mob that had descended on them at dawn, snarling like dogs, firing their homes, snatching an innocent young girl. He had bloodily butchered the man responsible; perhaps he wanted the girl for himself....

He held up his arms. 'My name is Khalil,' he called in ki-Swahili. 'You have nothing further to fear. I wish to speak to your chief. Let him come forward.'

The crowd stared back at him; only a woman's sobbing broke the silence. *No outsiders could have come here, otherwise they would understand ki-Swahili like every other tribe in eastern Africa. But what language do they speak? How can I explain matters if they cannot understand what I say? Who taught them to build such fine huts? Clearly they are skilled farmers; they couldn't have learned to sow crops and breed animals in isolation from the rest of the world. They have tools and cooking pots, wear clothes. Can they spin and weave?*

The crowd parted and a man strode forward and stopped immediately in front of Khalil. Dressed in a gleaming white ankle-length *kanzu*, he was tall and slim with a noble, aesthetic face. His shock of white hair was in striking contrast to his ebony skin. He stood silent, staring at Khalil.

'*Hamjambo*,' Khalil said; smiling with relief. He held out his hand.

'How dare you greet me in friendship?' the man retorted, his voice filled with contempt.

Khalil stared at him in amazement; the man had spoken not in ki-Swahili but in classic Arabic! Lacking a modern vocabulary, it had not been used in speech for centuries, surviving only in ancient poems and stories.

'Your men have burned our homes, destroyed our village. A young girl was brutally assaulted and a man bloodily killed in front of our women and children. Yet you choose to greet me as a friend! May you suffer the eternal torments of the damned.'

'You speak Arabic!' Khalil gasped, in his astonishment he ignored the curse just delivered on him. 'Are you a Muslim?'

'No, we are not Muslims. We are Christian Copts,' the man replied coldly. 'We do not speak ki-Swahili. Amharic is our language.'

'Copts! Amharic! Then you are Ethiopian! And far from home.'

'This valley, which you have destroyed, is our home.'

"The people of Ethiopia claim descent from King Solomon and the Queen of Sheba. Is that your belief?'

'We do not simply believe: we know it to be a fact.'

Khalil stared at this strange man. *Every word Tippu and Abdul uttered was true! These people are, or believe they are, Sheba's descendants*!

'You are chief of these people? What is your name?' he demanded. He spoke abruptly; aware that the askaris behind him would not understand what was being said he had to show an assertion of superiority.

'We have no chief, but I speak on behalf of the people. My name is Joseph.'

Khalil turned to Oriedo. 'This man is called Joseph,' he said rapidly in ki-Swahili. 'He is the leader of these people. They are from Ethiopia, their language is Amharic. He claims they have no knowledge of ki-Swahili but he might be lying. He and I are speaking an ancient form of Arabic. They'll not have words for many of the things we take for granted and they can have little knowledge of the world beyond this valley. Tell the men what I've told you and to have a care what they say in their presence.'

He turned back to Joseph. 'Are there other villages in this valley?' Joseph shook his head. 'None. Our community is alone here.'

'Very well. There are certain other things you must understand. For the moment you are free to do what you can for your people. My men will assist in putting out the last of the fires and beginning the repair of your village. The fighting is over, they have nothing to fear.'

In a remarkably short space of time the village was bustling with activity. There was no sign of Juma's corpse which Khalil assumed had been thrown over the cliff as he had ordered. There was a noticeable lightening of the spirits among the *askaris*. 'The men will be glad the hyena is dead, *mzee*,' Oriedo had said and it seemed he spoke the truth. Using sign language they had organized the villagers into a human chain to pass gourds filled with water from the stream to dowse the last of the smouldering flames. Others climbed onto the damaged roofs and were throwing down bundles of charred thatch to those below to sort out reeds which could be re-used. Work had started on weaving new panels to repair the ruined fencing. The escaped animals had not gone far; herded together by the children they were taken up the slopes to graze. Women began tending the fires, others settled down to prepare food.

Joseph stood alone at the top of the compound watching the activity. Khalil walked across to him. 'We must discuss the future, Joseph,' he said.

'What is there to discuss? You will do as you wish.'

'There is much I need to know. And much I need to explain.'

Joseph led the way to one of the open-sided stores. It was undamaged, dozens of woven baskets filled with grain stood on the raised floor. Joseph pulled a wooden bench forward and they sat down.

'Firstly, how did you come to be living here?' Khalil asked, when they were settled. 'Tell me something of the life you lead.'

'Two generations ago there was a minor disagreement amongst our people,' Joseph replied; his voice was weary, without warmth. 'To avoid unpleasantness twelve families, about eighty men, women and children, led by my grandfather, left our traditional village in Ethiopia. After two years of wandering and great hardship they finally reached this place. It was remote, fertile and uninhabited. Here they settled, continuing to observe their ancient religion, language and customs as we do today. We have not mixed with other people. Our people are farmers by tradition, growing produce and keeping cattle, goats and fowl. The women are fine cooks and weave cloth. Together, men and women work the fields and we have a small forge for forming iron implements. Every five years a number of people from our old country travel south to visit us. We welcome them and some stay to replace those who have passed on. Some of the younger ones marry so new blood enters our community. Our children are born healthy.'

How peaceful, until this morning, life must have been in this beautiful valley.

'Do all your people speak this form of Arabic?' Khalil asked.

Joseph shook his head. 'I am the last. I was taught by elders of the tribe.'

'Thank you. As I have already said, my name is Khalil. I am a master mariner, the captain of a dhow trading between Zanzibar and Musqat. I am here by order of my ruler the Sultan of Zanzibar.'

'I understand very little of what you are saying. My knowledge of the world beyond this valley is slight. Most of what I know comes from old writings and stories passed down without alteration from one generation to the next. You must be what is called a sailor. This sultan you speak of must be very wicked to send you here to destroy our homes. You are his servant and equally wicked. I fear my people will suffer even further harm in your hands.'

'Provided they do as they are asked they will not be abused,' Khalil said. 'I have given orders to that effect to my men.'

Joseph shrugged. 'I saw you kill a man this morning. How can I trust you?'

'I had no choice. He disobeyed my order to release the girl.'

'It was still murder. You could have injured him instead.' Joseph looked steadily at him for a long time. 'How did you find us?' he asked.

'Some time ago a Muslim traveller saw smoke coming from your valley. He investigated and even from a distance saw your people were tall and handsome. He died soon after he returned to Zanzibar but news of his discovery reached the ears of the sultan. He sent me to confirm the truth of the story.'

'I have long feared this would happen.' Joseph's voice was bitter. 'The smoke the man saw came from the burning of the old crop. Unfortunately it was a signal that summoned the Devil to us.'

'I am not the Devil, Joseph.'

'I say you are. The evil you have done to our valley will never be forgotten. I curse you. I know a little of other religions. Your Holy Qur'an says only Allah must be obeyed. Why then do you take heed of this sultan of whom you speak?'

'Because he threatened to harm my family if I did not obey him.'

'You saved your family by destroying our valley.'

'I am sorry. I will do all that I can to protect you from further harm. I have read something of your Coptic religion. I know it is early Christian, and that you have wonderful churches, carved out of solid rock but filled with light.'

Joseph nodded, looking at him keenly. 'You speak like an educated man yet act like a barbarian. Why is that?'

'I hope I can show you I am not barbarian. I have been ordered to

take back fifty of your young women for the sultan's pleasure ...'
Joseph gasped in horror and Khalil quickly held up his hand. 'Please
listen to what I have to say before you speak. I do not intend to obey
that order. But you must help me.'

'I will listen to what you have to say,' Joseph said. 'There is
nothing else I can do.'

'You must understand your peaceful existence in this valley is
over,' Khalil began; he spoke quietly but with firm authority. 'Your
former life has gone for ever. I can understand why you blame me for
that, but if I had not come someone else would have done so, eventually.'

Joseph nodded. 'I realize that.'

'That could still happen, if I were to obey my orders. Were I to
return to Zanzibar and report what I have found in the valley, there
are those who would waste no time in coming here. They would take
everyone, you, your men and your women, even the smallest children, into slavery. They would be tied together by ropes and forced
to march on a horrific journey lasting weeks, driven by brutes
wielding sticks and whips. Those who survived to reach the coast
would be sold like cattle and face yet another terrible journey, across
the sea to unspeakable fates. You have no real understanding of the
wickedness and cruelty that exists in the world beyond your valley.'

Joseph showed no reaction, gave no sign he understood anything
that had been said.

'Such evil can only be stopped by a force mightier than itself,'
Khalil continued. 'You must agree to surrender your valley to me.
You will then be given protection from those who would do you great
harm.' *This is like talking to a child. But how else can I explain the
world to a man who knows so little, who is so innocent?* 'Do you
understand what I am saying, Joseph?' he asked. 'There can be no
return to the past. If you do not agree to surrender the valley to me,
slave traders will soon come and drag your people away. They will
suffer the fate I have described, far worse than anything that has been
done to them today.'

'How can you offer us protection from such people? You will go
back to where you came from, taking your men with you.'

Khalil shook his head. 'I shall leave them behind to protect you for the next few months. I will return to Zanzibar on my camel and arrange for other men to come in peace to strengthen their numbers. Trust me. You have nothing to fear.'

From his notebook he tore out the surrender document he had prepared. It was a simple statement in Arabic script.

My name is Joseph, leader of the people in the valley captured by Khalil. I surrender the valley to him in return for protection from further attack.

The wording was vague, intentionally so, but it met the requirements laid down by the colonel. And, if the plan failed, and the document fell into Tippu's hands, it gave no hint of the existence of the Hamerton plan. Khalil laid the document on the bench and held out a pencil. 'Make a mark to show you agree to my proposal,' he said. 'Your people then will be safe for ever.' He watched Joseph add a wavering line below the words.

Khalil walked back to the lower end of the village where Oriedo was sitting on the ground with the six *askaris* eating a midday meal; a group of curious, solemn children stood watching them.

'All well, Oriedo?' Khalil asked.

'All well, *mzee*.'

'I wish to speak to you in private.'

They moved out of earshot of the men. 'There are several things I have to tell you, Oriedo,' Khalil began. 'First, you have shown exemplary conduct on this expedition. You have been an example to the men, and I am aware of the additional burden Juma's behaviour placed upon you. I am therefore promoting you to lieutenant with immediate effect.' He held up a hand to prevent Oriedo speaking; there was no time for that. 'The second piece of information is that Joseph has surrendered the valley to me. I'll go back to Zanzibar and report our success while you remain behind with the *askaris*. Your orders are to hold the valley until reinforcements arrive from the coast to relieve you.'

'Thank you for my promotion, *mzee*. I am honoured to accept it. With regard to remaining here I can see certain difficulties arising.

First, you say we are to hold the valley, possibly for some months until relieved. Seven of us can't fight off attacks by determined raiders, or even mount a proper guard. I might be able to call upon men from the village, but they aren't fighters as we've seen. And they'll need training but there are no spare weapons and very little ammunition.'

'I'm aware of the difficulties you face. You've forgotten Chakula, the *askari* left guarding Kirru. When I get back to base camp I'll send him to you. That will make eight, and he's an experienced campaigner. But it's unlikely there'll ever be a raid. This place was difficult to find as you know. Like the trader who made the original discovery, it was only smoke that revealed its presence to us. I suggest you forbid the burning of vegetation, and order cooking fires to be kept small. Your men can patrol and ensure these rules are followed.'

'Yes, *mzee*. The men are the next problem. Some of them could prefer to stay here, become farmers, marry women from the valley. There are signs of this already. If we are left for more than a few months all discipline will be gone. I will no longer be in a position to enforce orders.'

'No one can be blamed if that happens, Oriedo. All I ask is that you remain on good terms with the people. You know the men well. Ensure as far as possible there is no abuse, that all dealings are open and fair. Juma would've spoiled the valley for ever, but we've prevented that. And the damage that has been done can be repaired. Do your best to maintain law and order and work with Joseph for the good of everyone.'

After supper he said goodbye to Joseph, Oriedo and the *askaris*. He had a strong sense of it being a final farewell; whatever the outcome of his journey it was unlikely they would ever meet again. Joseph would never leave the valley and it was improbable Oriedo or any of the *askaris* would ever make the long journey back to Zanzibar. And he could not envisage himself returning. The men he was leaving behind would be amazed to be relieved by red-coated British soldiers but their commander would explain the full story.

Dawn was not far off. Khalil lay on his back, hands behind his head, staring into the darkness of the hut. Today he would start the long journey home. He tried to form a picture in his mind of Umma and the Jewels but they appeared only briefly, smiling silently at him before slipping away. This did not greatly trouble him. They were too far off, in time as well as distance, to catch and hold. It would be different when he reached home.

But why do I not feel elated? Where is the pride at all I have achieved? The completion of a long difficult journey, the capture of the valley, the treaty signed by Joseph exactly as Colonel Hamerton asked for. I am the king, just as Umma said, ruler of all that lies around me. So why don't I feel happy? Perhaps Allah is telling me I don't deserve it, that this isn't a moment of triumph but one of shame. Instead of attacking the village, I could have simply marched in. The people would have suffered shock but their homes and animals would not have been harmed. All I can do to make amends is keep my word to protect the valley's future. That means preventing the sultan from ever seizing it. What Abdul called my new harbour light has been lit; all my efforts now must be aimed at reaching Zanzibar and handing the treaty to Colonel Hamerton. And seeing my beloved Umma, my Jewels and the children.

He slipped away from the village as the eastern sky began to lighten.

Chapter Fifteen

Descending the rope into the chasm alone, hand over hand with his feet braced against the cliff, was an unpleasant experience. Shamba had plunged down this same face when the rope, almost certainly cut by Juma, snapped; he had died on the rocks below and was swept away. And yesterday Juma's bloody corpse was thrown off the cliff at the end of the valley into this same torrent. Khalil thrust aside a sudden image of the two bodies, victim and murderer, entangled in the dark churning water, whirling partners in a macabre endless dance. He was relieved to reach the bottom.

The return crossing of the stream was less difficult than before; he had to jump the yawning gap for the fourth time but the far boulder was the lower from this side and the leap was easier. He scrambled up out of the chasm into the brilliant morning sunshine above. The path he and Juma made was already becoming choked with new vegetation and at times he was forced to struggle through bush before reaching the ancient lake bed. Two hours after crossing the stream, he was striding up the slope to the camp. It had been an easy start to the homeward journey. Chakula, the camp guard, would be keen to hear how the battle had gone, how many slaves were captured, who did the most fighting. *He'll be disappointed there wasn't a more bloody encounter.*

I'll send him off to the valley without mentioning Juma is dead; he'll be a welcome reinforcement. Oriedo will explain to him. He'll find himself a village woman and settle in happily with the other askaris. *And Kirru will be pleased to see me though, camel-like, I doubt if he'll show his true feelings....*

He was only yards from the camp when he heard the first scream,

170

a howl like that of an animal in pain. He quickly took the two pistols from his pack; as he checked the priming the silence was broken by the same sound. What could it be? If it was an animal, why hadn't Chakula shot it? The howl was repeated, different this time, sounding more like a human cry; perhaps Chakula was injured! He hurried forward, a pistol in each hand. *If Kirru is seriously hurt I'll have to walk back to the coast! I'd never do it. I'll have to go back to the valley....*

Reaching the trees, he pushed aside the leafy branches and immediately recoiled in horror. Chakula was standing naked with both arms raised, his face and body smeared with grey mud in crude twisted patterns. He was at the centre of a circle bounded by upright sticks, each sharpened to a point on which a small bird was impaled. Some were still alive, fluttering helplessly. *This is Juma's work. He must have planned to kill me and take command of the mission. Before leaving he gave Chakula a narcotic to derange him. 'Remember to do what I told you,' had been his last words, meaning take the drug. This vile scene was meant to greet the* askaris *and their captives when they got back from the valley, a demonstration of his magical powers, a warning to all who were thinking of plotting against him....*

To Khalil's relief there was no sign of Kirru. It was likely he had escaped and was grazing not far away. Finding him may be a problem, but dealing with Chakula was his main concern at this moment. The *askari* wailed again, the piercing cry of a soul in agony. In his tortured imagination he must believe the ring of dead and dying birds was protecting him from nightmarish spirits.

I have to shoot him; I have no choice. I can't take him prisoner, or wait until he recovers. The range is too great for a pistol, I would need a musket. I'll rush him, a pistol in each hand, get close enough to wound him with my first shot then finish him off with the other....

He was surprised how cool and detached he felt, unconcerned at the prospect of killing one of his own men. *Juma was right about one thing: there's no law here in the wilderness, no right or wrong. Kill or be killed, my life or my enemy's.*

He gave the priming of his pistols a final check, pulled the branches apart and charged headlong into the clearing, cursing and yelling at the top of his voice to further bewilder the wretched *askari*. He had covered half the distance to the circle when a blurred yellow and black shape bounded out of the bushes on the opposite side. his left. He flung himself to the ground as the leopard reached Chakula, reared on its hind legs and with a snarl struck him with its slashing front paws. He fell to the ground, the cat pounced and gripped his throat with her teeth. She glared at Khalil, rumbling a warning growl to keep clear. He backed away, keeping his pistols levelled at her as he retreated into the scrub.

The sun was directly overhead and the silence was oppressive. Khalil waited a couple of minutes before pushing the branches aside and saw the clearing was empty. He pulled up the sticks, grinding the skulls of the still fluttering birds under his heel. He found Chakula's loaded musket. Half a mile off to the west lay a low scrub-covered hill. He walked to the crest and, with his telescope scanned the surrounding bush. A mile or more away Kirru was grazing with a herd of small gazelle, a giant among pygmies. It took Khalil an hour to reach the spot, forcing his way through the thick trackless scrub. On his approach the camel raised his head and gave a snorted greeting. A length of rope hung from his halter and Khalil led him back to the camp.

He rummaged through the supplies left behind when the *askaris* left for the valley, picked the best six muskets and the remains of the shot and powder, packed the last of the biscuit and some dried meat. He saddled Kirru, hung the bags from the pommels and rode round the perimeter of the clearing to check he was leaving behind nothing likely to be of use on his long journey. Then he turned Kirru's head south and set off for home.

Anxious not to tire Kirru, Khalil allowed him to chose his own pace. When he sensed he was beginning to tire he stopped for the night. As a result it was almost a month before they reached the vast area of silt and uprooted trees that marked the flood plain of the Mutumwa river. A large herd of zebra came into view and Khalil steered Kirru in their direction.

Constantly peering through his glass he finally picked out a dark dot which, as they drew nearer, hardened into the rectangular shape of the abandoned raft. He dismounted and tethered Kirru to a fallen tree. Zebra milled about, strangely reluctant to move out of his way; some snorted at each other, nostrils flaring, twisting and wheeling whilst others reared on hind legs, pawing at the air. A few simply stood stock still, staring at nothing in particular. In the bright afternoon sunlight the contrasting stripes of their coats shimmered oddly.

Khalil checked two of his pistols and thrust them back into his belt then shouldered a loaded musket before striding across to where the *Likilo* lay, 300 yards from the river-bank and half-buried in wind-blown sand. With the dry season well advanced the Mutumwa was several feet below the level at which it had stood when the expedition crossed on the inward journey. He saw at once it would be impossible for him to launch the raft single-handed; it would take at least a dozen men to dig her out and drag her to the bank.

He walked to the water's edge and stood gazing over the river which ran sluggishly at his feet. The far bank was less than 200 yards away, reaching it would be a simple matter. He remembered standing on the far side watching Kirru swimming across behind the *Likilo*. Later that night, by the camp-fire everyone laughed when Teso repeated his joke about a ship of the desert taking a swim. Now Teso was dead, taken by a crocodile that next morning. *All I have to do, he told himself, is sit in the saddle and steer Kirru into the water. Once out of his depth he'll float and start moving his legs as if walking. The current will sweep us downstream but it's not too strong. Pulling on the rein will keep his head turned towards the far bank and a kick now and again should encourage him to paddle in that direction. Once his feet touch bottom he'll wade out. In three minutes we'll be on the far side.*

As he was about to turn away his confidence turned to dismay. What he had thought was a stranded log suddenly came to life and, detaching itself from the opposite bank, it moved out into the main stream. Perfectly camouflaged in the turgid brown water, the almost submerged crocodile cruised in a wide arc across the river. Khalil lifted his telescope and scanned the far shore. It was no longer the innocent muddy slope he had assumed, instead the opposite bank was made up of the scaly bodies of seven monstrous crocs, basking in the sun. Khalil snapped his glass shut; had they attempted to cross he and Kirru would have been swept straight into the reptiles' great snapping jaws.

He walked back to Kirru and stroked his nose before mounting him. The zebras had mingled with a large number of wildebeest, whilst on the outer fringes a dozen large antelopes moved in to swell the numbers. Bunching together would cut the risk of being snapped up by a pack of hunting lionesses. Khalil used his knees to guide Kirru through the mass and reached the river-bank. Scanning the opposite shore to find a crossing place free of crocodiles, he had ridden some 300 yards downstream when he became aware of a commotion behind him and looked back. Making their way across the river in a broad ribbon line abreast, a dozen zebras were swimming strongly, led by two big stallions. Their striped coats glowed brightly against the dull flowing water. Plunging down the bank after them, throwing up great curtains of spray, came the rest of the herd. They were followed by the bulky shapes of the wildebeest, mixed with the brown and brilliant white antelopes. It was a living stream, an unstoppable tide migrating to summer grazing in the east.

Khalil pulled Kirru's head round and urged him back along the bank towards the crossing place. The flow of animals had turned into a stampede; a solid ribbon now spanned the river. In places six zebras were swimming line abreast and, on reaching the far side, scrambled up the steep muddy bank to the safety of the green turf above. As Khalil watched, the desperately clawing hoofs began breaking down long stretches of the bank; escape from the river now meant a desperate scramble over deep glutinous mud before climbing the slippery face to the safety of the pasture. Some animals became trapped and wallowed helplessly in the mud whilst others, failing to complete the climb, fell back on those emerging from the river. Many were swept away, some gained footholds downstream and managed to scramble ashore. But a new horror now emerged. A pair of open scaly jaws reared out of the water and clamped the muzzle of a zebra swimming at the edge of the herd. There was a momentary flaying of her striped legs before the crocodile dragged her down. Another zebra, ears back and eyes staring, was suddenly swimming backwards; the water around him turned black with blood as he was disembowelled and pulled below the surface. Not every crocodile attack was successful; one zebra stallion having almost completed the crossing kicked his heels back against a reptilian head rapidly approaching from behind. The crocodile turned away, thrashing its tail. Another zebra dived beneath its impending attacker then reared, lifting the reptile on her neck and throwing it sideways before it plunged on to reach the safety of the bank. Perhaps it was the noise, or the smell of blood, that made Kirru panic. He snorted and reared, ears laid back, eyes bulging with fear. In that instant Khalil made his decision. He drew a *panga* from the saddle-bag and wrenched Kirru's head round towards the crowd of animals massing on the river-bank.

'Go, Kirru!' he yelled, above the noise of crashing water and thundering hoofs. 'Go, Kirru, go!' He smacked the flat face of the *panga* blade hard against Kirru's rump and kicked his heels viciously into his ribs. The camel snorted angrily and jerked his head against the rein then lunged forward into the charging mass careering down into the water. Khalil hit him again with the *panga*, screaming encouragement. The water rose past his thighs then the ride became smoother as Kirru began swimming, hemmed in all around by the herd. Ahead and to their left the throat of a wildebeest was seized by one crocodile, at the same moment another bit deeply into her flank. The struggling animal was dragged down in a froth of blood and muddy water. A large wild-eyed zebra stallion took her place. Khalil caught a glimpse of a line of zebras standing safe on the pasture on the far side, ears pricked as they watched the bloody spectacle intently. Then, quite suddenly, the desperate frightening journey was over. The saddle gave an enormous lurch backwards as Kirru's long front legs reached up to the top of the bank followed immediately by his rear; he had leapt upwards like a cat.

Khalil clung to the pommel; between his knees Kirru's ribs were heaving with his efforts. He leaned forward and hugged him round the neck.

'Good boy,' he shouted. 'Good boy. Never again, Kirru. You'll never have to do that again.'

He grabbed a handful of the camel's ginger mane and tugged it hard. *If only Abdul had been watching, It must have been a great spectacle?*

The effects of the long journey were beginning to show; in the course of the next few days Khalil's health deteriorated alarmingly. A painful crop of boils developed on his face and back, his tongue and lips became badly ulcerated. He itched in numerous places, particularly where the insides of his legs continually rubbed against Kirru's sides. At times his vision became blurred; an especially worrying symptom since he was anxious to keep a look-out for tribesmen and avoid contact if at all possible. Inevitably they would assume all Arabs were slave traders, and there were many old scores to settle.

He realized his medical problems were related to poor diet. Scurvy was rare on ships in the Arabian sea as voyages were comparatively short and there were plentiful supplies of vegetables and citrus fruits to prevent it. But he was aware of the symptoms and recognized his were not dissimilar. Ever since setting out alone he had eaten almost nothing but under-cooked gazelle meat. During the march to the valley the *askaris* had foraged the surrounding bush for edible plants and fruits. The nutritious roots of wild cassava were common and mixed with meat had made nourishing stews. Khalil had not supplemented his meals in this way and was now suffering as a result. Physical problems were not his only concern; sometimes during the day, and often at night, he was disturbed by memories of the recent past. His killing of Juma recurred times without number in his dreams; the disembowelled zebra swimming backwards in a river of its own blood appeared in nightmares that woke him to the sound of his own screams.

Kirru was also at a low ebb, drained of energy. He had not recovered from the enormous effort of crossing the Mutumwa and the terrors he had endured were having a further weakening effect. He trudged along wearily, head held low. Frequently he stopped for no apparent reason, gazing ahead for long periods as if unable to comprehend the interminable journey he was making. Khalil let him make his own pace since nothing could be gained from trying to hurry him.

*

A week after crossing the Mutumwa they reached a delightful valley set in a fold of low hills. It was an inviting spot, verdant with a sparkling stream, an ideal place in which they could both relax and recover. By good fortune, a young buck wandered out of the scrub just as Khalil finished cleaning and reloading his muskets. He took aim and the buck toppled with a ball through the head.

Khalil had no butchery skills; he had barely spared a glance as the expedition cooks deftly skinned, gutted and jointed animals shot for the pot. It was an omission he now deeply regretted. Since beginning the journey home his efforts at preparing carcasses for cooking had been bungled failures; his only sharp knife was too small and the panga was blunt and unwieldy. With the newly killed buck he fared no better. He sighed as he placed the hacked-off lumps of raw meat on the fire and left them to roast while he went in search of edible greens to add to a stew.

How long the warriors had been watching him he did not know; his heart sank when he suddenly noticed them standing under a tree only a dozen paces from him. He was sure they had not been there a moment before, it was as if they had materialized out of the air. Four of them were tall and young, naked, each clutching several spears. Their faces were ghostly white, decorated with streaks of clay. Standing in front was, presumably, their chief. He was small, elderly and unsmiling with a rough blanket fastened over one shoulder. He carried a carved stick as his badge of office.

Khalil walked up to him and held out his hand. '*Hamjambo*, Chief,' he said. The old man merely nodded; holding the tips of Khalil's fingers for only a moment before releasing them.

'You will want your *hongo*, naturally,' Khalil went on pleasantly. He had little that would be of interest, except perhaps a musket, so there was need for caution. 'I am sure we can settle matters quickly,' he went on. 'But first, please, you must dine with me.'

The chief shook his head. 'You are travelling alone with your camel?' he asked in ki-Swahili.

'Yes,' Khalil replied. They would have seen him arrive so there was no point in pretending otherwise.

'Why is that?'

'I am a man of God. I have been visiting my brethren far to the west. My two companions became sick and died. That is why I am alone. I am returning to my home in Zanzibar.'

'Where are your slaves?'

'I am a man of peace, Chief. A man of God. I do not take slaves.' It was a point to emphasize as the old man might have a score to settle. 'I believe all men are equal. No man should be taken as a slave.'

'Do you have medicine?' the chief asked.

'Medicine?' queried Khalil. 'Yes, I have a little medicine.'

He had brought a few potions from the expedition's chest, treatments against diarrhoea wrapped in leaves, and quinine in a bottle in case of malaria.

'Are you sick, Chief? What is wrong with you?'

'It is my wife who is ill. She is with child but it will not come out of her. She is in great pain.'

Khalil stared at the old man. *Surely he cannot expect me to play midwife! Haleema had taken charge of all deliveries, even her own ...* On the few occasions he had been home when she was giving birth he had been banished to the courtyard to await the outcome. He cleared his throat. 'Surely there is someone in your village who can help? A woman who has had children herself? Or a witchdoctor with some skill?'

The chief shook his head. 'Our women are all young, except for my senior wife, Lambi. Old Bibi knew what to do but she died and her secrets were buried with her. We have no witch doctor now. Mganga went out one day and never returned. Perhaps a wild animal took him.'

One of the warriors jabbered vehemently to the chief in the local dialect, jerking his chin aggressively in Khalil's direction.

'My son says you Arab people are known to be skilled in medicine,' the chief said. 'You must help my wife. That is why I have come to you.'

I must be careful in what I say as they could become aggressive. If I get involved, and the woman dies, as she most probably will, they'll blame me and I'll be on the ends of their spears. But if I don't help her and she dies, they'll say it was my fault for doing nothing and I'll be killed just the same. What a mess! Allah! Help me!

He turned back to the chief. 'A woman having a child does not need medicine, Chief. It is something she has to do herself. I am sorry but I cannot help you.'

The old man stood with tears welling in his eyes. 'My wife is young,' he croaked. 'It is her first child. I am too old to father another. She and the child will both die if you do not help.'

'As I told you, I am a man of God, Chief. A Muslim. I believe that whether one lives or dies is not in the hands of man but in Allah's.'

The chief shook his head. 'I do not understand. If your Allah has the power to allow a woman and her child die, why can he not let them live?'

'I have no answer to that, Chief. All I know is His will must be accepted.'

The warriors clustered round the old man. There was a great shaking of spears and what appeared to be much plain speaking. *They're telling him to force me to do something, to threaten to kill me if I refuse.*

'Chief,' he called hurriedly. 'Let me speak. Please hear what I have to say. I want your fine sons to listen also. I have children of my own, a young boy was born to one of my wives recently. I understand the pain you are suffering.'

'Say what you wish. We will listen.'

'I will come with you and see your wife. But you must all understand that I am not a doctor. I know nothing of spells or of magic. If your wife has already lost too much blood, or become too weak, or if the child is wedged and cannot be brought out, no one on earth can save her. Or the child. Each of you must understand that. I will do what is in my power. I will pray to Allah for His help. But I cannot promise all will be well. You must not expect a successful result. All you can only do is hope Allah answers my plea.'

The discussion that followed was short. The chief spoke with great authority while his sons stood silent. He turned to Khalil. 'I understand what you say, Arab. You will not be held responsible if my wife or child dies.'

There were about two hours of daylight left as the party set out for the chief's village. Khalil brought up the rear riding Kirru; he could

179

not risk leaving him alone. The path wound along the foot of the low hills. The journey took twenty minutes, ending where eight circular mud huts stood on the perimeter of an earthen compound. Two women stood outside the doorway of the largest hut and one of them hurried across and spoke briefly to the chief.

'She is Lambi, my senior wife,' he said. 'She says my wife is almost dead. We have wasted much time and arrived too late.'

'Let me see your wife, Chief,' Khalil urged. 'If she is still alive I might be able to do something.'

The chief nodded and spoke tersely to the senior wife. She beckoned to Khalil and led him across the compound. He had to stoop to enter the hut which was dark and filled with woodsmoke, forcing him to stand until his eyes stopped stinging. The woman lay almost at his feet on a jumble of rough gory blankets. She was naked, knees drawn up and spread apart. Lambi cackled something to the chief, her voice shrill, irritatingly sharp. He turned his watery old eyes on Khalil. 'She says my wife lives but the child is dead.'

'Your wife will die soon too, Chief. There is nothing I can do.'

'Lambi says the child's body must be removed from her. It was being born the wrong way round. They have knelt on her belly and tried to push the child back and pull it out the proper way. But it was impossible.'

'Farmers are skilled in such matters,' Khalil muttered. 'They turn goat kids round.' He felt totally helpless, mouthing meaningless words as he stood looking down at the woman.

Lambi began cackling again, a grating, inhuman sound. The chief seized Khalil by an arm, his grip was amazingly strong. 'Lambi says you must cut my wife's belly open and take out the child's body.'

Khalil pushed the old man aside and walked out of the hut. The sun was beginning its descent towards the serrated western horizon, the searing heat of the day had gone. He gulped the cool clean air, filling his lungs like a swimmer coming ashore after crossing a treacherous tidal rip. He forced himself to think of what he had been asked to do. Someone Haleema had known had been cut open in pregnancy. She was too small to deliver the child normally so her wealthy husband had paid an expert Arab surgeon in Cairo to carry out the task. The pain of the knife sawing her open had been beyond description, she had felt the warm blood streaming across her body. The child was removed but lived only minutes. The gaping wound was sewn together with needle and thread. The woman had lived in constant pain ever since and was never able to bear another child.

Khalil stood watching the sunset. *Will the dilemmas I face never end? Am I being tested by Allah for some purpose not yet made clear to me? How can I, a simple humble sailor, cut open an already near-dead woman? This morning I couldn't cut a gazelle carcass into butcher's joints!*

The chief came to stand beside him, looking expectantly into his face. Khalil shook his head. 'I cannot do it, Chief,' he muttered. 'Your wife is weak and would not survive such a terrible ordeal.'

'You must do it.' The chief gripped his arm again, shaking it. 'Lambi says the child's dead body must be removed. If not my wife will die.'

Khalil shook the hand free and he turned savagely on the old man. 'Chief, I have told you,' he shouted in his fear and anxiety. 'I cannot do the impossible. I have no magical powers. Your wife will die whether or not the child is taken out. She is beyond all hope.'

'Take it out, Arab. It is dead and she still lives.'

'She is going to die and it is better she does so naturally. Cutting her open will only add to the agony of her last minutes.'

'No harm will come to you if she dies.'

'I have no skill in such work. Your men are able to cut up a wild animal for food far better than I. Yet you are asking me to do it to a living human being!'

'The Spirits forbid my people doing such a thing. They were friendly with Old Bibi, she was in league with them. But you are Arab. They will not harm you.'

'My God would punish me. He would not agree to me taking a knife to a woman dying in childbirth.'

'Perhaps, Arab, it was your God who sent you here to save my wife.'

'You do not know that, Chief. And I cannot believe it is so.'

'You do not know that I am wrong.'

No choice! God in Heaven, I have no choice! I could try to ride off, leave this pathetic old man to his misery. But his sons would chase me, kill me with their spears. If I cut the woman her blood will be on my hands for evermore. She'll join Juma, the spies, and all the other men I have killed. She'll haunt my dreams, I'll never be free of her. But I have no choice.

'Very well, Chief,' he sighed. 'I will do as you ask.'

'Thank you, Arab.'

'The hut is too dark. Have your wife brought into the daylight.'

The cluster of huts was already casting long shadows; the sun was sinking towards a bank of dark cloud. The woman was carried out, lying in the blanket, and gently laid on the ground. The news of what was to be done to her had spread and a knot of villagers pushed forward to view the coming drama.

'These people must be removed, Chief,' Khalil ordered. 'I cannot do this thing in front of them. Lambi and one other of your wives can stay.'

The old man spoke rapidly to his sons who thrust the onlookers back twenty or more yards. Khalil placed a consoling arm around the shoulder of the old man. 'Do you wish to stay, Chief?' he asked in a quiet voice. He nodded wordlessly and they walked forward together to stand by the woman on the ground. She lay on her back with her head supported on a bundle of ferns. Her eyes were closed, she breathed laboriously and it was impossible to tell if she was still conscious. The second wife squatted at her head, wiping her brow and murmuring words of comfort.

Khalil knelt at the woman's side, holding his knife. He murmured a short prayer, then with a trembling hand drew the point down the centre of the woman's swollen abdomen. The stretched skin parted easily; blood quickly flowed along the cut edges. The woman's uterus, a great pale balloon streaked with blood, bulged through the incision. She gave a choking cry and struggled to sit up; the women gently but firmly held her head in place on the fern pillow. Khalil, his hand strangely steadier than when he began, incised the uterus. As he drew the knife along he suddenly worried he may cut into the child lying inside before he remembered it was dead.

Bloodstained fluid gushed out, spilling over the woman's body. Lambi pushed Khalil aside, slipped her hands into the gaping slash and lifted out the lifeless child. She bit through the umbilical cord and laid the tiny body gently on a corner of the blanket. A long wail came from the watching crowd. The mother was bleeding heavily, unless the flow was staunched she would be dead in a minute, probably it was already too late. Khalil closed his eyes. *Allah! Allah! Allah! Please help me! Help this wretched woman! Help! Help*! He turned his head, unable to look at what he had done.

Lambi was babbling again; intrusive, insistent. She dug her skinny elbow painfully into his side. Wearily he glanced at her. To his utter amazement, in her upraised bloody hands, she held a second infant, a boy who until that moment had lain unsuspected in the womb. The mother's eyes flickered open, perhaps she caught a glimpse of her son, Khalil could not be certain. But he was sure she heard his lusty first cry as death finally came to her.

Chapter Sixteen

A week later, with the steep eastern face of the Rift Valley towering ahead, Khalil rode through a thick plantation of thorns near the foot of a vertical cliff. A jumble of large boulders, the remains of an ancient landslide lay, in his path. As he came up to it he noticed the remains of a half-grown elephant calf. It had been dead for some time, the body was reduced to a shell of ribs and hide, streaked with the thick white droppings of vultures. The entrails had been torn out, the tough skin of the haunches hung in strips and the great muscles they once covered had long since been devoured by scavengers. The head was sun dried and curiously shrivelled; the trunk was a mere withered appendage and the eyes had been pecked out by birds.

Khalil took all this in with a single disinterested glance and rode on. Within a few yards he came to another carcass, similarly ripped open. Beyond that lay yet another, then a fourth. He dismounted and scrambled on top of the rocks. Looking along the base of the cliff to his astonishment, for as far as he could see, there were dead elephants, some piled on top of others. He jumped down and walked past them, counting. The tally came to forty-three of which no less than thirty, possibly more, bore ivory. He walked back, rechecking his first count; there was no doubt that over forty elephants lay dead at his feet. He sat on a flat rock, suddenly the world was unreal. Chance had brought him to the exact spot where the elephants had plunged over the cliff during the inward march. An unexpected fortune lay at his feet, the ivory was his! He was rich!

*

He began work the following morning as soon as it was light. The first adult carcass was that of a cow lying on her side. The shrivelled skin of her head had peeled back to where the root of a two-foot long tusk grew out of her skull. A few blows from his *panga* splintered the bone and the tusk was free. The other was under her skull but she was too heavy to roll over. He moved onto a young bull lying on his back with all four legs held rigidly upwards. His tusks were both in perfect condition and almost three feet in length. Next to him was a cow whose skull was flattened where it had smashed onto a broad slab of smooth rock. The impact shattered the bone around her left tusk, breaking it loose. It lay beside her, undamaged and half-buried in long grass.

By mid afternoon he had collected forty tusks, more had to be abandoned. Two carcasses were inaccessible, lying on narrow ledges high above the valley floor. Some tusks could not be chopped out, others, broken on impact, were of little value. He stacked the good specimens at the base of the cliff. It was a valuable hoard; each tusk was worth at least 200 thaler per foot.

It took the rest of the day to find a cave in which he could safely leave the collection. It was so well hidden he saw it only when the rays of the setting sun were at the right angle to cast the opening into deep shadow. It was a hundred feet above the valley floor, over a mile from where the carcasses lay, and could only be reached by scrambling up a series of narrow crumbling ledges. The cave entrance was barely wide enough for him to squeeze inside. By then the sun was too low to light the interior but the walls felt dry and the floor solid enough. The tusks would be safe and well protected from the weather. If he failed to come back to retrieve them they could lie here for centuries. Discoveries had been made of ancient hoards of tusks and bones, gathered by men who had walked these plains hundreds, possibly thousands, of years before. He roped the tusks into compact bundles, slung them across Kirru's back and led him along the base of the escarpment to a point below the cave where he left them for the night. The following day was spent carrying the tusks, one or two at a time, up to the cave entrance. It was an exhausting task and he soon lost count of the number of ascents and descents the task entailed.

When the last one was stacked inside, he collected rocks and small stones and built a wall across the opening. To finish the job he pulled up plants and clumps of coarse grass by their roots and carefully replanted them in soil pressed into the joints of the new wall. Some of these were certain to become established and grow. In a few months the entrance would be completely sealed, obliterating all traces of anyone ever having been there. Looking up from the bottom of the cliff it was impossible to identify the cave so he built an odd-shaped pyramid of stones on the valley floor as a marker. He took a long final look then mounted Kirru and rode away.

It was Kirru who first knew the coast was near. It was late afternoon when his ears pricked and he gave a short snort. Another hour passed before Khalil caught his first scent of the sea and heard the distant thunder of surf. The final range of dunes gave way to a band of scattered windblown palms above a beach only a mile south of Bagomoyo bay where an incoming tide was washing up the salt-white glittering coral sand.

Khalil sat in the saddle for a long time, absorbing a sight that for so many months had been a mere dream. It was a while before he noticed the distant figure, far to the north, standing on top of a small outlying dune. Through his telescope he saw the man, framed against the sky, was looking in his direction with a hand raised to shade his eyes from the setting sun. He was in Khalil's intended path so an encounter was unavoidable. He drew a loaded musket from the saddle-bag and rested the barrel between the pommels. If the man saw these preparations he gave no sign; he stood his ground as Khalil approached.

When they were twenty yards apart he called in an instantly recognizable voice, '*Assalam-o-alaikum, effendi*! I see my old friend Kirru has served you well!'

Khalil grinned and slipped the musket back into the saddle-bag. '*Assalam-o-alaikum*. It's you, Omah, my old friend! Yes, he has been very brave!'

Omah hurried forward, took hold of Kirru's bridle and squinted up at Khalil with his one eye. 'I see you have both travelled far. I sold him to you too cheaply! He was worth at least another ten thaler. But where are the rest of your men? How many slaves have you brought? How much ivory?'

'That I cannot tell you, Omah,' Khalil said. 'I must first report to the sultan. I need to cross the channel tonight.'

'Tonight, *effendi*?' Omah shook his head. 'There was a schooner in the bay this afternoon but she has gone. You have had a long journey and must be tired. Come and spend the night at my house. I keep a good table and have comfortable beds for guests. Other ships will call in a day or two.'

Khalil shook his head. 'I thank you for your offer of hospitality, my old friend. But apart from the necessity of reporting to the sultan I am anxious to see my wives and children. They will be worried about me and it would be cruel to keep them waiting a day longer than is necessary. Surely there are fishermen at Bagamoyo? I will pay well for the hire of a boat.'

'I have a boat, *effendi*. But it will soon be dark and the crossing is very dangerous at night.'

'You have forgotten that I am a sailor, Omah. I have known these waters thirty years. The tide is almost full and I can put to sea without delay. In return for the loan of your boat, I return Kirru to you. See that you look after him well. He is not to be put to work again. I have promised him that.'

'Thank you, *effendi*. I have recently bought two fine young female camels who will make fine concubines for him. They shall be his reward. But your hire of my boat exceeds his value. When you return it, we shall agree a fair charge.'

'Agreed, Omah. I shall come and visit him regularly. He saved my life numerous times. I shall remember him for the remainder of my life.'

He slipped his arms round the camel's neck and rested his cheek against it. 'Goodbye, old friend,' he whispered.

In Bagamoyo bay a wide sandbank, half a mile from the beach, was exposed at low tide. Beyond that was a submerged coral reef, parallel to the shore, which broke the incoming swell. Omah, splashing ahead through the shallows, led Khalil out to where his *zaruk* lay on the sandbank, canted over on her side. She was a traditional Arab open boat, pointed fore and aft, with a steep sloping stem which gave her a distinctive shark-like appearance. A long yard, carrying a loosely gathered sail, hung from her single mast and two spars athwartships braced the gunwales. A tiller bar and block and tackle arrangement operated her tall, narrow rudder.

'As a master mariner you will appreciate at once her fine condition,' Omah said, ever the salesman. 'I have sailed her three times to Madagascar loaded with ivory, she knows this coast as well as I do myself. She was overhauled recently, some planks and her rigging were renewed. She'll carry you across the channel to Zanzibar and your wives as swiftly as a flying carpet.'

They shook hands, Omah picked up the lower folds of his *kanzu* and hurried off on his spindly old legs before he was cut off by the rising tide. Eddies lapped at the last stretch of exposed sandbank and the night breeze ruffled the surface of the sea. The *zaruk* shifted uneasily as the water rose about her, sweeping in strongly and churning up the sand. The keel bumped one last time and she floated free. Khalil stowed the saddle-bag under the stern thwart, hauled up the sail and took the tiller, feeling the rudder bite as the boat began to move.

The sea, piling in against the steeply shelving sand, lifted the bow high. As the wave passed beneath it sank and her stern rose, seconds later it dropped into the following trough and water cascaded into the boat. She rose with foaming sea pouring over her gunwales, soaking Khalil to the skin. He held grimly to the tiller, the pressure on the rudder was enormous as the *zaruk* tried to turn broadside on. Khalil knew if he failed to hold her, or if a rope in the steering gear gave way, disaster would quickly follow. The noise of crashing waves became deafening as the reef neared; a new danger loomed. If the boat were to roll over now he would be swept away by the undertow and smashed against the razor-sharp coral. Ahead an immense wall of dark water rose perpendicularly, the noise was mind numbing, a frightening, thunderous violence. The bow rose almost vertically to meet the mountain before it crashed over the *zaruk*. It seemed impossible for her to survive such a fearful blow; her slender ribs and planks must surely be torn apart.

But she had been built by Arabs who were tenth generation master shipwrights, men who well knew the poundings she would receive in the wild seas and high rolling surf of the East African coast. The graceful sweep of her sides, the sharp backward angle of her bow and pointed stern were born out of the experience of centuries of boat building. They gave her not only beauty, but also the strength to carry her through seas capable of smashing any other vessel of comparable size to matchwood. The immense wave filled the boat to the gunwales but she shouldered through. The surge of water picked her up and she was pitched well beyond the coral jaws of the reef.

Khalil was exhilarated. It was almost six months since he had last been in a vessel of any sort, the longest period he had spent out of a ship in the past thirty years. The sea was his true element: the wind in his face, the beauty of the ocean, the perfect order of the stars, these were his true loves. *I'll go to sea for as long as I am able. And, when I'm old, I know wherever I stand on Zanzibar, I'll always hear the surf.*

Night closed in on the *zaruk*. The sea became kindly, smooth with an even swell. The wind was steady but gentle, filling the sail sufficiently to carry the boat across the twenty miles of channel. There was no compass on board, so Khalil steered by a familiar star. Nearing the coast he glimpsed the first welcoming glow of the beacon marking the entrance to the port of Zanzibar. It was lit at sunset and kept burning all night for the benefit of returning fishermen. The passage through the reef was narrow and full of hidden dangers but he knew it well and adjusted the course towards the beacon. The familiar surge of excitement at the end of a voyage ran through him. Umma and the Jewels would be keenly looking forward to his return, longing to hear his adventures and to tell him about their own little episodes of excitement during his absence. *Is Khadija pregnant? Even Umma is not yet beyond childbearing age. And little Ali will have grown out of all recognition* ... He concentrated on these delights, thrusting aside all thoughts of the problems waiting to burst upon him the moment he stepped ashore.

The dhow carried no lights. With her lateen sail spread wide, she swept down out of the night, blotting out the stars, a black monster with outstretched wings. A towering wall of planks, close enough to touch, was suddenly alongside. The port side of the *zaruk* smashed against it and Khalil was flung headlong into the sea. The corner of a sail and a loop of rope became wrapped round his legs, pulling him down. He grabbed the knife from his belt and slashed wildly until the entanglements dropped away and he was able to kick upwards to the surface. Spluttering and gasping he called for help but his weakened voice was lost in the slop of waves among the wreckage. The dhow had vanished into the darkness, the crew probably unaware they had run a boat down.

Dazed and shocked, he trod water and tried to gather his senses. The sea, which had looked smooth and gentle from the boat, was choppy for a swimmer. He could only see the harbour beacon when the swell lifted him. He was more than a mile from shore. These were highly dangerous waters where sharks abounded. They were reputed not to attack shipwrecked sailors although cynics pointed out none had ever survived to prove the theory. Khalil had often watched them from the safety of *Salwa*'s deck, great dark silent shadows gliding through the clear green water. A giant amongst them, local sailors called him *Akbah*, meaning 'great', was said to have once circled a slave ship from Zanzibar round the Cape of Good Hope and across the Atlantic to Brazil, feasting on the bodies of the dead and dying thrown overboard.

Khalil began swimming slowly towards the coast, creating as little disturbance as possible, trying not to think of a man-eater silently rising from the depths with jaws agape to snap off his body from the waist down. *In time Abdul will hear from Omah that I reached the coast and borrowed the zaruk. He'll tell Umma and the Jewels I was lost at sea but no one will know how.*

When the *zaruk* sank, the saddle-bag went down with her. In it was the prayer mat, the log and the map of the route to the valley. And the document bearing Joseph's mark agreeing to the surrender of the valley. The colonel had stressed its importance and without it the Hamerton Plan was dead.

All I can do now is report my return to the palace and hope for a fair hearing. I captured the valley, the main reason for the expedition, and can report the inhabitants could be Sheba's descendants. His highness must be told that as soon as possible. Tippu will be present, sharing in the glory of the news. Perhaps that will be sufficient to spare me punishment for not being back in time, and for failing to bring the women back for the sultan, or ivory for Tippu. I may have to tell him I hid it in the cave for safety. That may persuade him to let me have the villa after all. But I really don't care about that any more. All I want is to get home, see Umma and my Jewels again, and forget everything else.

Hours seemed to pass before he felt his bare feet touch the shoaling bottom. He staggered through the surf and collapsed exhausted on the sand. It could have been as long as an hour before he summoned sufficient strength to move. He had no wish to be found in such a wretched state. He yearned for time to think, to assess his new situation, but that was impossible. He forced himself to his feet and began to walk inland. Over to his left the town was a blur, only slightly darker than the night sky.

The mosque doors stood open as always, lamps burning at either side of the entrance. Inside the *imams* would be eager to help him with prayer and spiritual guidance, but it was practical advice he needed. In the entrance hall hung a variety of clothing and shoes left by the faithful now at prayer in the main hall. He quickly made a selection, dropped his stained wet *kanzu* on the floor and dressed, then left as silently as he had entered. It was a minor achievement and he felt invigorated as he hurried through the dawn light towards the palace.

Slouching against the outer gates were two *askaris* in untidy uniforms and filthy boots. Khalil remembered how smart his men had been before setting off for the raid on the village; by contrast these guards were a disgrace.

'Bring your commanding officer at once,' Khalil demanded.

'What's it about?' one of the *askaris* grunted.

'Just smarten yourself up and tell him I wish to see him.'

'Go away,' the man retorted. 'You have no business here.'

'You will regret it, and so will your officer if he doesn't come here at once,' Khalil snapped. 'I am an emissary of his highness and I demand his immediate presence.'

The guard stared insolently and Khalil guessed demands for entry to the palace by beggars and madmen were a common occurrence. But an Arab, respectably dressed and speaking with authority, should be treated with courtesy.

'Clear off before I stick my bayonet up your rear end,' the *askari* snorted.

'Call him at once,' Khalil retorted. 'Otherwise I'll see you both suffer.'

The threat had some effect as the guards now muttered together, peering at him suspiciously. Finally one of them shuffled off and some minutes later a dishevelled lieutenant stumbled up to the gate, a bottle clutched in one hand. His unbuttoned jacket was dirty and crumpled, his eyes bloodshot. He glared through the gate at Khalil, the foul smell of his alcohol-laden breath wafting through the ornate iron bars. 'How dare you tell one of my men to fetch me!' he shouted. 'I give the orders here!'

'Stand to attention when you address me!' Khalil roared back.' I am a captain in his highness's service and your superior officer. Take me to the chief minister at once!'

The lieutenant took a long drink from the neck of the bottle. 'Don't speak to me in that tone, *bwana*,' he sneered. 'This is my gate and I decide who gets through. Dirty Arabs never do!' He grinned at the two *askaris* who appeared to enjoy the joke.

'I order you to open this gate!'

The lieutenant turned to the two *askaris*. 'Let him in. Then throw him in a cell. I'll deal with him when I come off duty.' He raised the bottle to his mouth, took a long draught and swaggered off. One of the *askaris* opened the gate, the other poked his musket in Khalil's ribs and jerked his head. 'You'll be sorry,' he said with a smirk. 'Quick march!'

The cell was filthy, bare except for a scattering of straw on the earthen floor, and the only light was a faint glimmer of sky through a barred opening at the top of one wall. Khalil slumped in a corner, shocked and dismayed. He told himself this was a temporary setback; with luck it would soon be realized a serious mistake had been made and his release would follow.

But until then I'm in a dangerous situation. What can I say if the lieutenant remembers to come? Be humble, beg forgiveness for my insolence? I need to get a message to Tippu, telling him I've been arrested and to order my release. But who can I bribe to take a note? I don't have paper or pencil. Or money. Everything I had went down with the zaruk....

It was several hours before footsteps sounded in the corridor outside. Orders were shouted, a key rattled in the lock and the door swung open. A tall, smartly dressed lieutenant strode into the cell.

'Who are you?' he barked. 'What's this nonsense about you being an emissary of his highness?'

He moved further into the cell and the faint light from the high opening fell across his face. Khalil involuntarily drew a sharp breath; the lieutenant had the same tribal markings on his face as Juma! And a strong resemblance in the scowling mask-like face and rigid military posture. Even the voice carried an echo of him.

'Do you know Sergeant Juma?' he asked hoarsely.

The lieutenant stared. 'He's my half-brother. What of it?'

'Do you know where he is now?'

'Absent on duty. On a mission to the interior.'

'My name is Captain Khalil. I was commander of that mission.'

'Come with me, Captain.'

The lieutenant snapped an order to the *askari* who stood aside. Khalil followed the officer down the corridor. He entered an office, sat at the desk and motioned to Khalil to stand in front of him.

'What proof do you have of your identity?'

'None. My boat was run down by a dhow as I crossed from the mainland during the night. All my possessions went down with her.'

'You know my half-brother?'

'I knew him well.'

'Knew? Is he dead?'

I can't say I killed him. 'I'm sorry to inform you he died of wounds received in the course of duty.'

'He was an ignorant bully,' the lieutenant snapped. 'I'll shed no tears.' *I remember him fighting the rebels hand-to-hand, diving into the Mutumwa when the crocodiles were near, jumping between the rocks in the gorge and holding out his hand to me....* 'He was a good soldier, and very brave.'

193

'My father had many wives, he was merely one of my numerous half-brothers. He was very jealous when I became a lieutenant while he remained a sergeant. He was buried in the interior?'

I ordered his body thrown in the river. 'Yes. With full military honours. The men were greatly upset.'

The lieutenant's lip curled in distaste. 'He owed me money.'

'His only possession when he died was his army equipment. It was shared between his men, following the usual practice.'

The lieutenant took a piece of paper from the desk drawer, scribbled a note and held it out. 'As his brother and a fellow soldier I am entitled to claim the pay he was due. Sign this paper certifying his death in action.'

Khalil signed and the lieutenant stuffed the note in his pocket. 'To see the Chief Minister you must first see the provost. I will take you to him.'

The provost was an elderly Turk, tall and ramrod straight in an elaborate blue and scarlet uniform, his legs encased in highly polished black riding boots. He stood with his hands clasped behind his back, staring out of the window. He turned and flicked a dismissive hand at the secretary who hurriedly bowed and backed out of the door. The provost fixed Khalil with a steely look.

'You are the dhow master who headed an expedition to the valley discovered by the slaver Muammar,' he said abruptly.

The statement could not have been more surprising or succinct; Khalil could only nod in astonishment.

'I read the confession made by Muammar's son,' the provost continued. 'I trust your mission was successful?'

'Everything Muammar told his son was true,' Khalil replied cautiously.

'Excellent,' the provost nodded approvingly.

Khalil took advantage of the pause that followed. 'You are commander-in-chief of his highness's army, Provost?' he enquired.

'I have that honour.'

'Then I wish to compliment you on the high quality of the training and discipline shown by the *askaris* on the expedition. I regret to inform you of the twenty who sailed from Zanzibar six months ago, only seven survived. Sergeant Juma was among the casualties.'

'Juma? I knew him well. Doubtless he died valiantly?'

'He did, Provost. In the battle to capture the valley.'

'That is good to know.'

'I had intended to inform his highness of the excellent service given by your men throughout the course of the expedition.'

'Pardon, Captain. You said "had intended". Is there a problem?'

'I am unable to express my appreciation without reference to the gross ill-treatment I received on arrival at the palace gates this morning. The lieutenant on duty was drunk and in a debauched state. In the presence of two *askaris* he called me "a dirty Arab". As his highness and the chief minister are fellow Arabs, I considered his comment as insulting to them as it was to myself. It was on this lieutenant's orders that I was locked in a filthy cell for several hours.'

The provost was visibly shaken. 'I am grieved to hear an important servant of his highness was met with such gross discourtesy. Such behaviour is rare in the army. The lieutenant will be severely dealt with.'

'Thank you. You will understand I am not concerned for myself, but for the insult to his highness and the chief minister. Happily I was later released by a lieutenant who was half-brother to Sergeant Juma. He was most courteous and immediately arranged for my release and this appointment with you.'

The provost nodded. 'I am pleased to hear it. There is of course no need for you to mention these unfortunate incidents to anyone else, Captain Khalil. I shall personally investigate and punish accordingly.'

'Thank you, Provost. Standards must be maintained.'

'Indeed they must, Captain. And rest assured I will see to it. I shall conduct you to the chief minster without delay. Please come this way.'

The provost led the way down a long corridor. The full light of the morning sun had not yet penetrated the high windows so Khalil was able to gain only a vague impression of the splendid frescoes adorning the walls. At the end of the corridor two lofty doors, magnificently carved, swung open. Two tall men, both ceremonial eunuchs to judge by their painted faces, in white turbans and scarlet uniforms, and carrying glittering scimitars, preceded them through an elegant ante-chamber. Another pair of doors, loftier and even more elaborate than the first, swung open. The provost stopped at the threshold and bowed deeply.

'Captain Khalil, Chief Minister,' he announced.

Abdul stepped forward, smiling, with his arms extended.

Chapter Seventeen

This cannot be happening! Abdul, the slave master, now chief minister? Ridiculous! Where is Tippu? If this isn't a dream, why did Omah not tell me? He must have known, unless he thought I already knew. But how could I? This must be a dream. Unless I've gone mad!

'It's wonderful to see you, Khalil, truly wonderful,' Abdul enthused, waving his empty sleeve excitedly.

'Abdul! You! Chief Minister? Can this be true?'

'It is, my friend.' He made an ostentatious bow. 'Tippu is dead. I am his successor. Allah rewards the deserving!' He bowed again and taking Khalil by the hand, led him to a long low couch with a covering of exquisite blue silk. His delight was great, and genuine.

'Sit with me, my friend. Wonderful! There's no other word for it. Wonderful! You're back. My God, Khalil, I can't believe it! I've got to say I had doubts when we sailed away, leaving you and your men on Bagamoyo beach that morning! Do you remember that British admiral's uniform I wore? Wasn't that a laugh! Yes, as I say, I had doubts. Only a few mind, but you were so innocent! The things you said to me, and the questions you asked! And yet you've survived! Come through it all unscathed! It's so amazing!'

Khalil struggled to adjust to the new situation. *Allah has struck Tippu down and avenged Haleema! Umma said he would receive just punishment. Abdul will explain to the sultan the situation I faced at the valley, why it was impossible for me to bring women back from him. All my worries will be over! With Tippu dead the villa is definitely mine.*

Abdul continued to gabble but Khalil cut him short.

'Was Tippu murdered?' he asked.

'Not murdered. Well, not exactly!' Abdul gave a cynical laugh. 'You'd only been gone a few days when Allah took our beloved chief minister from us. He went blue in the face and collapsed in the arms of a new concubine!'

'May his soul rest in peace,' Khalil murmured, hoping it did not.

'Yes, indeed. The whole business was most upsetting for his family of course,' Abdul went on solicitously. 'To spare them further distress, I had the woman concerned immediately moved into my own harem. There's no doubt she was the cause of Tippu's sudden demise. My God, Khalil! I could tell you things you'd never believe possible. She seems such a demure little thing too. Someone bought her off a street trader and gave her to Tippu as a mark of respect.'

Khalil could barely contain his astonishment. Abdul was undoubtedly talking about the slave-girl he had rescued from the procession! *It's thanks to me you're now chief minister*!

'And you stepped into his shoes?' he asked, hoping his voice sounded natural despite this latest shock. 'How did that come about?'

'Pure good fortune, my friend! One of my slaves has a brother who was senior eunuch in Tippu's harem and was on duty when he died. He had been watching through the spy hole and actually saw his master go blue and collapse on top of the girl! She was very shocked of course, sat up and screamed and screamed! The eunuch bundled her back to the harem, laid out Tippu's body then ran round to my house to tell his brother. You know how his sort love to spread gossip. Naturally he immediately told me so I was the first senior official to hear of the tragedy. Tippu wasn't yet cold. I knew immediately his highness would need support so I ran all the way to the barracks and ordered the army out onto the streets. That bully of a provost was there and tried to stop me, but I shouted that I was acting on secret orders which shut him up.'

'He's not the sort to be intimidated, Abdul. You were very brave.'

'Bah! I wasn't slave master all those years for nothing! I can handle his sort. And he's got too many enemies to be a threat to me. I keep him on my staff to scare the underlings. He's good at that.'

'I can imagine. Go on, please! This is an amazing tale!'

'Not as amazing as yours, I'm sure. I'm dying to hear it! The army kept things quiet for the rest of the day while I waited at the palace to be on call for his highness should he require my services. He happened to see me – I was careful that he did. I told him all that I had done and he thanked me for the promptness of my action. When I offered him my services in any capacity he made me chief minister on the spot.'

'Congratulations! But it must be a daunting task, even for you.'

'My friend, it is a labour of immense proportions. I've employed dozens of clerks to start putting things down on paper, something Tippu never did. With that phenomenal memory of his, he saw no need for written records. There were no registers or proper accounts, nothing! He kept all shipping movements in his head so nobody knew when what ships were due to arrive or sail. Dhows kept appearing without warning and leaving without clearance. It's been a nightmare trying to collect harbour taxes from the captains.'

'You're the perfect man for the job, Abdul! You always arrange matters perfectly, regardless of how complicated they seem to the rest of us. I have only to think of what you did for the expedition.'

'You're very kind, Khalil. But yes, I admit to having a flair for organization. My market ledgers were always in perfect order. My successor is having difficulty maintaining the same high standards.'

'Is the slave trade thriving?'

'An expedition is getting ready to go out in the next few days. But traders are finding it more and more difficult to get supplies. It's their own stupid faults. I warned them for years but they took no notice. Take a reasonable number, and leave the rest to breed another batch I kept saying. But you'll have seen for yourself how few there are left. Instead of being satisfied with making a decent honest living, the fools stripped the country bare.'

'I saw dozens of abandoned villages.'

'Exactly my point. That's why this new source you have found is so very valuable. The price of quality merchandise like that will be enormous.'

'I'd better explain what happened.'

'Oh, yes, Khalil, please do. I'm dying to hear the details. I've been so busy I've not yet read your message saying you'd reached the coast.'

'I didn't send a message, Abdul. I'll explain why later. But first I must thank you for the excellent job you did in fitting out the expedition. Your advice was excellent and I had everything that was required. I could not have succeeded without your help.'

'I'm glad I was of some use.'

'Your notes were invaluable although you should have warned me about the crocodiles in the Mutumwa.'

Abdul shrugged. 'You would just have worried in advance. I knew you'd find a way to beat them. The old slavers used to say all you have to do is get on your knees and bite their noses. They can't stand it and soon clear off.'

'I was nearer getting my own nose bitten off, Abdul,' Khalil replied, drily. 'But how is my family? Did you call on them whilst I was away? It must have been an additional burden when you became chief minister. They would enjoy your visits. I told the Jewels you would make them laugh.'

'Ah, your precious Jewels, Khalil. And that lovely Umma! My God, how I envy you.' Abdul's eyes sparkled. 'You must be desperate to get back to them. I would be, in your shoes.'

'All three are a great joy to me, Abdul,' Khalil replied tersely. 'I'm blessed by Allah to have them.'

'You are a man with divine pleasures here on earth, Khalil, as well as those awaiting you in Paradise,' Abdul murmured mournfully. 'Some of us are much less fortunate.'

'Let's move on,' Khalil said briskly, the conversation had gone as far as he wished. 'I'll answer all your questions in detail later as it will take some time to give the full story. Already it's beginning to seem like a dream, I cannot believe that some things really happened. Briefly, Muammar spoke the truth. His map made sense, and the valley he described exists. The people living there are unusual to say the least, quite amazing in fact, and are probably descended from Sheba as his highness thinks.'

'That's wonderful news, Khalil! Where are the women? The sultan is anxious to see them. Since the time of your return has got nearer, not a day has passed but he mentions his Sheba princesses. He thinks of little else.'

'The mission was successful but perhaps not quite in the way that was anticipated, Abdul. Once again I need your help.'

'I remain at your service, my friend. What do you wish?'

'First, I must tell you I am the only one of the expedition to return.'

Abdul gaped at him in horror. 'My God, Khalil! What are you saying?'

'Hear me out, Abdul, please. Sergeant Oriedo and six *askaris* are the only survivors out of the twenty to survive. I have left them guarding the valley.'

'What happened to the others? Where are the women?'

'It's a long story, Abdul. I told you I needed your help.'

'And I've said I'll do whatever I can.'

'Thank you. I want you to arrange an audience with his highness for me as soon as possible.'

Abdul stared. 'I smell trouble, my friend. What has gone wrong?'

'There has been an important turn of events and I need to see the sultan most urgently.'

'Is his life in danger?'

'No, it is politically important. I will speak frankly, Abdul. I assume his highness retains his aspirations to rule Africa from coast to coast?'

'He mentioned it only yesterday. He is still convinced he has been chosen by Allah to do so.'

'That goal is now within his grasp.'

'My God, Khalil, tell me at once what has happened!'

'It's a complicated story to tell now and repeat again before his highness, Abdul. May I, with respect, postpone the telling of it until he is present?'

'You are quite right, my friend. Such an important matter can only be divulged in the presence of the sultan. I shall inform him of your return at once, before his morning visit to the harem. He will be delighted with the news, and is certain to grant you an audience without delay.'

The audience was held in a small elegant room where his highness, clad in his most elaborate and costly *kanzu*, sat on a raised chair with Abdul and Khalil standing before him. It was the first time Khalil had seen him and it was a most disappointing experience. He had an almost god-like status on the island yet he was short and stout with a fat, bad-tempered face. His small piggy eyes darted continually from side to side; they flickered on Khalil for only a moment then were gone.

This is the man who has caused me so much agony, keeping me from my family, and making me a murderer. He has an annual income of millions of thaler from slaves and ivory, his harem is numbered in hundreds, and his hands are steeped in blood. Now he sits in judgment on me. How can Allah permit such a thing?

Abdul cleared his throat noisily to indicate the audience was about to begin. He turned to Khalil. 'His highness has offered a prayer of thanks to Allah on your safe return,' he began formally. Khalil was sure the sultan had done nothing of the sort. 'You were sent on a mission to which were attached certain special tasks.' Abdul continued. 'His highness wishes to know if these have been achieved.'

'Your Highness, I beg to—'

'Please address me, Captain,' Abdul said sharply. 'And confine your replies to essential facts. There are more weighty matters awaiting the attention of his highness.'

The ladies of his harem, for instance, Khalil thought. He was surprised how much at ease he felt, not in the least intimidated by the presence of the two men who held his fate in their hands. He recalled how the *askaris* had addressed Juma, standing stiffly at attention whilst staring straight ahead and shouting. He now did exactly the same.

'The mission I commanded was sent to find and capture a certain valley,' he barked at the wall above the sultan's turban. 'I was ordered to take the valley in the name of his highness and return to Zanzibar with fifty female inhabitants for his pleasure.'

'They are the only matters of concern. Carry on.'

'On crossing the Mutumwa river the expedition turned north,' he continued, in the same manner. 'I interpreted the map given to me by the now chief minister the Honourable Abdul and reached the location of the valley, one hundred and ten days after leaving Bagamoyo.'

'You were asked to prepare a new map,' Abdul pointed out.

'I did so. On the return journey I also took the opportunity to check the directions and distances. The map is accurate.'

'There is no need to shout, Captain,' Abdul snapped. 'His highness is three yards in front of you, not on a dhow out in the harbour. Carry on.'

'Yes, Chief Minister. After reconnoitering the valley I drew up a plan of campaign in consultation with my two sergeants. A successful attack was carried out at dawn the following morning.'

'Your attack was successful!' Abdul exclaimed. His surprise was false since Khalil had already informed him of the fact so his apparent glee was expressed for the sultan's benefit. 'His highness congratulates you on your most glorious victory,' he said.

The sultan had not moved a muscle or spoken a word since the audience began. 'In appearance the inhabitants are exactly as described by the slaver Muammar,' Khalil went on. 'Without exception they are tall and dark-skinned. Among the prisoners was their leader, a man called Joseph. He spoke only Amharic, and an ancient form of Arabic. He had no knowledge of ki-Swahili. I interrogated him at length and gained much information.'

At this the sultan leaned forward, hands on knees. 'Did you question him on his ancestry?' he demanded. 'Did he mention Sheba?'

Khalil paused a second before replying. 'Joseph informed me his people were Copts, from Ethiopia, Your Highness. He assured me they were descended from Prince Manilek, son of King Solomon and the noble queen.'

'By God, I knew it! Have I not said so, Abdul?'

'You have indeed, Your Highness. Many, many times.'

'Go on,' the sultan snapped. 'The fifty women. Where are they?'

'I found myself in great difficulty. The expedition had suffered much as a result of disease, accidents and attacks by crocodiles and bandits. I was left with only seven men, including one sergeant, out of the original twenty. Sergeant Juma and twelve *askaris* lost their lives honourably.'

'Yes?' The sultan expressed no concern at such heavy losses, made no enquiry into the nature of the deaths or the suffering involved. 'What about the women?' The piggy eyes were fixed on Khalil.

'It was impossible to march fifty prisoners five hundred miles back to the coast with only myself and seven men to guard them.'

An eerie silence fell across the room; Khalil kept his gaze firmly to the front but felt the sultan's stare. When Abdul finally broke the silence, his voice was cold and threatening. 'The Honourable Tippu had made you aware of the importance his highness placed on that part of the mission?'

'Yes, Chief Minster.'

'Yet you have returned empty-handed?'

'Not empty-handed, Chief Minister. On behalf of his highness, I accepted the unconditional surrender of the leader of the inhabitants, Joseph the Copt, grandson of the Grand Vizier of the Noble Kingdom of Ethiopia, descendant of Menelik, descendant of Their Majesties King Solomon and Queen Sheba.'

The imagined titles rolled glibly off his tongue. 'The valley is now formally a territory of Zanzibar, owned by his highness. the inhabitants are his loyal subjects. It is being defended by his army of occupation, commanded by Acting Lieutenant Oriedo. I have returned alone to inform his highness of the situation.'

He remained stiffly to attention, still staring to the front. The silence that followed was more than an absence of noise, the air itself seemed to pause for breath, awaiting the acclaim Khalil was certain would follow. The stillness was finally broken by the rustle of the sultan's *kanzu* as he swept out of the gilded door behind his chair without a word or glance.

'His highness is most disappointed, Khalil,' Abdul said sternly. 'You should have warned me of your failure to bring back the women. You made a serious error in not bringing even a few for his pleasure. I told you how he's been looking forward to them with great anticipation. And the man Joseph should have been brought back for close examination about Sheba. These are serious failings on your part, and cannot go unpunished.'

Khalil remained at attention during this reprimand. *Abdul is angry, but he's still a friend. Had Tippu been chief minister, I'd now be under sentence of death.*

'Consider yourself fortunate it is I who am chief minister and not Tippu,' Abdul went on, echoing his thoughts. 'He would not have hesitated in ordering that you be fed to the sharks. I'll take a lenient view and lock you up until I can persuade the sultan you've been adequately punished. I must warn you that may not be for some time.'

'Lock me up!' Khalil exclaimed. 'I was shipwrecked last night and had to swim ashore! I came straight here to make my report. I have not yet seen my wives and children. Can I not be held under house arrest? I am sorry to have disappointed his highness but I found the valley and captured it for him. I understood from Tippu that was the main purpose of the mission. I had lost too many men to bring the women back, as I have explained. I myself was very fortunate to return.'

'In the eyes of the sultan you have failed, Khalil, and that's what matters,' Abdul said sorrowfully. 'I will do what I can for you. House arrest is not possible, in view of the gravity of your offence. However, I shall order that you are to be detained in the palace, not the prison, for which you ought to be grateful. I will inform Umma and the Jewels you are not in immediate danger. Unfortunately they will not be permitted to visit you. After an appropriate time has passed I will inform his highness you have suffered enough and request your release. He may order you back to the valley in order to collect the women.'

Abdul clapped his hands and two of the scarlet-turbaned guards entered. With one on either side Khalil was marched out of the room. This time there was no opportunity to examine the fine décor, no stately walk along elegant corridors. He was thrust into a bleak stone passage and roughly pushed into a tiny room. The lock grated behind him.

The only light entering the cell came through an iron grille. Khalil slumped to the floor in despair. This was the reward for all he had done, locked alone in near darkness, totally cut off from his beloved wives and children. He felt no anger towards Abdul who had no choice but to obey the whims of the crazed sultan. *With luck he'll soon persuade him to let me go. He owns the valley now, his stepping stone to ruling Africa. And the women are still there, ready for collection by the next expedition.*

Tippu was dead so the original aim of the Hamerton Plan, to destroy him, no longer existed. But as the hours passed, Khalil began to recognize a new cause for vengeance to replace it. *In spite of all I've done, the anguish and dangers I faced, the sultan has imprisoned me. What greater blow could I deliver him than have Colonel*

Hamerton snatch the valley, even at this stage! He's a clever man, and may be able, with my help, to revive the plan, despite the loss of the paper Joseph signed.

Lying in the dark on the earthen floor, Khalil laughed aloud.

Thanks to Abdul his confinement in the palace was not onerous. The food was eatable and he was allowed out for exercise and to attend to calls of nature twice a day. He worried continuously about the distressing effects his absence must be having on Umma and the Jewels; he received no news of them.

He was in prison for a month and it was the provost who brought him the glad news that he was being freed. 'The chief minister is busy and has asked me to inform you of this most gracious gesture on the part of his highness,' he announced formally.

'I am most grateful, Provost,' Khalil exclaimed.

'You are fortunate the chief minister is your friend,' he replied. 'A stay in prison would have been much worse. I will escort you to the outer gate.'

They walked through a maze of dark passages, turning this way and that until they arrived in a small courtyard on the west side of the palace. There was no one else present; the provost turned on his heel and spoke quietly.

'I have a message for you from Colonel Hamerton,' he murmured.

The statement sent a shiver through Khalil. How could the provost possibly have a message for him from the Resident? It was inconceivable he was one of his agents. This must be a trap! He assumed a deep frown and shook his head. 'Hamerton?' he echoed. 'I know no one of that name.'

'He is the British Resident, as you are well aware,' the provost said with a smile. He stood in front of Khalil, hands clasped behind his back in his usual formidable stance. 'Before leaving on the expedition you surreptitiously visited the Residency and came to an arrangement with him concerning the future ownership of the valley.'

Khalil shook his head. 'You are mistaken, Provost. What possible arrangement would I make with a foreigner?'

The provost smiled. 'Your discretion is admirable, Khalil. But would we be having this conversation if Abdul knew the truth? He is as anxious as the sultan that the valley is annexed to Zanzibar. For it to fall into the hands of the British would be a disaster for them both. If he thought for a single moment that you had placed that intention in jeopardy, even though you are a friend you would be now hanging by the neck with your eyes pecked out by birds.'

'I am sorry, Provost, I know nothing of this matter.' He turned away, needing time to think, to assess this sudden and dangerous situation.

The provost moved quickly, stepping in front of him to bar his progress. 'The treaty, Khalil! The colonel must know what happened to the treaty! The secret word you agreed to was 'Boleyn', the name of an English queen. Tell me quickly! We may never have a better moment to talk than this. Even now someone might be watching. We cannot stand chatting much longer. The treaty! Where is it?'

The secret word, the urgency in the provost's voice and the steadiness of his gaze, left Khalil with no choice but to answer truthfully. He had not mentioned the treaty during the audience with the sultan, so the provost could only have heard of it from the colonel himself.

'Lost,' he replied, his voice hoarse with trepidation. 'My boat was run down by a dhow as I was crossing the channel. The treaty was in a saddle-bag stowed on board.'

'The sultan and Abdul know nothing of this?'

'Nothing.'

'But the valley truly exists, and the chief marked a document agreeing to surrender sovereignty to you?'

'Yes, Provost.'

'Thank you. That is the information the colonel needs. I shall release you now. There is something I must show you. As we walk towards the gate I will slip a piece of paper into your pocket. Read it when you get home then destroy it. The time will come when you can use it to great effect. Meanwhile say nothing of it, make no mention to anyone of this conversation.'

Khalil reached home, opened the door and stepped into the courtyard. A servant sweeping up leaves looked up and dropped the broom when he saw Khalil. He ran into the house, loudly calling out his name. There was an excited babble, followed by shouts and squeals then his three wives had their arms about him, all laughing and crying at the same moment.

Chapter Eighteen

'I'm sorry, there's no hope of you ever owning Tippu's villa,' Abdul said, visibly downcast. They were sitting in the courtyard of Khalil's house. He had been dozing in the morning sunshine when the outer door was suddenly flung open and through the opening he saw the chief minister, in a flowing scarlet gown and tall white turban, stepping down from a richly decorated sedan chair carried by two muscular eunuchs.

'The sultan has refused the transfer of the villa you were promised. He's still very angry at your failure to carry out his orders in full.' Abdul held up his hand to stem the protest Khalil was about to make. 'Tippu left no record of his promise to you; there's no proof he ever spoke to you. My clerks have searched everywhere; but there's nothing in writing to show the expedition was ever sent. The only record of its existence is the notes I made of our meeting at the slave market. As you may know, Tippu kept information in his head rather than commit it to paper. He was never a literary man.'

'He promised his lawyer would transfer the villa to my name!'

'Well, he didn't issue the instruction to him. What's more important is that his senior widow, Jubella, is very fond of the villa and means to keep it.'

Khalil shook his head. 'She must have inherited a fortune when he died, including a dozen other houses. Why does she still want the villa?

'Sentimental reasons, my friend. You know how stupid women can be over such trifles. It was where Tippu took her on their wedding day, and it was their home until he made enough money from slaving to buy a larger property.'

'But it's so unfair, Abdul! I was reluctant to go on the expedition as you know. Tippu asked what I wanted most of all in the world and the villa was the perfect thing to ask for. I'd gone there for years to pay the *Salwa*'s harbour dues so I knew the place and really liked it. I was sure Haleema, who through the mercy of Allah was still alive at the time, and the rest of the family, would feel the same.'

'Well, I'm afraid nothing can be done. First, there is nothing to show Tippu promised it to you. Second, his widow is determined to keep it. And third, you cannot expect the sultan to intercede on your behalf, not after you let him down so badly. Forget about the villa, my friend, it can never be yours.'

Tippu's failure to keep his word regarding the villa had another unfortunate consequence. He had promised to inform Khalil's employers, the Wafulu brothers, of his departure to the interior and order them to ensure his job as master of the *Salwa* would be available on his return. However when Khalil approached the brothers' local agent he denied all knowledge of any such instruction. As far as he was concerned, Khalil failed to report after his month's leave and a cargo of rhino hides awaited shipment to India. He had promoted the bosun Raschid to captain, and put him in command of the brig *Bahira*. He returned as the monsoon was changing; Khalil had still not appeared so he took *Salwa* to Muscat, one of the first dhows of the season to sail north.

Khalil sat with Umma one afternoon and together they composed a letter to the Wafulu brothers. It explained his recent absence was due to his carrying out an important mission on behalf of his highness which the chief minister would confirm. He had now returned to Zanzibar and was ready to sail as master again whenever required.

He took the letter down to the port next morning where a friendly captain leaving for Muscat promised to deliver it to the Wafulus as soon as he arrived. Khalil stood on the quay and watched the dhow's departure. The lines were let go and the foresail hauled to fill before the fresh breeze. She edged away from the quay, swung across the harbour and, heeling gently, headed out into the channel. Khalil ached at the thought of being on board her. He could feel the planks under his feet, hear the creak of her gear, smell her fresh tar and paint. But reality quickly returned. Until he received a new contract from the company all he could do was come down to the port every few days in the hope of finding a temporary berth with some other ship owner. The sight of the dhow decided him to accept a lower position as bosun if it became available.

He sauntered along the quay and, rounding the corner of a warehouse, saw an English frigate tied up alongside. Such ships were a familiar sight in the Arabian Sea, guarding British trade routes to Imperial India. On the quay, directly opposite the ship, was a café with tables and chairs neatly arranged along the pavement outside. Khalil sat down and ordered coffee. It was still early morning and there were as yet no other customers. It was the perfect spot from which to study the English ship. He realized, with sudden surprise, this was the café at which he and Abdul had taken coffee the morning *Arafat* sailed for Bagamoyo.

I'm sitting at exactly the same table and the waiter is the man who'd lost a leg to a crocodile. I was so happy that morning. Haleema had gone, but I had Umma and the Jewels. Tippu had promised I could have the villa, and I was master of the Salwa. *I had made the agreement with Colonel Hamerton and knew nothing of the horrors I was to face on the expedition ...*

He tried to recapture the joy of that morning but it eluded him. It was like trying to find his way back into a house, once welcoming and friendly, but now closed and shuttered against him. Grim memories, swirling like mists, returned to haunt him. *The renegade whose face he had shot away. The agonizing screech of the only cow elephant to survive the bloody stampede. The crocodiles seizing the Arab spies. Juma with blood gushing from his chest ... I was responsible for all these wicked things. Through my negligence eleven askaris died. I committed dreadful sins to become owner of a small villa, but in the end I failed to do even that. It's Allah's punishment on me. I'm useless, my life is over.*

'*Salaamu! Jambo!* Can you hear me?' The voice, speaking a mixture of Arabic and ki-Swahili greetings, dragged him back to consciousness. He jerked his head, his chin had rested on his chest and his neck was painfully stiff. One of the ship's officers, in a blue uniform with gold epaulettes, and wearing a cocked hat, was leaning over *Elspeth*'s rail, waving across at him.

'Are you are speaking to me, Captain?' Khalil called in ki-Swahili.

'Yes. Do you live here, in Zanzibar?' The officer elaborated the question by jabbing his forefinger downwards. He spoke hesitatingly, lacking confidence in his ability to speak a foreign language. 'Do you understand English?'

Khalil shook his head. He walked across to the ship, the quarter deck on which the officer stood was above the level of the quay.

'Want do you need, Captain?' he called up. 'I am a dhow captain. I may be able to help.'

'Ah! A sailor like myself! But I'm not the captain. I'm first lieutenant, and second-in-command of this ship. She's HMS *Achilles*. We came in on the morning tide. My name is Polycarp and I have important papers to deliver to the British Resident. Do you know where he can be found? Can you take me to him?'

'Yes, I can do that.'

The lieutenant swung his leg over the rail and climbed down the side-ladder onto the quay.

'It's only a few minutes' walk,' Khalil said as they set off. 'The Residency stands just above the harbour, near the sultan's palace.'

He could hardly believe his good fortune. *At last I have a legitimate reason to see Colonel Hamerton. I'll explain the loss of the treaty and what we can do to resurrect the plan. All is not lost after all!*

'Thank you,' Polycarp was saying. 'It's three years since I was last here and I find it hard to remember the little ki-Swahili I knew then.'

They walked together up the path to the door of the residency where one of the messenger boys stood up as they approached. 'I have brought this officer from the British ship *Achilles* which has just arrived,' Khalil informed him. 'He must see the Resident immediately.'

'Come inside, *bwana*. I will let the Resident know you are here.'

Colonel Hamerton came into the hallway. Ignoring Khalil, he held out his hand to Polycarp. 'I trust you made a swift voyage, Lieutenant?' he enquired with a smile.

Without waiting for a reply he turned to Khalil and said curtly in

Arabic, '*Assalam-o-alaikum*, Captain Khalil. Thank you for bringing the lieutenant here You may go.'

The Resident took Polycarp by the elbow in a friendly gesture. 'Yes, Lieutenant, your voyage was troublefree, I trust?'

They went into his office, the door closed behind them, and Khalil was left standing in the hall. *He treated me as if I was merely a messenger. The provost has reported the loss of the treaty to him and he has decided the plan is no longer possible and I am of no further use to him. But there was no need for him to be so rude.*

The Jewels remained in a state of excitement at having him home. Every whim he expressed was eagerly catered for, nothing was too much trouble for them. He was pampered and cosseted as if he had been an infant. He enjoyed their attentions even though at times he found them a trifle cloying. He told them stories about his journey, embroidering some of the incidents, and avoiding mention of anything unpleasant or likely to scare them.

Only Umma heard the true horror of his experiences. By speaking of them to her, their effect gradually lessened; his nightmares faded and the frightening images came to mind less frequently. Umma mentioned Haleema several times which he recognized as a signal he was not to feel inhibited about speaking of her. But she had gone for ever and nothing of hers now remained in the house. His memories of her lay only in his thoughts and he had no wish to disturb them.

Umma was aware of the new worries he was facing although he never spoke of them. Failing to be awarded the villa had hurt him deeply although the loss was of small concern to her. When one of the Jewels timidly raised the subject, Umma remarked it was much too near the harbour and the smell of rotting fish would be a constant problem. The loss of his job was more serious, but she saw it as a blow to his dignity rather his pocket since financially they were comfortably off and the loss of income was no hardship. She was upset at the unfairness of his treatment by the colonel. She, too, considered his curt dismissal at the Residency, in front of the naval lieutenant, extremely rude. She assured Khalil there must be a reason but it was several days before the truth emerged.

'*Bwana, bwana!*' Simba's urgent call a few mornings later, and his repeated banging on the bedroom door, dragged Khalil from sleep. Umma lay cradling her head on his shoulder; as he carefully disentangled himself she rolled away from him with a sigh.

In his nightshirt he tiptoed to the door. 'What is it?' he hissed.

'Men from the palace are here, *bwana*. They have brought a chair for you. They say you must go with them immediately.'

He dressed hurriedly, wondering what crisis had brought this sudden call. He was not being re-arrested, that was certain, a sedan would not have been sent to transport a prisoner to goal. Juma's brother, the *askari* lieutenant, came smartly to attention as Khalil came down the stairs.

'Good morning, Captain Khalil. The chief minister has sent me to fetch you. I have brought a sedan to get you to the palace as quickly as possible.'

It was an uncomfortable journey. The lieutenant, who had been carried in the chair from the palace, now trotted alongside, constantly urging the two *askaris* between the front and rear shafts to keep up a good pace. The sedan jerked and swung as they made their way along the rutted track; the elegant upholstery and gilded corner pillars did nothing to alleviate the lack of springs. Khalil clung to a leather strap as the seat bucked, tipping him this way and that, reminding him of *Salwa* tossing in a choppy sea. The palace gates swung open as the chair arrived and a moment later Khalil was able to step down in the courtyard beside the main entrance. The provost stood on top of the steps, hands clasped behind his back.

'Good morning, Captain,' he called. 'Thank you for coming.'

As Khalil came up to him he said quietly, 'There has been an important development and his highness will welcome your views. You've nothing to fear, I assure you. All you have to do is tell the exact truth. The exact truth, and nothing more. Remember that.'

The provost turned and led the way with his great strides down the long corridor to the elegant room in which Khalil had delivered his report on return from the valley. The tall doors swung open and he stepped inside with the provost at his side. The sultan sat in his raised chair; in front stood Abdul and beside him, resplendent in white suit and scarlet cravat, was Colonel Hamerton. A discussion must have been in progress for some time as Abdul swung round and snapped, 'At last!' as Khalil and the provost appeared.

'Khalil!' he barked without introduction. 'You commanded an expedition to a valley in the interior discovered by the slaver Muammar?'

'Yes, Chief Minister.'

'After an armed attack the leader of the inhabitants, a man called Joseph, surrendered the valley to you. Is that so?'

'Yes, Chief Minister.'

'Leaving the Zanzibar Army of Occupation in control of the valley, you returned to report your success to his highness?'

'Yes, Chief Minister.'

'Did the man Joseph say he had surrendered the valley to anyone else?'

Abdul had grown more and more excited as he put the questions and his face was now flushed, his dark eyes wide and staring on either side of his great hooked nose.

'No, he did not,' Khalil answered.

'There!' Abdul exclaimed, throwing his arms wide in triumph in front of the Resident. 'Muammar, a loyal subject of his highness, was the first to reach the valley. The next to arrive was Khalil, and Joseph surrendered the valley to him. On every count the valley is the property of his highness, and an outpost of Zanzibar. You have no case, Your Excellency!'

'Thank you, Chief Minister,' Colonel Hamerton said in his precise Arabic. He turned and looked at Khalil, frowning a little but not unfriendly. 'Captain Khalil,' he began, 'you heard the statement made by the chief minister. I have only two questions to ask and I want you to answer them in all honesty, without fear, or hope of favour. In your presence, did Joseph make his mark on a document agreeing to surrender the valley to you?'

Khalil stared hard at the Resident who looked back at him firmly. 'The truth, Captain Khalil. Only the truth,' he said quietly.

'Yes, Your Excellency, he did.'

'Thank you, Captain Khalil. And where is that treaty now?'

'It was lost when my *zaruk* was run down by a dhow as I was crossing from the mainland to return to Zanzibar.'

'Thank you, Captain.'

The colonel took a scrap of paper from his jacket pocket. 'I have here a document, written in Arabic, on which Joseph has made his mark,' he said. 'Please read it out aloud.'

Khalil was stunned; how had the treaty been recovered from the bottom of the sea? His hand shook as he took the paper but he saw at once it was not the document he had received from Joseph.

'Read it out aloud please, Captain Khalil,' the colonel repeated. 'Word for word, in Arabic.'

Khalil found it difficult to speak in his normal voice. 'On behalf of my people I agree to accept British rule.'

'I agree to accept British rule,' Colonel Hamerton repeated. 'Thank you, Captain Khalil.'

He took the document from him and, holding it aloft, turned to face the sultan. 'This is a legal document, Your Highness. It is unambiguous, and carries the formal mark of Joseph. It cannot be disputed.'

'Where did it come from?' Abdul shrieked the words.

'It reached me from Gibraltar,' the Resident said calmly.

'Gibraltar? Where's that?'

'It is a port, a British possession, at the western end of the Mediterranean Sea.' The colonel turned to face the sultan again. 'If I may offer an explanation, Your Highness? An English explorer searching for the source of the Nile came upon the valley in question some months ago. It was peaceful, free from raids by slavers, and the inhabitants were anxious it should remain so. The explorer had with him an Egyptian guide, who of course spoke Arabic, and through him the explorer suggested to Joseph that he sign a paper seeking the protection of the British Government. This would prevent future attacks from slave traders and others who would cause great suffering to his people.'

There was silence in the room, all eyes were fixed on the Resident. 'Joseph had long feared invasion and willingly agreed to this offer,' the colonel continued. 'This paper bears his mark and confirms his acceptance. The explorer left the valley, headed north and eventually reached Khartoum in the Sudan. From there a boat on the Nile took him north to Alexandria where he gave the paper to the British

Resident. His excellency immediately realized its importance and sent it by the first available vessel leaving Alexandria for Gibraltar. There it was read by the governor whose first intention was to send the paper to London, but by chance the next English ship to call at Gibraltar was HMS *Achilles*, which was bound for Zanzibar. As I was the nearest British Resident to the valley in question, it was an opportunity for the governor to inform me of the situation. He therefore gave the paper to the captain of *Achilles* who delivered it to me on his arrival a few days ago. Before it left Gibraltar, the governor made a copy of the document and told the captain he would send it on the next ship leaving for London.'

'It's all lies!' Abdul was almost weeping, and trembling with rage. 'The valley belongs to his highness. It is part of Zanzibar. Muammar, then the expedition led by Captain Khalil, reached it before anyone else!'

Colonel Hamerton shook his head. 'I disagree, Chief Minister. We do not know who arrived at the valley first. The slaver, Muammar, may have caught a glimpse, but never set a foot in it. Captain Khalil may have made an arrangement of sorts with Joseph, but there is no documentary proof of it.'

'His highness is the proper person to rule the valley,' Abdul screamed. 'What right has your English Government to do so, far away in London?'

'We rule India, Chief Minister, and that is much further from London than Africa. It began with the East India Company and we rule very well. We have brought peace where there was conflict. Built roads, hospitals and schools where there was jungle. Introduced justice, law and order in place of tribal oppression. We shall do the same in Africa. The British East Africa Company already exists, and will soon establish itself across the country. I have no doubt in time it will have a strong presence here on Zanzibar.'

'His highness will not allow that to happen,' Abdul snarled. 'This is his island. He already owns the coastal strip and has plans to extend his rule across the entire continent.'

The Resident moved to one of the tall windows and drew aside the curtain with a flourish. 'If you would care to look down in the harbour, Chief Minister, you will see His Majesty's frigate *Achilles* lying broadside on to the palace. It was her captain who brought the paper to me from Gibraltar. Her guns are loaded and run out, ready for action. I have only to signal and this palace will be reduced to rubble in minutes. The captain has a duty to defend the colonial possessions of His Majesty King George, wherever they may be. The valley, formerly ruled by Joseph, is the latest addition to that long and honourable list.'

He let the curtain fall and walked to the foot of the steps where he gave the sultan a formal bow and said, 'I bid Your Highness good morning.'He turned, nodded briskly to Abdul and murmured, 'Chief Minister.'

Finally, casting a knowing glance at Khalil and the provost, hat in hand, he strolled nonchalantly out of the room.

The sultan swept out of the door behind his chair without a word whilst Abdul remained standing with his head bowed.

'You will excuse us, Chief Minister,' the provost said after a short silence. 'There are certain matters I wish to clarify with Captain Khalil.'

Abdul gave no sign that he heard as the two men left him.

It took Khalil an hour to describe to Umma the events of the morning. She grew concerned for him as she listened, worried that by supporting the Resident's case he had placed himself in danger.

'I am quite safe,' he assured her. 'Colonel Hamerton put both the sultan and Abdul down firmly. They are in no mood for a fight, both are more worried about their own futures than seeking retribution from me. The Hamerton Plan, your plan, Umma, worked to perfection. And there is something else I have to tell you ...' He showed her the paper the provost gave him as he left prison.

He arranged a meeting with Abdul; they met in his office at the palace the next day. 'His highness is devastated, totally exhausted,' Abdul said mournfully.

'His harem must take a lot of his energy,' Khalil remarked.

'The great plan is in ruins,' Abdul went on. 'It was his life's ambition.'

'A gravestone, not a stepping stone,' Khalil murmured.

The grim humour was lost on Abdul. 'The whole business has caused nothing but heartbreak and worry to everyone, yourself included,' he said mournfully. 'It grieves me, Khalil, that you lost the villa you longed for. And your job. I have written to the Wafulu brothers confirming your absence on duty for the sultan and demanded your reinstatement. Whether they take any heed is out of my hands.'

'Thank you, Abdul. That was kind of you.'

'What are your plans if they refuse to take you back?'

'Oh, I'm not in the least bothered! Now I have recovered from the shock of everything that has happened, I'm looking forward to a bright future. I'll build a large new villa, Umma is drawing the plans. And I've ordered the building of four new dhows. My sons will be their captains once they become master mariners.'

Abdul stared at him across his wide desk. 'Have you acquired a fortune I know nothing about?'

'In a way, Abdul. A friend of mine has a great deal of money. He doesn't know it yet, but he's going to help me.'

'You're fortunate to have a friend like that, Khalil.'

'You are that friend, Abdul. You'll pay for my new villa. And the dhows.'

Abdul gaped, open-mouthed. 'Have you gone mad, Khalil? I have nothing! How can I possibly pay for a villa and dhows for you?'

'Actually, the sultan has already paid for them. The money will come from the fortune you have stolen from him over the years.'

'Me? Steal from his highness? You have indeed gone mad!'

Khalil smiled and shook his head. 'No, Abdul, I'm not mad. And you are undoubtedly a thief. Here's the proof.' He laid a sheet of paper on the desk. 'This is a statement signed by the provost. His appointment allowed him access to every room in the palace, except the sultan's private apartments of course. For some months, in the evenings after you went to your quarters, he systematically searched the offices looking for items of interest.'

'The villain! How dare he?'

'In his days as quartermaster-general in the Turkish Army, he learned the mysteries of Arabic book-keeping, a qualification he neglected to mention to you. He was impressed by your meticulous accounts, particularly the second set you keep in your secret blue book. It shows every penny you deducted for yourself over the years from slave sale taxes, collected on behalf of the sultan, and more recently the vast amounts you have taken since becoming chief minister. Well over one hundred thousand thaler. Tippu probably stole as much, but he wasn't stupid and didn't put it in writing. As you said, he was never a literary man.'

For a moment Khalil felt sorry for Abdul as he visibly shrank to become nothing more than a terrified old man. 'Khalil, my friend,' he whispered, 'Do not speak of this. Please, I beg of you. I will do whatever you ask if only you promise me your silence.'

'It's too late, Abdul. The provost knows and he will not be silent. He was about to inform the sultan of your deceit when I returned, hoping to succeed you as chief minister. We became friends and he sought my advice on the best way of achieving his ambition.'

Abdul sat hunched in his chair, trembling.

'You know how I was robbed,' Khalil went on. 'Of the villa, of recognition of the responsibilities I undertook. You know the dangers I faced on the mission, yet because of it I lost my job as dhow master and cannot find another. The provost agrees that I'm merely regaining what is due to me and, in taking this action, I am being properly compensated for my losses.'

'I am doomed, Khalil. His highness will have me executed.'

'Not before you are tortured, Abdul. But there's still time to escape. Bring the money to my house tonight and you can go free.'

'Tonight! That's impossible!'

'In that case the sultan will be informed of your actions immediately.'

'No! Wait. Suppose I do as you say, what then?'

'After you hand over the money I'll allow you three days in which to flee, taking whatever you can carry. At the end of that time the provost will show his highness written proof of your treachery.'

'How much do you want?' Abdul mumbled.

'Fifty thousand thaler will be enough.'

'Fifty thousand? In coin?' Abdul gaped. 'Do you know how much that weighs?'

'Yes, I've calculated it exactly. Six hundred thaler weigh one *farasza*. Sixty-five *farasza* weigh one ton. Fifty thousand Austrian silver thaler in bags weigh a little over one and a quarter tons. That's only six ox cartloads!'

'Khalil, I—'

'Shut up, Abdul. You have more than enough to pay what I ask. It's less than half of what you have stored in the dhow you have moored in the private dock off the main harbour. The provost knows all about that too! And, if you are thinking of sailing before paying me, you should know that three of his men are outside this room, waiting for my orders. They will not leave your side until you fulfil your promise to me.'

A month later Khalil sat under a tree at the Residency taking afternoon tea with Colonel Hamerton. Umma was included in the invitation, but had regretfully declined as both Jewels were heavily pregnant and much too nervous to be left. Their delicate condition had become apparent a few weeks after Khalil had left with the expedition.

The conversation was polite and formal during tea. The colonel questioned Khalil on aspects of his journey which would be of interest to the commander of the two companies of troops soon to arrive from India and proceed to march to the valley and form the garrison of the latest addition to the British Empire.

'Your lieutenant and his seven men will be stood down,' the Resident said. 'As Africans I am afraid they are not permitted to join the British Army.'

Khalil smiled. 'I suspect they've already thrown away their uniforms and become farmers, with Sheba princesses as wives.'

'I wonder what Holy Joseph thinks of that!' the colonel remarked and they both laughed.

'May I crave a favour, Your Excellency?'

'Of course, Khalil. My government is greatly indebted to you. If there is anything we can do, please ask.'

'Thank you. During my return journey from the valley I found the remains of the elephants we had driven over the cliff. As I explained, they were killed on Tippu's orders which I was forced to obey. He robbed me of the villa so taking his ivory was fair compensation. I hid the tusks in a cave and would like to retrieve them. Would it be possible for you to seek permission for me to accompany the soldiers on the march inland? I shall take men and camels to transport the ivory to the coast.'

'Of course, my friend. I'll do better than that. I'll tell the commander to send a platoon to guard you back to the coast. They'll protect you against attacks by fugitives.'

'I am very grateful, Excellency.'

Later they strolled together along the beach at the edge of the surf. 'Do you think the provost will be a success as chief minister?' Khalil asked.

'Well, he's honest, which makes a change after Tippu and Abdul. As a Turk he'll not be popular with Arabs, your people grew weary of Ottoman rule long ago. And military men tend to be over-rigid in matters of administration. It will be interesting to see what develops.'

'Yes, indeed it will.'

'You have no doubt heard Abdul has fled the island.'

'It would be impossible to keep that a secret,' Khalil said, smiling.

'I found it strange that he resigned as chief minister. It wasn't his fault the sultan's dream of ruling the continent failed. I know of no reason why he should have decided to go. Do you have any ideas?'

'Perhaps, when he lost the argument with you over the valley, the sultan no longer had confidence in him.'

'Maybe. There are some quite ridiculous stories circulating of course. For instance, I was told he kept a dhow permanently ready for sea. Whichever way the monsoon was blowing, north or south, he could leave port at any time and go wherever the wind took him.'

'Some dhows are kept in readiness for a sudden voyage. Abdul's would have been registered in someone else's name, in his position it was a wise precaution. The sultan's not to be trusted, as I know to my cost.'

'I also heard he had a fortune in coin stored near the docks, and there was much coming and going of ox carts at dead of night, shortly before his departure. I suppose you know nothing about that either?'

'He never discussed it with me, Excellency.'

'No, I don't suppose he needed to.'

They stopped, looked at each other and smiled, sharing a diplomatic understanding before strolling on.

'Incidentally, may I congratulate you on your good fortune? I believe the four dhows at present under construction have been ordered in your name.'

'Thank you. Perhaps you would honour me by attending the launchings and naming one of them?'

'I shall be delighted. Especially as Tippu will be paying for them with his ivory. There's a certain justice in that.'

After a further silence, Khalil said, 'I've been wondering, Colonel, why you adopted such an unfriendly attitude towards me when I brought Lieutenant Polycarp to the Residency. It was very much out of character for you.'

'My apologies for that, Khalil. I guessed you were hoping to explain what had happened but by then I knew from the provost that your boat had been run down and the treaty lost with it. I kept you in the dark on purpose, it was better to let you think our plan had failed although I was already working on the amended version. I knew Abdul would call you to the palace when I claimed possession of the valley for my government, and decided it was better you came unprepared. You played your part perfectly, innocent and totally truthful! The arrival of *Achilles* added a nice finishing touch, giving me a plausible explanation as to how I came by the note. Ordering her captain to anchor in front of the palace with his guns run out was the final straw. Abdul didn't dare provoke a bombardment!'

'Something else has been puzzling me, Colonel. Do British explorers really come to Africa, searching for the source of the Nile?'

'Oh yes, it's an obsession! The Royal Geographical Society in London spends large sums trying to solve the problem. They call it the Great Enigma.'

'You British are indeed strange people. I have only one more question. Was the mark on the document I read out really made by Joseph?'

The Resident smiled. 'That, my dear Khalil, is what we may call the Second Great Enigma!' He reached inside his jacket pocket and took out the crumpled paper. 'The valley is safe now, thanks to you. This treaty has served its purpose.'

He tore the paper into tiny pieces and threw them in the air. They stood watching in silence as the monsoon wind scattered them across the island.